FLESH AND BONE AND WATER

Brazilian-born doctor André Cabral is living in London when one day he receives a letter from his home country: a letter he keeps in his pocket for weeks. The missive prompts him to remember the days of his youth: afternoons on the beach with his teenage friends; parties in elegant apartments; his job at his father's plastic surgery practice — and, above all, his secret infatuation with a maid, the intoxicating Luana . . .

LUIZA SAUMA

◆

FLESH AND BONE AND WATER

Complete and Unabridged

ULVERSCROFT
Leicester

First published in Great Britain in 2017 by
Viking
London

First Large Print Edition
published 2017
by arrangement with
Viking
Penguin Random House
London

*A catalogue record for this book is available
from the British Library.*

ISBN 978–1–4448–3516–8

Published by
F. A. Thorpe (Publishing)
Anstey, Leicestershire

Set by Words & Graphics Ltd.
Anstey, Leicestershire
Printed and bound in Great Britain by
T. J. International Ltd., Padstow, Cornwall

This book is printed on acid-free paper

SPECIAL MESSAGE TO READERS

THE ULVERSCROFT FOUNDATION
(registered UK charity nu~~/ICES~~   )
was ~~established in 1972~~   date stamped below   r
research, d~~~~   ~~a of eye diseases.
Examples of major projects funded by
the Ulverscroft Foundation are:-

- The Children's Eye Unit at Moorfields Eye Hospital, London
- The Ulverscroft Children's Eye Unit at Great Ormond Street Hospital for Sick Children
- Funding research into eye diseases and treatment at the Department of Ophthalmology, University of Leicester
- The Ulverscroft Vision Research Group, Institute of Child Health
- Twin operating theatres at the Western Ophthalmic Hospital, London
- The Chair of Ophthalmology at the Royal Australian College of Ophthalmologists

You can help further the work of the Foundation by making a donation or leaving a legacy.
Every contribution is gratefully received. If you would like to help support the Foundation or require further information, please contact:

THE ULVERSCROFT FOUNDATION
The Green, Bradgate Road, Anstey
Leicester LE7 7FU, England
Tel: (0116) 236 4325

website: www.~~~~croft.com

F 202 04496 X 1234

Luiza Sauma was born in Rio de Janeiro and raised in London. After studying English at the University of Leeds, she worked at the *Independent on Sunday* for several years. She has an MA in Creative & Life Writing from Goldsmiths, University of London, where she was awarded the Pat Kavanagh Award in 2014. She has also been shortlisted for the Commonwealth Short Story Prize.

Visit her website at: www.luizasauma.com

Twitter @luizasauma

1

André,

A few weeks ago, I looked you up online for the first time. It was easy to find you. There are many André Cabrals in the world, but not in Londres. I saw a photo of you. You look the same — just old. I am old too, unfortunately. I found your work address and your email, but it didn't seem right, after so many years — email is too instant. So I'm writing you a letter.

Do you ever think of us? Probably not, but you should.

I know you've lived in Londres for many years and that you're a doctor. Of course you are. You have two daughters, don't you? That's what I heard from your father, before he died. Two inglesinhas — who could have imagined it? It must be cold over there.

I've never been to Europe. I've never even left Brazil, but that's OK — I never expected to. How could I complain? Look at where I'm living. It's beautiful and safe. Children grow up wild, like Indians. You can smell the jungle wherever you go. I'm not at home at the moment, though. I'm in Belém, visiting my daughter.

One day I will come and see Europe: Paris, Londres, Ireland, Germany. My daughter, Iracema, would love that. (She's training to be a doctor, too. Isn't that funny?) Those are the ones that appeal to me, the cold places, because I've never been cold. Let's see. Though the few gringos who come here tell me not to bother — they prefer Brazil. Our country seduces them, makes them crazy. They don't know what it's really like.

I will write to you again. I have a lot to tell you. I will make you wait, just as you made us wait.

Luana

That was the first letter. I didn't tell anyone about it. Not even my wife, Esther. The paper smelled woody, humid, faintly tropical. The past has a certain scent, don't you think? To me, it smells like Brazil. I held the letter to my face, inhaled and felt the years dissolve. I could be seventeen again, just a boy. I hadn't seen Luana in almost thirty years. There was no return address.

2

I read the letter at work, between patients, read it again several times and stuffed it into the pocket of my blazer. It stayed there for a few weeks. Sometimes I would reach for it in my pocket, touch its edges and feel my skin go numb. I wanted to look her up on the internet, but I couldn't remember her surname — or did I ever know it? Papai would have known, but he was long gone. To me she was just Luana. Luana Costa? Luana Santos? I tried some common surnames. Dozens of other Luanas stared back at me from my screen, posing in mirrors, pouting, younger than Luana would be now, older than she was back then.

If Mamãe hadn't died, none of this would have happened. I would still be in Rio de Janeiro, married to a Brazilian woman from a good family, living in our old flat, overlooking the beach. My wife and I would raise our children the way we had been raised — by benevolent black women who slept in a small bedroom behind the kitchen. Dinner parties in Ipanema, Leblon and Copacabana, week-ends in Teresópolis and Búzios, and holidays in Europe, where we would dream of living.

Instead, I'm living alone in a one-bedroom flat on Albion Road in Stoke Newington, London. Esther still lives at our house on Winston Road, two minutes' walk away

— the house we bought after we got married twenty years ago, when it was still relatively cheap around here. Her family is nothing like mine — English and Jewish, or Jew-ish, as she used to say. We have two daughters, Beatriz and Hannah. Beatriz is named after Mamãe. I call her Bia; everyone else in England calls her Bee. She wouldn't exist if Mamãe hadn't died. Every day I walk to the practice, I walk home, I eat alone. My life is small and compact. My bedroom faces the road and I hear cars in my sleep. You wouldn't believe the rent I'm paying for this shithole. Being a GP — tending to all those mad people and their non-illnesses — keeps me occupied for around forty-five hours a week, but what about the other hundred and twenty-three?

Mamãe died in a car accident in January 1985, on the street where I grew up. Everything was subsequent to that. The dictatorship ended that year, but I don't remember how I felt about it. Mamãe was dead. What more was there to feel? Papai went back to his surgery. My brother, Thiago, and I went back to school. People remarked on how well we were coping. But we weren't. Her absence was quiet and constant, like mild tinnitus. Our flat felt empty, even with five of us living there. Sometimes I thought I could hear her calling our maids — 'Rita! Luana!'

— her voice bright and rasping, or I'd see a flash of pink and orange in the corner of my eye. She loved bright colours. She was always smiling. At night I could hear Thiago, who was six years old, crying in his bedroom, being sung to sleep by Rita. Crying was for women and children, so I didn't cry. In my eyes, I wasn't a child. I was a man without a mother. My seventeenth birthday came and went.

The last time I went to Brazil was for Papai's funeral — he had a heart attack on my fortieth birthday. We cancelled the party and flew to Rio, the whole family. It did make me wonder: did he do it on purpose, to get my attention? I hadn't been back for a while. That was six years ago. London is my home now. It's been my home for a long time. I'm a British citizen — have been for years. It didn't occur to me, when I left Brazil, that I would miss the place. I was only eighteen; what did I know? I wanted to get away from all the stupid things I'd done, and the people who knew about them. Now I find myself thinking, several times a day, about the green wildness of the trees on any street in Ipanema. Thin vines snaking around telephone lines. The sting of the Atlantic in my eyes. The people, their breezy manners.

In my dreams, everything about Brazil is

exaggerated. The leaves are so green and the sea so blue. In one dream, it was raining and the sky was a stark grey. I was on Ipanema beach in my swimming shorts, feeling the downpour. All I knew was that I had to swim to the Cagarras, the uninhabited archipelago that you can see from the shore. I waded into the water and swam towards the islands, my eyes open in the saltwater. I climbed on to land, lay down on the rocks and felt the sun sizzle my skin, like bacon in a pan.

The Cagarras dream isn't the important one. I've only had it twice. The important one is about our maid Luana, Rita's daughter. Even before she started writing to me, I had been dreaming about her at least once a week. It was maddening. It goes like this: we're swimming in the river, in the Amazon, trying to get to the other side. An impossible task, because the river is too wide. I'm seventeen years old again. My arms are slim, my chest hairless, my stomach flat. My young body is miraculous to me. Luana is swimming ahead, and I can't keep up. I can see her black hair bobbing ahead in the distance. I sink to the riverbed and cool water enters my lungs.

I first had that dream a year and a half ago, last July, after my forty-fifth birthday party. I didn't want to celebrate my birthday, but

Esther insisted. We were still together then. She was always good at parties, just like Mamãe. She organized the guest list, the Brazilian catering — salgadinhos, churrasco, caipirinhas — and booked the band, who played Brazilian songs in our living room. The musicians arrived an hour before the guests: two men and a woman, carrying instruments and amplifiers. Esther was upstairs getting ready, so I welcomed them into the house and performed the ritual of being Brazilian among other Brazilians — I was out of practice, it took some effort — laughing and joking, complaining about the weather, talking about where we were from. They were impressed that I'd been here for so long, that I was a British citizen. I told them that when I arrived, in the eighties, I rarely saw other Brazilians in the street — not even tourists.

'And now we're taking over Londres!' said the woman.

Carolina, that was her name. I looked at her, she smiled, and it hit me: she looked so much like Luana. Carolina had brown eyes, not green, and she wore her hair in long braids, not in a bun; her skin was darker, perhaps, and her lips didn't have that deep curve, but when she smiled, meu Deus! She was talking about where she was from (Recife) and where she lived (Walthamstow)

7

and I carried on nodding, responding, performing, but my body felt weak, my hearing muffled.

Luana. Our empregada, our maid. I hadn't thought of her in years. OK, that's not true. Of course I thought of her — how could I not? — but only briefly. Her face was just one of the hundreds that flipped through my mind on any given day: ex-girlfriends, dead relatives, long-lost friends, patients and colleagues — but I tried not to linger on my memories of Luana, of what happened between us. When I met Esther, I locked those memories away at the back of my mind.

'Where should we set up?' said one of the male musicians, interrupting my thoughts.

That night, Esther wore a shimmering navy dress, her curly dark hair was pinned up, her body slim and graceful; she walked, in heels, from group to group, making sure that everyone was having a good time. A few hours in, when everyone had been fed and greeted, I was nicely drunk. I spent much of the night in the kitchen, away from the band, from Luana's double, but I could still hear her sweet voice, singing old Tom Jobim songs. Esther's friend Nina dragged me back to the living room, shouting, 'Stop hiding, André!' I gave a speech in which I declared my love for Esther and thanked her for throwing the party, and then retired to the end of the garden to smoke a cigarette.

'Where have you been?' said Esther when I returned holding an empty glass.

'Just getting some air.'

I took a bottle of Prosecco from the table and refilled my glass. She sniffed.

'Have you been smoking?'

'I've only had one.'

'But you told me you were giving up.'

Next to us, on the makeshift dancefloor, our daughters were dancing and singing along to the band's rendition of 'A Minha Menina' by Os Mutantes. Carolina was playing an egg shaker and singing backing vocals, but I kept my eyes on the girls. They didn't speak Portuguese but knew the words to a few songs — I raised them on Mamãe's old records. Hannah was fifteen and Beatriz almost eighteen, not a child any more. Beatriz resembled my mother, her namesake, with her mercurial smile and long, thin limbs. Hannah wore thick glasses, like I did at her age, but the rest of her was pure Feldman, from her pale skin to her curious, headstrong nature.

'Look, Esther,' I said. 'Look at them.'

Hannah pushed her glasses up her nose and waved at us. Esther laughed, her face radiant. I put my arm around her and she turned to kiss me. Everything would be fine. The night would end, the singer would go home and Luana would return to the depths of my mind, a small bedroom behind the kitchen.

But I woke from that dream the next morning covered in sweat, my mouth dry, Luana's face imprinted in my mind. Her face, not Carolina's. We had been swimming in the Amazon, just like when we were teenagers. Esther had her back towards me, wearing a white vest, her skin tender and pale. I stroked her arm and she murmured.

'Good morning, querida,' I said.

She turned to face me, her eyes still closed and smudged with makeup, a small smile on her lips. Her dark curls were loose, spread across the pillow. Yes, life was better then.

'How's your head?' I said.

'Not bad. And yours?'

Luana was from a different time and place, so far from London in 2013. More suited to dreams.

'Strangely enough, I feel fine,' I said. 'Maybe I won't when I get up.'

'Urgh, do we have to get up?'

We had stayed up till 2 a.m., long after the band had left and the girls had gone to bed. A few friends had lingered (let's be honest, they were more Esther's friends than mine) to drink whisky, smoke cigarettes and even, at one point, a joint. What had we talked about, for all those hours? I wasn't sure, but I remember a lot of laughter. I had played along, despite feeling like I was elsewhere, watching the scene, from another room, another continent.

'You look beautiful,' I whispered, trying to lock the memories back in their vault.

But they kept coming. I remembered another birthday: my eighteenth, in Rio; the party I threw, with Rita and Luana's help, at our flat.

'Hmm, I bet I don't,' said Esther, her eyes open a slit.

Luana in the river. Luana serving our meals, day after day. Luana after my party. Luana laughing like a child. She was a child and so was I.

Esther put an arm around my body and her lips to mine. Her eyes were now open.

'Come on,' she said, 'before the kids wake up.'

I put my hand under her vest. We made love quickly — we knew exactly what the other wanted — but every few seconds, my mind wandered. To that birthday party, twenty-seven years before. Esther arched her back, her legs locked behind me. Finally, I returned, for a minute or two, and belonged solely to the present.

But it didn't last. She left me earlier this year, in June. It's now December.

2

Winter in Rio de Janeiro barely exists, but there is some respite in July, when the humidity gives way to a distant coolness. Twenty-two degrees Celsius: that was our respite. In July 1985, our grief, like the temperature, also seemed to break. It had been six months since Mamãe's accident. We started talking more during meals. Papai asked ordinary questions, like 'How was school?', and told us stories about his work: plain girls made beautiful, a cardiac arrest on the operating table, a nipple lost during a breast reduction and found in the bin — that one made us laugh. Thiago stopped crying every night, his tears replaced by dull acceptance. Papai began talking about the Amazon again.

He had always wanted to take us to the city of Belém, where he was born and raised. A return to our roots, to the Amazon, to the state of Pará — that's how he sold it to us. During my childhood, he had visited the city two or three times, always alone. A family trip would never have been possible while Mamãe was alive; just the word 'Pará' was enough to make her wrinkle her nose in distaste. Papai's parents were dead and he was an only child — what was his obsession with the place?

'It's all organized,' he told us in August, over Sunday lunch. 'I'm taking a month off work and we're spending Christmas in Pará.'

He spooned some feijoada into his mouth and looked up at us, smiling, waiting for a reaction. The steam from the food clouded his glasses.

'Pará?' said Thiago. 'What's that?'

'It's where I'm from, which means you're from there, too.'

'What about Vovô and Vovó?' I said.

We usually spent Christmas with Mamãe's parents in their country house in Teresópolis, an hour or two from the city. Even in summer, it was cool and quiet there — the opposite of Rio. Papai would come for a day or two, before returning to work.

'Teresópolis? We're talking about the Amazon, not some hill town.'

'What will we do there?' I asked.

'See relatives,' he said, with a slight grimace — my father was antisocial, like me. 'Walk around the city, eat good food, swim in the river. There's an island, Marajó, in the river — we could go there. I haven't been since I was a boy. It'll be an adventure.'

'I want to stay with Vovô and Vovó,' said Thiago.

'I've already told them about it,' said Papai, 'I've bought the plane tickets.'

'What does Vovó think?' I said.

My grandmother was recovering from a facelift. Grief had aged her. Papai had performed the surgery himself. The previous weekend, when we had visited her, Vovó had been jubilant — probably drugged — and grotesquely swollen. I understood then why Papai always told Mamãe that she shouldn't get anything done herself — not until she was old, and needed it.

'She thought it was a good idea for us to spend some time together,' said Papai. 'Just the three of us, the Cabral men.'

I wondered what she really thought. This would be her first Christmas without her youngest child, my mother. Surely she wanted to keep the family together?

'Luana's coming, too,' said Papai.

'Great,' said Thiago, 'then I'll come.'

'André?'

'Sure, it'll be fun,' I said, trying my best to please him.

★ ★ ★

I was dreading it. I wasn't used to spending time with Papai. Before Mamãe died, he was never around — always at the surgery, hammering noses into shape, stuffing breasts with silicone and tightening faces. When I remember Mamãe, though, I always think of her at home: talking to the maids, eating lunch with us, her jewellery jangling as she ate. Swishing her long, black hair over our shoulders as she kissed us, chatting about parties, people and her shop, where she sold north-eastern folk art to tourists. But this was our new life — might as well get used to it. At least Luana was coming. By December, the hell of summer was back and, with it, the long school holidays. Papai shut the surgery and we caught a plane north. There were four of us: me, Papai, Thiago and Luana. Rita stayed at home to look after Fifi, our cat. Really, she had been Mamãe's pet. Her real name was Filha, which means 'daughter', but only Mamãe called her that. Since the accident, Fifi had lost her mind. Gone on hunger strike and punched out razored paws when we tried to stroke her.

Belém is the Portuguese word for 'Bethlehem', but those long-dead explorers from the old world must have named it when it was abundant, full of hope. In 1985 it was a city of broken pavements, colonial buildings gone green and mossy, torrential rain and burning sun. The people were shorter and darker than in Rio, with small eyes, like me and Papai.

16

(Thiago was more like Mamãe: spindly and white.) It took only seconds to sweat through a fresh set of clothes. We stayed at a cracked, pale yellow colonial house with tall, shuttered windows near the Pará River — the southern part of the Amazon, where it meets the Atlantic. The house belonged to one of Papai's cousins, Eduardo, who had moved to Miami. It was half empty, ready to be sold, and the air conditioning was broken.

'Meu Deus,' said Papai over breakfast on our first morning in Belém. He took a bite out of a bread roll as sweat trickled down the sides of his face. 'I just had a shower, and look at me. André, where's your brother?'

'Still in bed.'

The sun flickered through the closed shutters. I could barely see the food on my plate. My glasses were slipping down my sweaty nose. Papai's were slipping, too.

'Can't we turn the lights on?' I said.

'No. It's too hot for lights!'

Luana came in, holding a plate of sliced fruit. Her curly hair was scraped into a bun and she was dressed casually, in knee-length shorts and a T-shirt. Not like Rita, who always wore a starched white uniform. Even in the gloom, I could see a light sweat on Luana's forehead. I had started to notice her, after many years of not noticing. The new curve of

17

her waist, her green eyes, her doce de leite skin — suddenly, there was a beautiful girl living with us, as though Rita's skinny, quiet child had been replaced. Between infancy and adolescence, we had sometimes played together, like friends. I still have a photograph of Rita holding us on our balcony in Rio, one toddler on each knee, with Fifi — a kitten, then — on the floor. On the back, in my mother's curled handwriting: *André, Luana, Rita e Filha, abril 1971.* Since then, a distance had grown between us. A silent acknowledgement that we were not the same. She had left school to work for us full-time, even though she was a good student.

'What do you think, Luana?' I said. 'Is it too hot to turn the lights on?'

She put the plate down in the middle of the table, smiled in that mysterious, closed-mouth way she'd recently taken to, and said, 'Whatever Doutor Matheus prefers.'

Papai gave me a smug look and mopped the sweat from his forehead with a napkin. She walked out of the dining room, back to the kitchen.

My relationship with Rita was less complicated: I loved her completely. She was dark and stocky, strong as a tree, with a north-eastern accent that had faded over the years. Embarrassingly, I can't remember which state she was from, because she never talked about it. Rita smiled rarely, but her face, in repose, had more kindness and warmth in it than any other I've encountered. She had wiped my bum, bathed me and made my meals seven days a week, with two Sundays off per month. She was my black mother, my babá. If anything, I was jealous of Luana because Rita would always be her mother, not mine.

But back to Belém, and the hot house.

'Why didn't we stay in a hotel?' I said to Papai.

'Stop this nonsense. Trying to make me feel bad.' He stood up and shook his shirt to let the air in. 'I'm going to walk around the bairro. Do you want to come?' I shook my head. 'What are you going to do, then?'

'Start studying for the Vestibular,' I lied.

Those were the university entrance exams, which I would take in a year's time. I was planning to go to medical school in Rio. Papai had decided I was going to be a doctor before I was even born. His father was a doctor, one of his grandfathers was a doctor (the other inherited a sugar-cane fortune), and so was one of his great-grandfathers, who was born in Beirut and qualified in Belém.

'Good idea,' he said. 'Want to watch the football later?'

'Who's playing?'

'Who's playing?' he said, in mock-exasperation. 'Jesus Cristo! Are you another man's son?'

★ ★ ★

It was too hot to go outside and explore Belém. I spent the day fanning myself in the house, sticking to furniture and opening windows to let the thick air inside, which made things worse. I read the first few pages of Jorge Amado's *Gabriela, Craw e Canela*, which I found on a shelf, but every time I focused on the print, my head throbbed and my eyes shut. I gave up and lay with Thiago on the sofa, in a stupor, watching TV. An old episode of *Tom and Jerry* was on. Tom was cleaning his house with a mop and bucket, while Jerry was doing everything to disrupt him: emptying ashtrays on to the floor, juggling eggs and throwing pies around.

'Isn't it funny, how you never see the humans?' I said.

'You see the legs of Tom's owner sometimes,' said Thiago.

'She's not his owner. She's the empregada.'

'How do you know?'

'She's black,' I said.

We watched the rest in silence. By the time

the maid came home, Jerry had filled the house, floor to ceiling, with coal. But the maid blamed Tom, and pelted him with it.

Thiago said, 'So, Rita and Luana, they don't live with us because they want to?'

'Well, they want to, but we pay them. Who wants to cook and clean for free?'

'I thought they just liked us.'

'They do like us.'

Luana came into the room, but she didn't seem to have heard us. She was working hard, despite the heat. I suppose she didn't have a choice. She mopped around Thiago and me as we lay on the sofa, as still as sloths. A few months before, she had been at school. Now, she was just an empregada.

'Come on, Lua, watch TV with us,' said Thiago.

He was the only one who called her Lua. Actually, so did Rita, when they were alone — I remember hearing it. I longed to use this nickname, but it was Thiago's thing, not mine. It means 'moon'.

She looked up from her mop.

'I'm working. Maybe later.'

'Later we have to go to meet our family,' said Thiago.

'That'll be nice,' she said.

It started to rain outside, hammering down like nails.

'No, I just want to watch TV.'

'You need to get out,' she said, suddenly sounding like her mother, like an adult. 'Get some fresh air. Both of you.'

'Look at the rain,' I said. 'And the air's not so fresh here. At least in Rio we have air conditioning.'

'You'll get used to it.'

I shifted my position a bit on the sofa, and felt my sweat pour. Better to do nothing. Better to remain still.

3

In Belém, it barely cooled down at night.
Papai looked us up and down, in our shorts
and T-shirts, and threatened to make us
smarten up. He was wearing beige linen
trousers and a white shirt, already sweating.

'OK. If my family thinks you look like
favelados, that's just fine.'

We were going to have dinner at his cousin
Camila's house. Papai hadn't seen her in
eight years. He seemed nervous. Not just
sweaty, but twitchy. Parties were Mamãe's
thing — not his. Outside, it had stopped
raining, but water still streamed into the
gutters. We got into Eduardo's car, which he
had left behind: me in the passenger seat and
my brother in the back.

'Turn on the air conditioning, André,'
whispered Thiago, leaning forward.

I looked at Papai and he said, 'Fine.'

When the cold air started blowing, all of us
sighed with pleasure, even Papai.

'When will we get there?' said Thiago.

'It will take a little while. They moved out
of the city a few years ago.'

Driving through Belém, I realized how little

of Brazil I actually knew — the state of Rio de Janeiro, and nowhere else. Yet I had been to Disney World in Florida, to New York, and on a tedious cultural tour of Europe that started in Rome and ended in London. (The city gave no indication that it would one day be my home — I would've paid more attention if it had.) But there I was in Belém, in the Amazon, for the first time in my life. Papai's city, before he moved to Rio for all the usual reasons: boredom, hubris, reinvention.

The roads were lined with people selling coconuts, popcorn or sweets, or just lying about on the pavement, begging for change. Papai pointed out landmarks, like the Ver-o-Peso market and the grand, pink Theatro da Paz. What kind of plays did they put on? The people in the streets didn't look like theatregoers. A few miles outside the city, we entered a gated community, after Papai gave his name to a guard with a gun strapped to his hip. It looked like a holiday resort: neat lawns, the gentle hills of a golf course, horses neighing in the dark. I looked at Papai to see what he thought of this strange place, but he said nothing. I couldn't see his expression. After a minute or two, he stuck his head out of the window and called out to another guard, who was standing by the side of the road under a streetlight.

'Hey,' said Papai, 'where's number twenty-one?'

'Just carry on, senhor. It's right at the end. The big, white house.'

He had a languid, friendly accent, not unlike my father's, but stronger.

We found the house at the end of a drive: a modern, floodlit mansion that looked like the home of a movie star. The front lawn was pristine. Evenly spaced palm trees reached towards the black sky. We parked in the driveway among several other cars and walked to the front door. Insects were humming all around us. The door was opened by an empregada dressed in black and white, like a French maid, but she was quickly pushed aside by a skinny blonde in a pink dress and white diamonds. Her skin was leathery and burnished. She had a cigarette in one hand and a drink in the other.

'Matheus!' she screamed.

'Camila!' said Papai, trying to match her excitement.

Beyond the entrance, we could hear music and voices. We thought we had only come for dinner, but it sounded like a party.

'Matheus!' she said again. 'How many years?'

'Boys, this is my cousin Camila. We grew up on the same street in Belém.'

'So you must be André and Thiago?' she said, looking from one to the other, obviously unsure who was who. We stepped forward, smiles fixed, and kissed her on both cheeks.

'I'm André, and this is Thiago.'

'Of course — I know! Meu Deus, what beautiful boys.'

She held on to my brother and gave his cheeks a squeeze, her cigarette hanging out of the corner of her mouth. I imagined taking it and having a quick puff. The thought of it made me laugh out loud. Camila's smile froze, as though I were mocking her, but she didn't drop the happy-family act. She took Papai's arm and led him inside. Thiago was rubbing his cheeks. The empregada shut the door behind us, like a gentle gust of wind.

We hardly knew anyone who lived in an actual house. In Rio's wealthy beachside district, Zona Sul, most of the houses had been knocked down before I was born to make way for high-rise buildings. I'd never seen a house like Camila's. Everything looked shiny, white and new, apart from the various folksy paintings of fishermen and village women, framed in gold.

'What a nice house,' said Papai.

'So much better than the one in Belém, né?'

Papai nodded.

'Yes, there's a lot more room.'

'And there's so much outside space, horse riding for the girls, tennis, restaurants — you name it.'

'Do you ever leave the community?'

'Once in a while. And Carlos still goes to work in Belém. Poor thing.'

'Carlos is Camila's husband,' said Papai, in a low voice, to Thiago and me.

A few seconds later, the man himself showed up: a big guy in length and width, with white hair, a booming voice and a handshake that could dislocate a shoulder. Thiago and I hung back as the adults caught up. They put on their sad faces when they talked about Mamãe, whom they had never met. She didn't even *want* to meet them. Papai told them that we were coping well. Camila moved her sad face on to Thiago and me. I didn't know what to do.

'Poor little things,' she said, with tears in her eyes.

'Fucking truck drivers,' said Carlos. 'I always said cariocas couldn't drive for shit.'

'Carlos!' said Camila, tugging his arm.

'Well, it's true.'

'You've been to Rio?' I said.

Carlos shifted a little, from foot to foot.

'Only for very short trips,' said Camila. Her jaw spasmed. She turned her gaze to Papai. 'I

27

think you might have been away?'

'Probably,' said Papai, his eyes on an empregada, who was walking past with a tray of drinks. She noticed him, stopped, and he took a caipirinha. 'Thank you.'

That was the end of the conversation. Camila took Papai's arm once more and led him into the dining room.

We were introduced to Papai's cousins, second cousins, elderly great-aunts and great-uncles — who all looked happy to see us, and whose names I instantly forgot. There were over twenty people there, many more than Papai had expected. Thiago and I were seated at the kids' table with Camila and Carlos's daughters, Alice and Regina, who were both wearing blue velvet dresses, knee socks and shiny black shoes, like they were going to the ballet. They were eight and nine years old. I had very little to say to them. I ate in silence: Lebanese starters, followed by a creamy fish stew that didn't taste as good as Rita's. Thiago fared better. He told the girls about our cat, Fifi, who was once beautiful but was now as decrepit as those Portuguese houses in Belém.

'She's very old,' he said. 'Ancient, in fact. Thirty years old at least.'

'Wow,' said the girls in unison.

Fifi was fourteen.

'I *love* cats,' said Alice, the elder. 'We have a dog, but I want a cat, too. Papai says Pará isn't good for cats. He says it'll run off into the jungle and get eaten by a snake.'

'Or a monkey,' said Regina. 'I want a monkey.'

'You wanna meet our dog? He's a poodle.'

The three of them scurried to the kitchen to find the dog, and I hung back, wondering why, at seventeen, I still had to sit with the kids. There was no one my age there. The closest was a beautiful, olive-skinned pregnant woman in her twenties, who was married to one of Papai's cousins. As people stood up from their seats, she quizzed me briefly about my university plans, with a delirious, maternal smile on her face.

The adults moved to a separate living room. I went along with them and sat on the corner of a sofa, drinking my Coke, failing at small talk. Luckily, there were enough people there, and enough alcohol, for no one to notice. They listened to music from their youth — Caetano Veloso, Gal Costa, Chico Buarque and a bunch of northern stuff I'd never heard before — laughed loudly and drank copiously. They ranted about the new president, that filho da puta, who wasn't even properly elected. 'Democracia brasileira!' someone shouted, over and over again. The three maids refilled the guests' cups, their faces blank. Everyone complimented Camila on the food she hadn't cooked.

'She's been planning it for weeks,' said Carlos.

'It's very kind,' said Papai.

'Anything for my darling cousin,' said Camila.

Darling? She hadn't even called him when she'd visited Rio.

I went back to the dining room, in search of alcohol. The empregadas hadn't yet cleared the table. I spotted a glass of beer, half full and tempting.

'You want some?' said an empregada, standing behind me.

She was a middle-aged woman with a hard, dark face and the same soft, stretched accent as the guard.

'You're a big boy — surely you're allowed.'

'OK,' I said. 'Maybe just a glass.'

She went to the kitchen and came back a minute later with a fresh, frosted glass of beer.

'Here you go.'

'Thank you.'

I could hear the children giggling in the kitchen with the other maids, and the adults singing and laughing in the living room. What is it with adults? I thought. During the day they're so grumpy and rushed, and at night they become the happiest people on earth. My mother was like that, too, when she held her dinner parties. By 11 p.m. you'd think it was Christmas, not just another Friday night. Alcohol helped, but it was something else.

I wondered what Luana was doing, alone in the house in Belém. Probably watching TV, her bare, brown legs stretched out across the sofa. Enjoying a few hours of peace.

My arms and legs were feeling numb, so the beer was doing its job. I walked through the back doors into the garden and retreated to a dark corner. Sat down on the preened, spiky grass. Leaned my head back on the wooden fencing, listening to the loud, buzzing cicadas. Drained the beer and wanted another. Thought about Mamãe. If I closed my eyes, I could almost hear her among the guests. Her throaty cackle. Heh heh heh.

'What are you doing, André — hiding?' she'd say, as she walked into the garden, nicking her long, dark hair, lighting a secret cigarette. 'Don't tell your father that I'm smoking.'

'Can I have one, too?'

'Fine. Oh, I'm a terrible mother!'

She would smell of heavy, flowery French perfume. I hated that smell, but now I sniffed

31

the air, hopefully. At seventeen, you still believe in a sort of magic. But when I opened my eyes I could smell nothing more than grass and air, and hear a dozen unfamiliar laughs, echoing in the night.

4

After Camila's party, Papai's wrinkles seemed
to have deepened. Maybe he was remembering why he had left Belém. Or maybe he was
just sick of the heat. That's what he told us, a
few days later — that it was too hot to stay in
the city. He announced that we would spend
Christmas on Marajó island, at the mouth of
the Amazon River, where he had holidayed as
a child.

'My grandmother was from Marajó — did
you know that?'

'Yeah, Pai, you've only told us a hundred
times,' I said. 'Where are we staying?'

'It'll be a surprise.'

We set off for the dawn boat: Papai, Thiago,
Luana and me. It was cooler in the morning
but hot enough to make us sweat. The air felt
dense, pregnant, like it was about to rain. As
the sun rose, pale pink and smoky, we caught
a cab to the harbour. A long queue for tickets
had already formed, even though we were
early. Bedraggled men clucked up and down
the queue, selling manioc pancakes and cups
of coffee.

'Want some?' said Papai, looking giddy.

'What is it?' said Thiago.

Papai called one of the men over with a slight nod of the head. A skinny, short seller sidled over, carrying a plastic container of coffee and a bag of food. He looked smarter than the rest, in his loose white shirt and beige trousers. He poured coffee from the container's tap into a paper cup, which he handed over to Papai. Then he took a paper-wrapped pancake out of his bag and gave him that, too.

'My sons, they've never tasted northern food.'

'Yes, we have,' I said.

'Well, not this stuff.' He looked over at the man again, as he shuffled through his pocket for money. 'We live in Rio, you see.'

'But you have a northern accent,' said the man, smiling. Most of his teeth were missing.

'I was born here,' said Papai.

'I've never been to Rio. What's it like?'

'Beautiful,' said Luana, and the man nodded at her, as if seeing her for the first time.

She was standing behind us, her small suitcase at her feet.

'I'd like to go someday,' said the man.

Papai paid him, and he was gone, further down the queue.

'It's beautiful here, too,' said Papai, passing

34

the pancake to Thiago, who held it for a while, sniffing it. 'Eat it, menino!'

Thiago took a bite.

'It tastes like nothing.'

I grabbed it out of his hand and took a bite. He was right.

'Yeah,' I said. 'Like paper.'

I thought of offering some to Luana but then thought better of it. Sharing your food with an empregada was definitely weird. Papai ate the rest of the pancake and didn't offer us any coffee, but he was still in a good mood. After buying our tickets, we boarded the ferry as the sun moved over the river, making the brown water glimmer like gold. Our seats were on the top floor, shielded from the glare by a roof, but with large, open windows overlooking the river, which was bigger than I had imagined. I had thought, at the very least, that I would be able to see the other side, but it stretched out like a murky ocean. Thiago took one look at it, said, 'Huh,' and started reading one of his *Turma da Mônica* comics. The comics followed the adventures of a gang of children, led by a buck-toothed tomboy. Papai always thought he should be reading something fancy and foreign, like *Tintin* or *The Little Prince*.

Papai put his bag on his seat and stood gazing at the water. His olive skin was smooth, all tension released. Luana sat on a chair near the side of the ferry, sometimes turning towards the river. In the sun, her eyes were the colour of lime flesh: acid green. She glanced at me, and we both looked away. I went and stood next to my father.

'Isn't it beautiful?' he said.

'Yes.'

'It's been too long. This is my home, André. You don't know how it is, to be away from your home for so long.'

'Why don't you visit more often?'

He screwed his face up.

'It's so far away.'

'It's not that far.'

'Your mother never wanted to come.'

'That's what you always say.'

'I meant to come back, but then I met your mother,' he said. 'It's easy to leave a place when you're young. Coming back is harder. That's my advice: stay where you are.'

It started to rain, so we sat back down, moving away from the seats by the windows. The trip took three hours. It was sunny when we disembarked on the other side, and Papai looked as peaceful as the Dalai Lama. The scrappy harbour was crowded with people taking boxes and suitcases off the ferry, shouting, talking, hugging hello to friends and family. The air smelled of chicken shit, jungle and sweat. To my amazement, they had taxis, even though it looked like the kind of place you could only travel by donkey.

We sat in the cab in silence, apart from Papai, who was telling the driver about his connection with the island. Thiago, Luana and I sat in the back, staring out at the stretches of forest and marsh, herds of buffalo and clusters of two-room shacks. All their windows and doors were open. Through them, we saw people lying on sofas and beds, watching television or listening to the radio. Music everywhere. I heard little bits, as we passed, but I couldn't put them together to remember the song. The sun was now blazing high up in the sky and there was no air conditioning in the cab. The insides of the car were stuck together with tape. Everyone had a shiny face. If it was cooler in Marajó than in Belém, it was hard to notice the difference.

We pulled up outside a blue house. Compared to all the bungalows, it had an old Portuguese grandness: tall windows, fresh paint, a garden sprouting yellow and purple flowers, and a porch. We got out of the car and stood on the lawn while Papai paid the driver. I watched Luana as she looked up at the house. Her full top lip curved down in the centre, in a deep Cupid's bow. I imagined tracing it with my finger. Down and up.

The cab rattled away.

'Is this the hotel?' said Thiago. 'Does it have a pool?'

'This is your inheritance, filho,' said Papai.

We stared at him, not understanding.

'This was my grandmother's house. I haven't been here in decades.'

'It's just been sitting here?' I said.

'My cousin Eduardo uses it sometimes, but it's mine. Meu Deus, it looks just like I remember, only smaller.'

Inside, the house was cool, spacious and clean. There were colourful ceramics on every table and on the sideboard, paintings on the walls, neatly made beds. Looking back, I realize that someone — an empregada — had tidied up ahead of our visit. But I didn't notice such things then. Meals appeared, houses cleaned themselves, beds were made.

Luana helped us to carry our heavy bags to our rooms, and then she went to the small maid's room behind the kitchen.

5

Papai took us on a tour of Salvaterra, a village centred around a strip of shops and cafés. Luana stayed at the house, doing whatever she did there.

'It's changed,' said Papai, as we walked down the street. 'When I was a boy, there was almost nothing here. We brought everything we needed from the mainland.'

He walked with his hands on our shoulders. I couldn't remember him ever doing that before. It was disconcerting. He pointed out a tree he liked to climb, a house where a beautiful woman had lived — was she the skinny old lady sitting on the porch? — and the church he used to attend.

'When I still believed,' he said.

Then he took us to a beach. It was a five-minute walk from the high street, but the sun was fierce and bright so it felt ten times longer.

'Look, they've got the right idea,' said Papai, pointing at two chubby women walking down the road under brightly coloured umbrellas.

The beach was virtually empty: two sunbathers, a coconut seller, a few stray dogs and, at the far end, a herd of buffalo, standing by the river. Papai went over to the coconut man, said hello and held up three fingers. The man took three green coconuts out of his icebox, chopped their tops off and handed them over, with a straw in each. We sat on the sand and drank them quickly. Ice-cold heaven. That's something I miss — drinking straight out of a coconut.

'Want to go for a swim?' said Papai. 'You've never swum in the Amazon before — there's nothing like it.'

I shielded the sun from my eyes and looked ahead at the water, which was pale brown, with gentle waves.

'I can't see the other side,' said Thiago.

'I don't have my swimming shorts,' I said.

'Ah, come on!'

Papai undressed to his boxers, wiped sweat from his forehead and strode into the river.

'He's gone mad,' I said.

'Has he?' said Thiago. He was too young to notice anything.

'Want to go in?'

'But you said he was mad.'

'Come on, idiot.'

We quickly undressed. I threw my glasses on to the pile of clothes, and we ran into the water, splashing it high with our feet, laughing. Papai had swum further out, maybe twenty metres away from us, but we could see his face sticking out of the water, his black hair slicked down. We swam out to meet him. In my mouth, the river water tasted almost sweet.

'It's wonderful!' shouted Papai. 'I told you!'

★ ★ ★

It seems like paradise now, those first days in Marajó. I barely noticed it at the time. Young people don't know the importance of things when they're happening, but when those images still play in your mind long after your hair's gone grey and your belly slack, that's when you know. As I swam in the slow-moving river, which was so different from the salty violence of Ipanema, I felt happy for the first time since Mamãe's death. Maybe life with Papai would be all right, I thought. Different, but fine. My joy quickly became tinged with guilt.

Remembering Marajó, I feel like I'm flicking through a filing cabinet, reading files written in a language I once knew but am out of practice in. The language of being young, of knowing nothing. I'm setting these memories out as though they came to me so simply. This happened, then this and then this. But that's not how it is. That's not how it was.

* * *

I left Thiago treading water with Papai and swam off, dismissing shouts of 'Don't go too far!' with a thoughtless 'OK, Pai!' When they were just specks in the distance, I stopped swimming. I couldn't touch the riverbed with my feet. I flipped on to my back, held my arms and legs far apart and floated. So this is where Papai is from, I thought. Does that mean I'm from here, too? How far back do you have to go to find your origins? Back to the Portuguese, to the Lebanese, to my native ancestors, who must have floated like this, hundreds of years ago, in the same river?

The sun baked the front of my body until it was nearly dry, while my wet hands shrivelled. The waves were almost nonexistent. Just a slight rocking, back and forth. I put my head up and realized I had floated far away from the beach. Papai was standing on the sand, waving his hands in the air, while tiny Thiago hopped up and down. Even without my glasses, I could see that they were still just wearing their underpants.

* * *

As we walked to the house, the sun was coming down and insects were clucking and purring, welcoming the night. All the houses still had their doors and windows flung open, their radios tuned in to the same station, playing songs I didn't know. In Rio I was always careful not to open my bedroom window at night, because that's when the mosquitoes get in. Maybe people here are immune to them, I thought. Then we passed a house that was listening to something else: a familiar swell of strings and horns. We stopped walking. Chico Buarque sang into the darkness about wanting to be a tattoo on the body of his lover — a desperate kind of love. It was strange to think his music existed there, in the middle of nowhere.

'Your mother's favourite song,' said Papai.

'I know,' I said.

She sang 'Tatuagem' often; sometimes whistled it. Its melancholy tune could be heard, distantly, all over our flat in Ipanema. From her bathroom, reverberating over the pounding water. From her bedroom, as she did her makeup. From the balcony, as she looked at Ipanema beach, at the islands. I remembered seeing her and Papai one Christmas Eve, dancing to it. She sang the words into his mouth. She knew them all, back to front. Papai merely smiled back, with a boozy look in his eyes. I must have been ten years old, sitting on the sofa. We had Christmas at home, that year, because Thiago was just a baby — he was asleep in their bedroom. It had taken them ten years to conceive again. The end of a happy year.

It was late. We'd had dinner and opened our presents at midnight. Our relatives — Aunt Lia, Vovô, Vovó and mad Uncle Gustavo, whose intense eyes made me feel uneasy — had gone home. Luana and Rita were still there. They had spent the morning with relatives in Vidigal, the favela, before returning to make our food. Mamãe paid them extra to work on Christmas Eve. They were standing in the doorway that led from the living room to the kitchen. Luana was smiling and had her arms around her mother.

Standing on the street in Marajó, I wondered what became of Luana's father. She was so much paler than Rita. He must have been white, or almost white. I once asked Mamãe, but she said he was long gone and that I should mind my own business. Don't go upsetting the empregadas. Having a father doesn't matter, she said, not to people like them.

The song drew to a close. We had stood there, on the dirt road, listening to the whole thing.

'Come on, boys, it's nearly time for dinner,' said Papai.

He walked too quickly for Thiago to keep up. I dropped back and strolled with my brother.

'What was that song?' said Thiago.

'Mamãe liked it a lot.'

We walked on a bit more, until the blue house appeared. In comparison to the surrounding shacks, it was as grand as the Copacabana Palace. Papai was already inside.

'I miss Mamãe,' said Thiago.

'I miss her, too.'

He stopped walking.

'André,' he said, 'sometimes I can't remember her face.'

'What do you mean?'

'When I'm lying in bed, I think of her face and I can't get it right. It doesn't look like her.'

'I know what you mean,' I said.

Though I didn't — I was a decade older and my memories were stronger. Even now, I can see my mother and hear her loud voice, her heels clicking on the floor. She's like a pop song, the melody and lyrics imprinted in my mind.

'Just look at the photos, and you'll remember.'

He nodded, his eyes downcast. I put an arm around his shoulders and ruffled his hair.

I didn't know what else to say.

Inside, our father had turned on the radio, which was still playing northern music. He was sitting on the sofa in the living room, flicking through a book. I could smell dinner cooking.

'You boys walk so slowly,' he said, looking up. 'You fit right in.'

It was true. Everything was slower in Pará. People walked slowly, talked slowly, packed bags in the supermarket slowly. Even time passed slowly. In London, I learned to walk fast, focused and blinkered like a racehorse. But in Pará, that three-minute Chico Buarque song seemed to last an hour. By the time it ended, the island was black with night.

Luana was in the kitchen, tending to a few pots on the stove, one hand resting on a hip, the other holding up a wooden spoon to her mouth to taste. I stood behind her for a few seconds without her noticing. She took her right foot out of her flip-flop and bent it behind her other leg, so that I could see its pale sole. The air was steamy with the comforting smell of a fish stew: coconut milk, peppers and lime.

I said, 'Oi, Luana,' and she immediately put her foot back into her flip-flop.

'Hi, André.' She turned her head. 'How was the beach?'

'It was great. You should go sometime.'

'Maybe.'

'You can come with me.'

She turned again and looked at me, but didn't say anything, then she rinsed the wooden spoon under the tap. The water fell heavily into the metal sink, loud and echoing.

'It smells good.'

'It's the first time I've made a moqueca without my mother.'

'I'm sure it's great.'

We stood there a while. I was thinking of something to say. Her lovely brown face, with those green eyes, showed nothing. No emotion. Her lips were closed. What would it be like to kiss them?

'Is there anything else I can get you? A snack, a drink? Dinner will be a while.'

Usually, it was Rita who made my snacks. I couldn't treat Luana like that.

'No, there's nothing I want. Thank you.'

When I closed the kitchen door behind me, I felt weak. My heart was beating in my throat. I hit myself in the chest and tried to pull myself together. In love with an empregada? I had lost my mind. I hadn't been interested in girls since Mamãe's death. I'd barely even masturbated, because it made me feel so guilty, like her ghost was watching me. I was practically a virgin, if you didn't count the fumbling fuck I'd had on the beach when I was fifteen, with a friend of a friend. But with Luana? No. That couldn't happen.

I went to the TV room, where Thiago was flicking between channels. I flipped on the ceiling fan, and it whirred above us.

'Well, that makes no difference.' I popped my head out of the door. 'Pai!'

No answer. I could hear him whispering with Luana in the kitchen.

'Paaaai!'

'What, what?' he said.

'Does this place not have air conditioning?'

'Of course it doesn't.'

'Why 'of course'?'

'Stop being so bourgeois. Wear fewer clothes.'

I was just wearing shorts, but he couldn't see me.

'Yeah, André, go naked,' said Thiago, giggling.

'Shut up.'

'With your willy dangling out!'

I jumped on him on the sofa, pinned him down and tickled him. He laughed gleefully, showing the little gaps in his milk teeth.

'Stop, stop!'

'Only if you admit that you're an idiot.'

'I'm an idiot, I'm an idiot!'

I stopped tickling him.

'You give up too easily.'

He looked rumpled. Sweat had dampened his wavy black hair. I was getting a bit old to be teasing my brother. I sat next to him and pulled my feet up on the sofa. Luana came in, still wearing her apron, and stood by the door. Sweat trickled down my face, making my glasses slip. She smelled like moqueca, which made my stomach rumble loudly.

'Are you hungry, André?' she said, laughing.

'Yes, it smells so good.' I'd already said that before. Say something else. 'Do you want to sit on the sofa? You'll get a better view.'

'Uh, no thank you, I'll get a stool.'

'Come on, it's more comfortable.'

'OK.'

We moved up, and Luana sat on the end of the sofa. I could feel Thiago's hot breath on my left arm and her denim shorts touching my right leg. I had never sat on the same sofa as her. I could feel the heat of her body, through her shorts. I hoped she couldn't smell my sweat.

Everyone stopped talking and looked straight ahead as the opening credits to the six o'clock novela, *De Quina Pra Lua*, began, soundtracked by a jaunty samba. In the credits, a shadowy male figure runs after a flying piece of paper: he rips a towel from a woman's body, ends up in prison and then flies to heaven. The show followed the story of Zezão, who dies after winning the lottery and is buried with his ticket, prompting his family to go on a madcap search for it. Sometimes, he appears as a ghost to give them clues.

It was the first time I had sat next to Luana and heard her laugh up close. In Rio she watched TV quietly, sitting by the door. But now she laughed quickly and loudly, like a machine gun.

'You laugh like a donkey!' said Thiago.

'Thi, don't be rude.'

She covered her face, still laughing, but embarrassed. I could have kissed her then. All of us were giggling. It was contagious. We laughed so hard that we missed most of the programme. Once we had calmed down, Thiago made us promise that we wouldn't ruin the next novela. The seven o'clock show, *Ti Ti Ti*, was about a rivalry between two former best friends in the São Paulo fashion world.

'I don't like this one as much,' said Thiago.

'Me neither,' said Luana.

'São Paulo's stupid,' I said, though I had never been there. My contempt for São Paulo had been passed down through generations, like an heirloom.

'It's the pit of the earth,' said Papai.

We all looked over at the doorway, where he was standing, wearing a grey T-shirt and jeans, leaning against the frame like a nerdy Marlon Brando. Luana immediately stood up, but he waved her away, tutting under his breath.

'Sit, sit,' he said. 'On the sofa.'

She sat back down.

'What's wrong with São Paulo?' said Thiago.

'It's ugly, dangerous and everyone is obsessed with money.'

'Don't we care about money?' I said.

'We care more about dinner. Luana, do you know . . . ?'

'Sim, doutor. It's nearly ready.'

She went to the kitchen, looking grateful to be leaving the room. She behaved differently towards Papai. He was her boss, and we were not.

'What is this shit?' he said, gesturing at the TV.

'*Ti Ti Ti*,' said Thiago. 'It's very bad.'

'We're going to eat now, so turn it off and wash your hands.'

'But *Roque Santeiro* is on next!'

That was the eight o'clock novela, about a saint who returns to his town to save it from money-grabbing landowners and politicians.

It was a popular show, partly because it had been delayed for ten years by the dictatorship.

'André, don't you have better things to do than watch this?' said Papai. 'Like thinking about the Vestibular?'

'Pai, we're on holiday. The exams are a year away.'

'You're not going to get into university with that attitude.'

He walked over to the mostly empty bookshelf, pulled out a heavy, dog-eared book and wiped the dust off it.

'*Anatomia Humana*,' he said, reading the cover.

He threw the book on to the sofa, where it landed with a thud between me and Thiago, who picked it up and started leafing through it.

'Your brother is more interested than you,' said Papai.

I wanted to throw the book at his head. Wipe that smirk off his face. For years he had been the invisible man, never asking how school was going, but now he was suddenly interested?

'It's ready,' said Luana, appearing by Papai's shoulder. 'Come and eat.'

At least I could delay reading the textbook for half an hour. Thiago had lost interest in it and was looking at the television, his eyes round and still. *Roque Santeiro* had started: the evil landowner and the mayor were cackling over their plans.

'You're too young for this, Thiago,' said Papai. He walked over to the TV and switched it off. 'Stick to cartoons.'

In the dining room, the mahogany table had been set with plates and cutlery, and bowls of rice and moqueca. We helped ourselves to the food.

'It looks fantastic, Luana,' said Papai, but she was no longer in the room.

'Thank you, doutor!' she called from the kitchen. 'I hope it tastes good, too.'

She must have already prepared her own plate, and been eating it at the kitchen table.

★ ★ ★

As I ate Luana's first moqueca, I remembered an incident a few weeks earlier, in Rio. I was struggling with my maths homework on the dining table, when I decided to take a break and get a drink. When I returned, with a glass of cold, sweet mate tea, Luana was looking at my maths exercise book. She saw me and jumped back.

'Sorry,' she said.

'How's my homework looking?'

'Well . . . '

'Go on.'

No way can this girl know something I don't.

She poked a thin brown finger at the book.

'That one's wrong,' she said, pointing at a sum. Something to do with quadratic equations. I don't remember exactly, but I remember her smile, which was two thirds shy, one third cocky.

'No, it's not,' I said, taking a sip of mate.

'Sorry, I shouldn't have been looking.'

She walked to the kitchen and turned on the taps. Washing the dishes, or whatever she did in there. I reworked the equation. How embarrassing — she was right.

Eating Luana's moqueca in the blue house, remembering that conversation, I felt ashamed.

6

I met Esther in December, twenty-one years ago, at the Fitzroy Tavern on Charlotte Street. The pub was covered in tinsel and fairy lights, packed with drunk students, the windows steamed up. Everyone was shouting, giddy with freedom, no more classes till the new year. I was with my friends from UCL, who were all foreign students, or the offspring of foreigners. I had lived in London for five years and knew, by then, that most of the natives kept to themselves. They were at home, after all. Some of them had been at home for hundreds of years.

I saw her a few metres away, sitting on a sofa: a girl with dark, shoulder-length curls, throwing her head back as she laughed. She had large brown eyes and a small mouth, painted red. A glass of red wine in one hand and a cigarette in the other. Silver tinsel around her wrist. My friend Matt noticed that I was looking at her.

'That's Esther,' he said.

'You know her?'

'Yeah, a bit.'

Matt was from Massachusetts and studied

economics. His mother was Chinese, his father was English and he had spent two years at an English boarding school, but he was American to the core: cocky and charming, everyone loved him. He now lives in New York. We never see each other.

'You like her?' he said.

'I don't know her.'

'She's a medic, too — you should meet her. Hey, Esther!' he shouted across the room. She looked up and waved.

'Come 'ere.'

She walked over, still smiling, but looking slightly uneasy. Maybe she fancies him, I thought. Of course she does. She was wearing a red tartan dress with knee-high black boots.

'Hi, Matt,' she said. 'How are you?'

'Happy Hanukkah,' he said.

'Thanks,' she said, laughing. 'L'chaim!'

They clinked glasses and drank.

'This is my friend André — he's from Brazil.'

She looked over and held out a hand.

'I'm Esther.'

We shook hands.

'Are you on holiday in London?' she said.

When I look back, there's a shimmering aura around her, like the room was blurred, with only Esther in focus. I was bowled over by her open, beautiful face and the jumpy way she moved.

'No, I'm studying medicine at UCL,' I said.

'Oh, me, too! What year are you in?'

'Final year.'

'Me, too! Do you know what you want to specialize in?'

'Maybe psychiatry,' I said. 'Or tropical medicine.' I didn't have a clue, but I thought that sounded impressive. 'How about you?'

'Actually, let's not talk about work, otherwise we'll never stop,' she said, bringing a palm up to her reddened cheek. 'Sorry, I know I started it.'

At some point, Matt moved away. I didn't notice — he just wasn't there any more. I bought another round of drinks: red wine for Esther and a pint of lager for me, plus a packet of salt-and-vinegar crisps. I was well versed in English customs and I enjoyed them.

'Is it summer in Rio?' she said.

'Yes. It's probably thirty-something degrees today.'

'Christmas on the beach — why would you leave that behind?'

'It's a long story.'

'I like long stories.'

'It's not the kind of story you tell someone

the first time you meet.'

'Another time, then.'

'OK.' I grabbed at a safe question, one that English people love asking: 'So what are you doing for Christmas? Or is it Hanukkah, like Matt said?'

'Oh no, we're terrible Jews and do the whole thing: Christmas tree, turkey, presents. We hide it from my gran because she'd have a heart attack.' Her eyes were shining. I wanted to kiss her. 'What are you doing?'

I was planning to spend Christmas in my bedsit off Holloway Road, eating a takeaway. Papai had offered to buy me a plane ticket to Rio, like he always did, but this time I refused. I had gone home for Christmas every year since I started university, and each trip depressed me more than the last. The city's familiarity felt alienating rather than comforting, especially at home, with that new maid working there. What was her name? Edilene — Papai's second-to-last maid. Friends seemed happy to see me, but it felt like an act. They promised to call the next day, but then they didn't, so I stopped calling, too. They didn't know why I had left.

'I might spend it with some friends in the countryside,' I lied. 'Not sure yet.'

'Sounds nice, but Rio sounds better.'

I lit a cigarette and offered her the pack.

'Want one?'

'Yes, thanks.'

After she lit it, she inhaled audibly.

'It's so hot in here,' she said, fanning her face. 'Want to get some air?'

We took our cigarettes and drinks outside, and stood on Charlotte Street, coatless. It was a mild winter, but still we shivered. The sky was green-black, lit by the city, but I managed to count three stars. Esther pointed out the brightest and told me that it was Venus.

'How do you know that?'

'Someone else pointed it out to me once.'

She drained her glass, no longer smiling. Her lipstick was fading, purpled by the wine.

'Isn't it sad, this time of year?' she said, looking at me and then back at the sky.

'Do you think so?'

'Yes, everything about it. The music, the carols . . . ' She was slurring her words, but trying not to. 'Every Christmas song just reminds me that I'm not eight years old any more, and I never will be again. Another year ending, time passing and we're just getting old.'

'We're not old yet.'

'But we will be. It'll be 1994 in a couple of weeks and, in six years, a new millennium. Can you imagine it? We'll be thirty and then fifty and then eighty, but Christmas will always be the same. The same songs, the same decorations, the same trees.' She shook her head and laughed. 'Sorry! I'm so drunk.'

'Don't worry, so am I. I see what you mean.'

I put an arm around her and she looked up at me, with those wide, brown eyes. She was tiny. She made me feel tall. A group of office workers walked by, wearing Santa hats, sharing a bottle of wine, shouting, 'Merry Christmas!'

'Merry Christmas,' we said.

When they had passed, I pulled her closer.

* * *

In those first sweet months, we told each other about our lives. Mamãe's death, my life in Rio, Ipanema beach, monkeys skimming along telephone cables. Esther's adolescence seemed impossibly exotic: the Victorian streets of north-west London, underage drinking by the Regent's Canal; her all-girls school, full of over-achievers. There had been other girls in London, but no one like her. She was clever, introspective and laughed more than anyone I knew. She studied too much and worried that it wasn't enough. It was always enough — she was a perfect student — but she also liked to drink red wine, smoke, talk and fuck. She told me about her exes and I batted away questions about mine. You're the only one who matters, I said. Let's forget the past.

We married in October 1994 at a registry office, with two guests, our witnesses: Matt and Nina, one of Esther's school-friends. Esther's parents were furious and so was Papai, down the phone from Rio, but we didn't see the point in waiting. We were in love. Esther breathed life into everything; she breathed life into *me*. When we got together, I realized how exquisitely lonely I had been. I had struggled with the speedy greyness of London, the drab food and the language, slowly translating myself into someone who could belong. More than anything, I had struggled with my memories. Esther gave me new ones: walking on Hampstead Heath, admiring the view of the city; Sunday lunch, weekends in Europe, marriage; waking up next to her every day, feeling that all would be well.

And then it wasn't. The euphoria of love dissolved as the years went by. We were no longer mysterious to each other. We had children. I suppose I didn't help out much. We had a series of cleaners — from Poland, the Philippines — who came weekly, but Esther did everything else. The complaints started small, after Bia was born: a creased forehead, a look of distaste, a sigh. I didn't spend enough time with the baby, I didn't like to change nappies, I didn't clean up after dinner, I didn't *make* dinner, ever.

'Don't men do anything in Brazil?'

'No, I told you — we had maids.'

'Maids!' she'd say, laughing, still in love. 'For God's sake.'

I tried to do better. I learned how to iron, which was a personal victory — my parents had never done housework in their lives. I put dishes in the dishwasher and pressed start on the microwave. Hannah came along, and I changed her nappy once in a while. But then Esther quit her job — she was a paediatrician — to look after our daughters, and ended up doing everything herself, even when she returned to work part-time, some years later.

She knew what she was getting into. She could have settled down with any of the affable English medics who were half in love with her — men who liked to cook, men who assumed pitifully sincere expressions when talking about feminism (I have nothing against such men, but I'm not one of them) — but she chose me, the unknown. She liked my foreignness, and I liked hers.

After a few years, the haze lifted. We were just people after all. We still loved each other, but it was a quiet sort of love, not the lunacy of youth. That's the nature of love; there's no way around it — time rubs away the shine, like gold leaf from wood.

But everything was fine until that singer, Luana's double, came to my birthday party. After that night, after we made love in the morning, I became frighteningly detached. I had breakfast, I laughed with the girls about the night before, I got dressed and went to the supermarket; I went to work the next day, saw my patients and talked to colleagues about our weekends — but my movements felt robotic, my mind slow and panicky, caving in like a blown-up building. Somehow, I held it together. I remember looking at a patient's records while she sat next to me, crying — her husband was dying of cancer and she wanted something for her sadness, to help her cope — so I told her, in my best caring-doctor voice, that I could write her a prescription, but she might be better off without it, because the grief was inevitable, something she had to work through, and she agreed and thanked me sincerely — but I was on autopilot, not really there; an anchor cut off from its boat, watching the world from below, through a mile of ocean. No one would notice, I thought, no one would know. And then the letter came.

'I think you should leave,' said Esther, that night in June.

'Leave?'

'Yes, for a few months. Or for ever. I don't know.'

It was a Monday. We were in the bathroom, getting ready for bed. The evening sky, through the half-open blinds, still had a touch of light in it. I tried to take her hand, but she withdrew it, behind her back.

'I'm not joking,' she said.

'Come on, let's go to bed.'

I was trying to be playful, jovial — anything to change her mind. It was all an act, of course. Almost a year had passed since my birthday, and three months since the letter arrived. I had transferred it from my blazer pocket to a shoebox at the back of my wardrobe, and read it several times a week. It still smelled like Brazil.

Earlier on, at dinner, I had drunk a few glasses of wine as Esther watched me, seething. We used to get drunk together — blindingly drunk, till the world disappeared — but now I was on my own. The girls were quiet, which was unusual, and at one point I caught Bia rolling her eyes at her sister. I was talking too much, too loudly, about work, my patients, things they weren't interested in. After the girls left the kitchen, Esther washed up while I finished off the bottle. I carried on talking, but the tap water drowned me out, gushing into the sink. Then she walked out, without a word, and joined the girls in the living room. I sat for a while, listening to the musical hum of the TV and their laughter — all three of them. I went upstairs and did a few hours' work.

'You didn't use to drink like this,' she said later, in the bathroom, as we got ready for bed.

'Not this again.'

'Seriously, you didn't. What happened?'

I considered telling her about the singer, the letter, the dream I'd been having, about Luana — but no, I couldn't.

'It just helps me to relax.'

'You don't look relaxed, you look drunk and mad. Why won't you tell me what's going on?'

Whoosh! went the ocean in my ears, blocking her out. Esther was above me, on the boat, sailing away. I was the lost anchor.

'There's nothing going on,' I said. 'We've been through this before.'

'You think I can't tell that you're hiding something? *I know you.* You're not really *here*; you haven't been for the past year. I mean, your body's here, and you're busy filling it with alcohol and talking nonsense, but your mind is elsewhere. Where have you gone to?'

'Esther, what are you talking about?' I said, laughing, though my heart was slamming against my chest. 'I'm right here.'

'It wasn't a literal question, for God's sake!'

'Don't shout, the girls will hear.'

'Like they haven't heard it a million times. The other day Hannah asked me if we were getting divorced.'

'And what did you say?'

She stared back.

'I told her not to worry,' she said, and then looked at the floor, 'but I've changed my mind. You, your secrecy — I can't deal with it any more.'

She turned her back to me.

'I'm not hiding anything,' I said.

She laughed bitterly. I tried to touch her shoulder and she shrugged me off. I could see us in the mirror: older and unhappier than we once were. She started to brush her teeth with an electric toothbrush.

'Esther,' I said. 'Turn it off.'

She stared straight ahead, into the mirror, and turned off the brush.

'Fuck my life,' she said.

'Esther.'

She turned the light off and left me in the dark.

★ ★ ★

A few weeks later, the second letter arrived at work. By then, I was living alone on Albion Road, but only on a short-term lease. I was sure that I would return home soon. When I saw the postmark — Marajó, Pará — my body went numb. A patient came in, so I put the envelope aside, but I was barely able to hear what she was saying. A fungal infection of some sort. I examined her foot and printed out a prescription. After she left, I read the letter.

André,

It's your birthday this month, isn't it? I'm afraid I've forgotten the exact date. Happy birthday.

I'm sitting on my front porch. It's Sunday. Children walk by, on their way to the beach. Some of them ride old bicycles with no brakes, so that when they want to stop they have to drag their feet on the wet ground. It has just stopped raining, but the heat is unbearable — that's how it always is. The air is so heavy I can almost touch it.

Sometimes I like to imagine what the gringos thought when they first arrived here, hundreds of years ago. When they first saw a red macaw flying overhead, or a naked Indian walking out of the jungle. When they first ate a sweet, ripe mamao. They must have laughed. Too much beauty, too much life. It threatens to take over. Sometimes I wish it would, that the jungle would grow over our cities, through the walls of our houses, round our necks. That it could go back to the way things were.

Sorry, I'm being silly. I've had a long time to think.

I don't know how much you know about me. Your father said that you knew about my husband, Jorge, and my children, Francisco and Iracema. He said you knew I was living here. I've waited years for a letter. I thought, André is a good man — one day he will write to me. I waited and waited and waited. I became angry. When I couldn't sleep at night, I would write furious letters in my head, but I never wrote them on paper. But then things changed. I felt compelled to write. So here I am.

You might know about Chico, but you don't know him. He was such a good child. Not like the others — the ones who spent all day and night at the bottom of the morro, guns slung over their shoulders, many of them dead before their twentieth birthday. Francisco was never going to end up like that. He was top of his class. He always did his homework. The other kids made fun of him for being the teacher's favourite. One day, when he was seven, he came home crying — another boy had grabbed his pencil out of his hand and snapped it in two. I told him that the kid was just envious. He would probably disappear from school in a couple of years, barely able to read and write, while Chico could do whatever he wanted, with that big brain of his. He looked so sweet and sad. It brings tears to my eyes, just thinking about it.

The bullying got worse. One day, Chico came home without his trainers — they had taken them, even though they were cheap, just to upset him. We had to leave Rio. He deserved a better life. He was better than those boys.

Francisco was like the other boys in one sense — he grew up without a father. The ones who did have fathers would've been better off without them. Like Leandro, his best friend when we moved up north. His dad spent most of his time by the river, sucking on a bottle of cachaça. Then he'd come home and kick the shit out of everyone. Chico was lucky. I'd have been better off without a father, too.

I will write again.

Luana

My hands shook as I read it. She was writing to me from Marajó, but why? Why was she there? It was odd to think that the island still existed; as though it should have melted into the river when we left in January 1986. Her son's name, Chico, made me think of Mamãe's song, how it echoed through Salvaterra a year after her death. I was glad to hear that she had children, that she had made a life for herself, but I had known nothing about it. My father never told me anything. I didn't know they had stayed in touch. My old anger rose up again, but it was pointless — he was dead. Perhaps he was afraid I would go looking for her.

Was I a good man?

I read the letter several times that evening, drank a bottle of wine and went to bed. I read it again before closing my eyes, but I couldn't sleep because the words were reverberating around my head. I listened to Chico Buarque's 'Tatuagem' on my phone and fell asleep when the room was half lit, woke an hour later and went to work.

My mind was cloudy that day. Sometimes I would think of Luana's face and her calm, soft voice. At other times, I couldn't remember the exact dimensions of her face. Chico's song was still in my head, but now it was just annoying.

In the afternoon I emailed Thiago, asking, 'Do you know Luana's surname?'

He replied, sarcastically: 'I'm very well, thanks for asking. No, I don't know it. Even if I did, perhaps I wouldn't tell you. Why are you asking? Will you come visit soon?'

7

On Christmas Eve morning in Marajó, the local radio station was playing American pop songs about reindeer and snow, which didn't really go with the forty-degree heat. Papai was at the beach on his own — an old habit of his. In Rio he sometimes swam early in the morning, before work. I skipped breakfast and sat on the porch, smoking a cigarette. I wasn't a real smoker yet. Sometimes I would take one from a friend or, when Mamãe was alive, from the pack in her jewellery box. That morning I had bought some from the shop. Luana was already making preparations for a Portuguese Christmas dinner, as requested by Papai. Hearing her humming along to the radio and smelling the buttery salt of her cooking was enough to keep me out of the kitchen.

Thiago popped his head around the door and I flicked the cigarette into a bush. But it was too late.

'Are you smoking?' he said.

'No.'

He walked out on to the porch. He was wearing a blue sunga — a pair of tight swimming shorts; his chest bare, tanned and ribbed.

'I'm going to tell Papai,' he said.

'What do you want, babaca?'

'You're a babaca! Can we go to the beach?'

'Let's go when he comes back.'

'I want to go now.'

'Look, there he is.'

Papai was walking up the road, looking hazy in the sun. He was dressed more casually than I'd ever seen him, in a T-shirt, shorts and flip-flops. He was even wearing a pair of aviator sunglasses instead of his tortoiseshells. Thiago ran towards Papai, making him break into a dazzling, gold-toothed laugh. He hoisted my brother into the air with some difficulty. Again, I felt a strange sort of guilt, that we were having a good time without Mamãe. It was our first Christmas since the accident.

'I saw Papai Noel last night,' said Papai. 'He told me he's bringing a special present for you.'

'Papai Noel is coming here?'

'Didn't you know? He lives in Marajó.'

Thiago looked thrilled, hugging his arms around Papai's neck like a much younger child.

'Hello, André,' said Papai. 'Had breakfast?'

'Yes. Thi and I are going to the beach.'

'Why don't you take Luana?'

'Luana?'

He made up some excuse: 'Yes, to look after Thiago.'

'I don't need looking after,' said Thiago.

'What if a bandido comes and tries to kidnap you while André is swimming? Luana can stop them.'

Thiago looked unsure.

'OK,' he said, 'but I think I could stop them by myself.'

★ ★ ★

We walked to the beach in single file — me followed by Thiago and then Luana — each carrying an umbrella to shield ourselves from the sun. Papai had found them in a cupboard. I gave Luana a blue one with lace edges, and I used the one that looked like it had been in a tornado. Thiago and I were wearing sungas, flip-flops and nothing else (a style I've thankfully renounced, since then), and Luana was in a lilac dress printed with white flowers. It was an old dress of Rita's. Once in a while, I would look back at her and Thiago. Each time, Luana flashed a smile and Thiago stuck his tongue out, and I would wish that I was walking behind her, so that I could see how the thin cotton clung to her newly rounded thighs.

Many of the villagers had dragged tables

and chairs into their front yards and were spending the day outside — smoking cigarettes, eating snacks, drinking beer and humming along to the radio. Several called out 'Bom dia!' and 'Feliz Natal!' as we walked past, smiling that peculiar, fascinated smile that everyone directs at outsiders, all over the world. (Apart from London, where outsiders are too plentiful to be fascinating.) We caught sight of the river as we passed a shabby blue bungalow. An elderly black couple was sitting in front of it, on plastic chairs.

'Feliz Natal!' called the man.

A black-and-tan dog sat between the couple, panting. It was of no discernible breed — probably a former stray. Saliva dripped hotly from its tongue. The woman rested her hand on its head.

'Feliz Natal!' I said. 'I wish you all the best.'

'Thank you,' said the woman. 'What a nice, polite young man.'

'And what a beautiful girl!' said the man. 'Are you cousins?'

Thiago and Luana giggled.

'Of course not,' I said.

'She's our empregada!' said Thiago.

'Thi, be quiet.'

He hadn't done anything wrong, but I wanted to shut him up. We shouldn't be flashing our wealth in front of these unfortunate people — that's what Mamãe would say.

'Feliz Natal to you, too, querida,' said the woman, looking at Luana and then at me. 'Give her some time off, won't you? She deserves it.'

We walked on and Thiago said, 'People around here are nice.'

I was about to disagree — I thought they were rude and intrusive — but Luana said, 'Yes, they are.'

★   ★   ★

The sand was too hot for us to go barefoot, but Thiago did anyway. He danced from foot to foot until he reached the shallows of the water, saying 'Ai, ai, ai!' Then he said, 'Ahhh!' with satisfaction, making us laugh. The beach was busier than usual, because it was a holiday. People were sunbathing, talking, laughing and kicking footballs around. Little kids were playing by the water, digging holes in the wet sand. Thiago and I were the only white people there.

'Are you going in?' I said to Luana.

Could she even swim?

'No, I'll just watch you two.'

She took a blue sarong out of her cloth bag

and laid it on the sand. I wondered when she would take off her dress. I could see orange bikini straps peeking out underneath. I left my flip-flops and glasses next to her sarong and did the same hot-sand dance Thiago had done until I reached the water. Luana giggled, so I clowned around even more — splashing Thiago with water and trying to do handstands. Then I walked into the river with my brother. He was a good swimmer for his age, but I swam out slowly so that I wouldn't lose him. He was ten metres behind, moving splashily through the water. Beyond him was the sandy shore. I squeezed my myopic eyes till they were almost shut, and could vaguely make out Luana: she was standing up, lifting the dress over her head.

'What are you looking at?' said Thiago. He stopped swimming and looked at the beach. 'Look, there's Luana. Lua! Lua!'

He waved frantically, struggling to stay afloat.

'Stop it, Thi, you'll drown.'

Luana was standing on the beach, in her orange bikini, waving back. Her hair was down — I hadn't seen her hair down in years. It trailed past her shoulders in dark ringlets. She sat down on the sarong, and Thiago caught up with me. We swam further out. The water was calm.

Back on the shore, Thiago rushed over to Luana and hugged her. I put my glasses back on. They steamed up against my damp face.

'You're all wet, Thi,' she said.

He pulled away and she laughed, shaking the water off her hands. In her bikini, you wouldn't know she was an empregada. She could have passed for one of my school-friends: well-spoken, slim and pretty. Though none of my friends were black. Maybe an eighth or a sixteenth, but not visibly.

'How's the water?' she said.

'Perfect,' I said. Like you. Perfect. 'Are you going in?'

That Chico Buarque song came back to me. My mother's song.

'Maybe.'

I sat next to her on the sand, just like I would with the girls from school.

'Do you like the beach?' I said, stupidly. 'You wouldn't imagine it, would you, a beach by a river?'

'It looks like a brown ocean,' she said.

'That's what I thought.'

'It's nicer when it's blue.'

'But the river feels so much better. There's no salt — no need to wash it out of your hair.'

'I don't mind the salt,' she said.

'Really?'

'I like how it feels.'

These days, I know what she meant. How it dries into a thin, white crisp on your hair and skin. You lick your lips several hours later and taste the ocean. The taste of home.

'Do you ever go to the beach in Rio, on your day off?' I said.

'No. Not any more. But I like to look at it from the living-room window. It's such a great view.'

She said it like a guest, not like someone who lived there.

'I'm so used to the view I think I hardly notice it.'

'It's important to notice things,' she said.

Thiago was digging a hole by the water's edge, talking to himself. Sometimes he seemed like he was four years old, not seven.

'I'm going to swim,' said Luana.

'I'll go, too.'

'What about Thi?'

'We'll keep an eye on him.' She looked unsure. 'Come on, he's not a little kid any more.'

We walked into the river. She was grinning, enjoying the lukewarm water. She could swim. Of course she could swim. We swam out and trod water, watching Thiago on the shore. I could see her shoulders, golden and slim, just under the surface of the river. I wanted to touch them.

'Was it weird,' I said, 'leaving school?'

'What?'

'You know.' I knew that I shouldn't have asked, but I couldn't take it back. 'How you left school to be an empregada?'

I couldn't see her face, because both of us were still watching Thiago. I was scared to look at her, to feel her contempt.

'Sorry, that was a stupid question,' I said.

'Is it weird being rich?'

'We're not rich. Some of my friends have boats, horses, designer clothes — we don't have any of that.'

She turned towards me, with hard, green eyes, and smirked.

'Did you want to go to university?' I said.

'No, I want to be an empregada until I'm old and grey — it's the job of my dreams. I shouldn't be talking about this with you.'

She was so close to me. Just ten inches away. All I had to do was float my hands towards her, under the water, and I would feel her hips. I felt a tingle in my penis as I imagined it. But she was looking away, at my brother. The silence stretched like a piece of chewing gum. Luana turned and swam back, without saying a word. Out of the water, she

sat next to Thiago and helped him to dig his
hole.

⋆　⋆　⋆

That evening we had Christmas Eve dinner.
Luana ate in the kitchen, by herself, and we
ate in the dining room, smilingly served by
her. Portuguese-style salt cod with potatoes
and vegetables. It tasted good, but I would
rather have had turkey and ham, the usual. At
least Papai let me have a beer. When he left
the room for a minute, I gave Thiago a sip.

He screwed up his eyes, stuck his tongue
out and said, 'That's horrible,' and then,
'Give me some more.'

I wondered what Rita was doing in Rio. I
liked to think that she was sleeping in my
parents' double bed and watching TV all day
but, most likely, she was cleaning the flat,
going to church, changing Fifi's litter tray and
missing her daughter.

'Proper Portuguese food,' said Papai, as
Luana cleared the plates. 'Well done.'

She nodded and said, 'Thank you, doutor.'

'We're going to church at midnight. Would
you like to join us?'

'We're going to church?' said Thiago.

'Are you going to start complaining?'

Thiago creased his face like he was in pain.

'Yes, I'd like that,' said Luana.

After dinner, it was time for presents. Papai called Luana from the kitchen and gave her a small, square package.

'Feliz Natal!' he said.

She opened it with a curious look on her face. We always gave small presents to Rita and Luana — bars of soap, hand cream, flip-flops — but this time, Luana gasped as she unwrapped a pale yellow box, with fancy gold lettering. She opened it and lifted out a bottle of perfume, her hands trembling because of all the attention.

'Thanks so much,' she said. 'This is far too generous.'

'I saw it and thought of you.'

She took off the lid — two glass birds in flight — and spritzed some on her wrist. The scent of flowers and musk filled the room. The smell of women.

'Let me smell it!' said Thiago. He got off the sofa, walked up to Luana and sniffed her wrist. 'Smells like Mamãe.'

'No, Mamãe wore a different perfume,' said Papai.

'I'm sorry I have nothing to give you back,' said Luana.

'Your presence is a gift to us,' said Papai, which I thought was over the top.

We opened a few more presents. Luana sat

on a wooden stool and watched as we unwrapped them. Thiago and I gave Papai a box of Cuban cigars, which he seemed pleased with. I wasn't expecting anything special, and I was right not to be: he gave me a small anatomical model of the human body.

'Thanks, Pai,' I said. 'I really needed this.'

His tipsy eyes were swimming with pride. He gave Thiago a copy of *Alice in Wonderland* in English. My mother would have given him a new record or a toy gun. Thiago hadn't yet learned how to fake gratitude. He threw the book on to the ground as though it were a grenade, said, 'I hate it!' and burst into hysterical tears. My father sat on the sofa, immobile and confused. Luana went to my brother and hugged him.

'I miss Mamãe,' he sobbed. 'How can we bring her back?'

'We all miss Dona Beatriz. Don't cry, Thi.' It was as if she had been possessed by Rita. It was exactly the sort of thing Rita would say, in that same low, shushing tone. 'I've heard that this is a great book, you know.'

He stopped crying and fixed his eyes somewhere in the distance. All of us were silent for a while. Papai drank a much-needed glass of whisky, and then we went to church.

* * *

After Pará, Luana took to wearing the perfume fairly often. Even when she was just cooking and cleaning, she smelled like a rich lady on her way to a party. The perfume was called L'Air du Temps. I didn't remember that until several years later, when Esther took me to Kentish Town to meet her parents for the first time. It was May, 1994 — a Saturday. Two months before my twenty-sixth birthday. We walked up Falkland Road arm in arm. Still wearing wool coats, even though it was spring.

'I'm nervous,' I said.

'Don't be!' said Esther. 'They'll love you. They love anything foreign and exotic.'

'You're the exotic one, gringa.'

Esther's childhood home was a Victorian terrace, three storeys high, with bumblebees clinging to the lavender in the front garden. The door was opened by her mother, Judith, a good-looking woman with short, dark hair and Esther's smile. We said hello, and then I smelled Luana in the air. Flowers and musk. Marajó. Our living room in Ipanema. Everything else. I kissed my future mother-in-law on both cheeks, answering her questions, laughing when she told me that I had a charming accent, that she had always wanted to go to Brazil. Soon her husband, Joe, was in the hallway, and I was shaking his hand and offering the bottle of wine I'd brought, but my body felt like it was closing in. After a couple of minutes, I excused myself and went to the bathroom. Splashed water on my face, looked up and saw it there, sitting next to the sink: L'Air du Temps.

8

It was the same church Papai had attended as a boy: small and white with a blue trim, and a sign saying 1911. All the seats were taken. The doors were open and half of the village was sitting outside, straining their necks to see the priest give his sermon, fanning themselves with prayer books. We were a few minutes late and he was already in full swing, droning away in Portuguese and Latin.

'There's nowhere to sit,' I said.

'Let's just sit here,' said Papai, gesturing at the people on the ground outside the church. They were all looking at us and whispering to each other, but in a friendly sort of way.

'Senhor,' came a voice from just inside the church. It was a thin old man sitting in the last row of chairs. 'Your daughter can have my seat.'

I looked at Luana to see her reaction, but she had turned away from me and was staring at the half-naked, gape-mouthed wooden Jesus.

'That's quite all right,' said Papai, rather loudly. 'We'll sit over here. Thank you.'

We sat on the floor, just inside the building.

People moved over to make room, and then offered us drinks and snacks. Cups of coffee ('It'll help you stay awake'), manioc cake and handfuls of buttery popcorn. After taking one bite of a cake, Thiago curled up on to Luana's lap and fell asleep. I felt jealous that he was young enough to get away with that. She looked sleepy, too. Her eyes were opening and closing, opening and closing. She put her arms around my brother.

I looked to my right and saw Papai's face in the darkness, looking at me, his eyes glinting. There was a tiny piece of popcorn stuck to his lip. I could barely hear a word of the service, other than the regular 'amém's that the crowd joined in with. Neither could the people sitting around us, it seemed; many of them were having quiet but animated conversations.

'Comfortable?' said Papai.

'Not really.'

'Me neither.' He seemed as bored as I was. Fidgety, barely watching. 'Maybe we should wake up those two.'

I gave Thiago a little shake.

'Mamãe,' he said, wrapping his arms around Luana. She was asleep, too, hugging him back.

'Thi-thi,' I said.

He opened his eyes.

'Where are we?'

'At the church.'

'Huh?'

'In Marajó.'

He looked up and saw that he was in Luana's arms, not Mamãe's. Luana opened her eyes and lifted her head.

'Come on, let's go,' said Papai.

We thanked everyone for their food and drinks, and they all nodded in return, saying, 'Prazer, prazer.' Papai had satisfied his nostalgia, so it was time to go home. Midnight mass, like Belém, didn't live up to his memories.

'Now I remember why I stopped going to church. It's so boring,' he said, as we walked home.

Luana and Thiago were trailing behind, hand in hand.

'Isn't it funny?' he continued. 'You yearn for things that you didn't even like at the time.'

'What do you mean?'

He turned to me, but I couldn't see his expression. It was too dark.

'Never mind. I'm just rambling — it's what you do when you get old.'

Inwardly, I agreed. My father was ancient to me. He was forty-three — younger than I am now.

It was too hot to sleep that night. I lay awake in bed, sweating through my sheets, feeling like I was on fire. The cicadas were screaming so loud it sounded like they were in the room. I opened the window, but it made no difference. The air was thick and unmoving. I reached for my glasses, but they weren't on the bedside table. I got out of bed and went downstairs, where it was cooler. The tiles were almost cold beneath my feet. I was walking to the kitchen to get a glass of water when I heard her.

'André?'

In my sleepless, half-blind haze, I thought my mother's ghost might be paying me a visit. I spun round to face the doorway of the darkened TV room and saw a shadow, sitting on the sofa. Her curly hair was loose. So different from my mother's, which was straight like an Indian's.

'What are you doing in the dark?' I said.

I reached for the light, but Luana said, 'Don't.'

'Have you become a vampire?'

I walked into the room and felt my way along the wall to the sofa. I sat on the other side, far from Luana.

'I couldn't sleep,' she said.

'Me neither. It's too hot.'

'The heat doesn't bother me.'

'What is it, then?'

'I don't know.'

'You don't know, or you won't tell me?'

'We shouldn't act like friends,' she said.

'Why not?'

'You ask too many questions.'

'Sorry.'

I was about to ask her if she missed Rita, and then realized that was another question.

'I don't know what to say now,' I said.

There was a silver halo of light around her hair — the only thing I could see of her. No features, nothing. Just black.

'You look like an angel.'

'What?'

'There's a halo around your head.'

A stupid thing to say — too intense.

'Were you thinking about Dona Beatriz?' she said. 'Is that why you can't sleep?'

'Kind of. When I saw you sitting there, I thought you were her ghost.'

'What gave me away?'

'Your hair.'

In the dark, she shook her curly head, and the halo shuddered over it.

I swallowed hard before asking, 'Do you think about your father?'

'No. I never knew him.'

'Who was he?'

'You and your questions. I don't know, some white guy from Vidigal who doesn't live there any more. Mamãe only mentions him when she's warning me about men.'

'What does she say?'

'Not to bother with them. Just to concentrate on work.'

But Rita loves *me*, I wanted to say, and I'm a man.

'That doesn't sound fun,' I said.

'I know.'

I knew then that I could kiss her. Outside could wait. There was nothing in the world apart from that room, the humming of the insects, Luana's halo and my erection, rising hopefully in my shorts. I moved closer to her. Cool sweat trickled down the sides of my face. She must have felt the sofa shift.

'What are you doing?' she said.

'Now you're asking the questions,' I said, in a serious, flat tone. The kind that men used in novelas when they were seducing women. I didn't mean it to be funny, but she laughed.

'André.'

I moved closer, so that our thighs touched. Her skin was cooler than mine. In the darkness I found one of her hands, resting on her lap. Our palms were sweating. Her breath was blowing hot and humid on my face.

Using it as a guide, I could just about work out where her lips were hiding in the dark. Those full, pink lips, with the deep Cupid's bow, like the letter 'V'.

I leaned in and she said, 'What are you doing?', but she didn't push me off.

My calculations were wrong. I kissed her on the side of her mouth, and she whispered a laugh. I laughed, too, nervously. Luana turned her head an inch and our lips pressed drily against each other, came away, and then pressed again. It lasted five seconds, no more, until she stood up, and her halo disappeared.

'I'm going to bed,' she said.

'Luana?'

'Goodnight.'

Back to her room she went, padding through the kitchen. My heart beat quickly, like that of a small animal. I went to bed and masturbated while thinking of Luana in her orange bikini, then fell asleep as the sun was rising.

* * *

The rest of our time in Pará passed quickly. We were in Marajó for two more weeks, including a quiet New Year's Eve, and then a few nights in Belém. I said all the right things to Papai, played with my brother, thanked

Luana for lunch every day, but inside I was lit up. When I went to the beach in Marajó, the river water crackled against my skin like electricity. Everything slowed down when Luana entered a room — though she seemed to avoid any room that I was in. She didn't acknowledge what had happened and I didn't know what to do about it. Getting her alone was impossible. She stuck to Thiago like a parasite: watched TV with him, took him to the beach before I woke up, took him to the shops and somehow convinced him to stay in the kitchen while she cooked. He sat on the little table, leafing through *Alice in Wonderland,* making her laugh the way I wanted to make her laugh. I would hear them from my room, feeling angry and sweaty with jealousy. There were no further kisses in Marajó, nor in Belém.

The night before we flew home, there was a farewell dinner at Camila's with all the same people from the previous party, and a few more. Wine, several courses of food and a three-piece band playing the same old songs. Thiago ate so much that he was almost sick. I rubbed his back as he retched in the garden. Nothing came up. Inside the house, he pulled two dining chairs together and fell asleep on them as the party carried on around him. Papai and I were told, time and time again, that we had to come back soon. That we should have stayed longer. That we could stay in any of their homes, any time.

I never saw any of those people again.

I went back to my hiding place, at the back of the garden, closed my eyes and thought of Luana. The curve of her lips, her moist hand, her breath.

9

On a Friday morning in September I received a postcard of Christ the Redeemer, arms spread, looking over the city and the sea — the classic Rio shot, too far away to see the ugliness.

'Looks nice,' said one of the receptionists, handing it over to me.

'It is,' I said.

Andé,

I'm visiting my mother in Rio. She still lives with her sister in the old bairro. I've asked her many times to join us in the north, but she always says, 'Maybe next year.' She won't even visit any more. She thinks the river is cursed. I feel the opposite. I can't stand to be in Rio. Can you? Graças a Deus, I will leave tomorrow.

Luana

I read it in a few seconds, while waiting for my first patient. I read it again during my lunch break, over a sandwich, and then several times at home that evening, over a microwaved curry and a bottle of wine, half watching a Danish TV drama that Esther had liked. I read Luana's letters from the beginning, from the first to the postcard. I got out of bed at dawn and read them again in the kitchen. Outside the window, London was dark blue. I closed my eyes and tried to imagine Ipanema beach, the ocean, the favela at the end. Then I opened them, saw a row of Victorian terraces and felt a shiver of embarrassment. I was far from home.

★   ★   ★

In the afternoon I trudged down the road, exhausted, to pick up my daughters from Winston Road. I rang the bell for five minutes before Hannah answered, wearing pink pyjamas, glasses and a dark nest of hair piled on top of her head. While she got ready I waited in the living room, sinking into our old leather sofa, resting my feet on the Persian rug Esther and I had bought together, a few months after we married. If I had closed my eyes, I would've fallen asleep in seconds — that's how tired I was. The same framed photos sat on the mantelpiece, including the one that Matt took at our wedding. Esther wore a short white dress and dark red lipstick. She looked eighteen, not twenty-four, and ridiculously happy, caught in mid-laugh. The smell of the place: plants, wood and dust, the smell of Esther, Hannah and Bia. A hundred years from now, we would all be dead, but a hint of us would linger in the house. I was sure of it.

I took the girls to our usual place. After three months of living apart, we already had a usual place: the Clissold Park café, which is housed in an old mansion. Once it had been the home of someone rich and important, but now it was a place to drink coffee and eat cake, for mothers with babies to congregate. It was close to the restaurant where Bia worked — she was saving up to go backpacking, before going to university to study medicine, the family business. We sat outside. It was one of those blue-and-gold early-autumn days that make you thankful for everything: sandwiches, coffee, various small dogs running around us on the grass. The girls ate with one hand, stroking passing dogs with the other.

'Bia,' I said, 'have you thought about where you're going to go?'

'Dunno,' she said, chewing. 'Maybe Brazil.'

'Brazil? Really?'

She narrowed her eyes and her upper lip twitched.

'Yes, really,' she said irritably.

It was so easy to get on her nerves, so easy for her to twist an innocent remark into an attack. There was an air of sadness around her, a nervous tension that made me feel like a failure.

'It's a dangerous country,' I said.

'Oh, come on.'

'Why *do* we never go to Brazil, Dad?' said Hannah.

'We've been a few times,' I said.

'Twice,' said Bia. 'Once when I was three, which I don't remember, and then for Grandad's funeral.'

Papai was sixty-seven when he died. His empregada found him, keeled over in the bathroom. I'm next on the list.

'I remember the view from Grandad's flat,' said Hannah. 'Of the beach?'

It was funny, how they called him Grandad, when they barely knew him. They had met him just once, when they were too young to hold on to their memories. The second time, he was a body in a coffin — his skin smooth and waxy with makeup, blushing like a doll. My atheist father had a Catholic funeral with an open casket. Thiago organized the whole thing.

'Your uncle Thiago lives in that flat now,' I said.

'We know, Dad,' said Bia. 'We know him.'

Thiago had stayed with us twice in London. A few days when he was a teenager, on his tour of Europe, and two months in his early twenties.

'Thiago's emails are so nice,' said Hannah.

'It's Chee-ah-gu,' I said, correcting her pronunciation.

'OK, Chee-ah-gu,' she said. 'He's always inviting us to come and stay with him and his boyfriend. What's his name, again?'

'Jesse,' said Bia and I, at the same time.

Bia laughed. I was surprised that she knew Jesse's name, that she had forged a relationship with Thiago without my knowing about it. What else did they talk about?

'We found some photos of you and Thiago recently,' said Bia, 'when Mum was clearing out the attic.'

'And photos of your maids,' said Hannah. 'I can't believe you had *maids*.'

'In their little white uniforms,' said Bia.

'Oh my God, it's like *Downton Abbey*.'

'Not quite,' I said. 'There were only two of them.'

'Only two?' said Bia, laughing. 'Can we get one, then?'

I remembered those photos. There was one in particular, taken at my grandparents' house in Teresópolis, weeks before the accident. My mother standing next to a small tree in the garden, where a hummingbird had made a nest and laid two eggs, as tiny as aspirin. The nest was just outside my bedroom, and I took the photo from inside, kneeling on a chair. You can just about see the mother bird's shimmering blue-green face, and Mamãe — looking at her — eyes downcast, with a small smile, her black hair pulled into a bun. Her face is Bia's face: wide cheekbones like an Indian, hooded eyes, pale skin. She's a ghost of my daughter from the past.

The girls moved on to other subjects — school, TV, friends. At one point I looked up at their laughing faces and realized that I had no idea what they were laughing at; I hadn't been listening for several minutes. I was somewhere else. I should get something to help me sleep, I thought — yes, I'll do that tomorrow. My daughters carried on laughing, somewhat hysterical. They dabbed tears from their eyes. I smiled, pretending to get the joke. The ground felt unsteady under my feet.

10

Like many apartments in Rio, ours could be entered through two doors: one opened into the kitchen and the other, the guests' door, opened into an L-shaped living-cum-dining room. My father unlocked the kitchen door as we stood in the hallway gloom. Thiago was expectant, waiting for a hug from Rita. Luana was staring straight ahead. She had mostly ignored me on the way home, but was just courteous enough for no one else to notice.

'Hello, everyone,' came a soft voice from behind the door, like a balm over a scratch.

'Rita!' said Thiago.

She was standing in the kitchen in her white uniform and white rubber flip-flops, that small, rare smile on her face. Thiago rushed inside and hugged her wide body.

She laughed, patted his head and said, 'How are you, Thi-thi? Did you miss Rita?'

'Yes,' he said, muffled by her uniform.

Rita was in her thirties, but to me she was as old as the earth. Not that she looked it. Her dark face was unlined, but she carried herself with weight, literal and metaphorical, as though she knew something you didn't know. At seventeen, I was too old and timid to merit a hug, but I still remembered the feel of her hands, roughened by two decades of cleaning. The hands that had bathed and fed me for so many years. I hid my jealousy with a grin.

'How are you, Rita?' said Papai.

'I'm well, and you?' She kept her eyes on Papai, Thiago and me, saving Luana's greeting for later. 'Did you enjoy your city, doutor?' she said to Papai.

'Very much so,' said Papai. 'Did you have a nice Christmas?'

'Yes, doutor, it was good.'

'Well, I'm going to unpack.'

He left the kitchen, and then so did we. Apart from Luana. She stayed with her mother.

As I walked to my bedroom, I heard her say, 'Oi, Mãe.'

Rita replied, 'Oi, querida.'

There was a silence. They were probably hugging. The silence went on for a long time, and then I shut it out with my bedroom door. Fifi was lying on my bed, staring at me with paranoid blue eyes, her shoulder bones jutting out under her skin. My sheets were covered with her moulted silver fur. I sat next to her and she emitted a small, deranged yowl.

'Hi, Fifi,' I said. 'Still crazy?'

She darted off the bed and out of the room.

Like most pets in Ipanema, Fifi lived indoors. That's the price they pay for living in high-rise luxury — no adventure and insufficient exercise. She slept all day, pooed in a box and liked to sit on the balcony, gazing at the people on the beach, probably wishing that she could walk among them. Sometimes Thiago took her to our building's playground and she would chase a lizard for a few minutes, before meowing for him to take her back. But she hadn't done that in a long time.

Later, we found her on an armchair in the living room, looking like a haunted, grey statue of a cat.

'What's wrong with her?' said Thiago.

Outside, the traffic on Avenida Vieira Souto was screeching, and waves were rolling and crashing on to Ipanema beach. I glanced at the windows, took in the view — the rough blue ocean, the sand clogged with sunbathers — and remembered what Luana had said about the importance of noticing things.

'She's old,' I said. 'That's all.'

I looked at the cat and tried not to laugh at her ennui. My brother was taking it very seriously.

'She missed us,' he said. 'She thinks we stopped loving her.'

'She doesn't think, Thi. She's a cat.'

'She does think!'

He tried to put his arms around her, but she said, 'Yeow!' and smacked him on the face.

'Aiee!'

'Are you all right?'

'You hurt me!' he said to the cat.

Fifi narrowed her eyes and gave him a 'so what?' glare. Then she settled down and turned her head. Thiago rubbed his cheek.

★　★　★

It was thirty-six degrees in Rio, but at least we had air conditioning. We shivered in our cramped, small TV room — it had a sofa, a wooden chair, a TV and nothing else — sometimes opening the window a notch just to check that, yes, it was still like a sauna outside, and then closing it before the precious arctic air could escape. Back to his old ways, Papai was working in his study and Luana had gone back to her usual TV-watching perch, the stiff-backed wooden chair by the door. I could smell her perfume.

In the days following our return, she had taken to wearing a starched white dress, like her mother's. The uniform overwhelmed her figure — it must have been two sizes too big — and it was terrible to see her wearing it. It erased her. Once, when we passed each other in the street, I didn't notice her until she said hello; she was just another empregada dressed in white. Who had made her wear it? I couldn't imagine Papai caring either way. It must have been Rita, wanting her to look more professional. I didn't ask. I was too shy to talk to Luana. Her eyes were as cold and empty as Fifi's, fixed on the TV screen. Maybe Marajó was just a one-off, and the heat had made her drunk. Not me. I would have kissed her again in a second. And more.

Soon I would be back at school. I didn't want to go. I wanted to stay at home with Luana. Watch her cooking with those slim brown arms, which would one day be as strong as Rita's, and her hands as rough. Get her alone, hear her say my name again. Remove that ugly white dress, to see what lies beneath. Doce de leite, dark hair, woman-hood. Fuck her, obviously. My mind was locked in a film about Luana — part porno, part romance. My eyes were on the TV, but I didn't even know what was on. I was playing my seedy little film, rewriting the script as I went along. Luana and I, our limbs entangled. My hands kneading her small breasts like dough (I had the sexual technique of a moron) and then grabbing her perfect, round bum-bum. That word is pronounced like a drumbeat — *boom-boom.* I was fucking Luana in my head and she was just sitting there, laughing at the TV. For one horrible minute I wondered whether she could read my mind and knew that I was a pervert. After all, she was the child of Rita, the all-seeing eye.

Right on cue, Rita interrupted my little reverie by poking her head into the room, looking spooked. Her head darted like a bird's. My penis instantly shrivelled. Nothing like a babá to stoke your guilt.

'You OK?' I said.

'Yes, it's nothing,' said Rita.

She moved away from the door and could be heard walking around the flat, moving furniture about and making kissing sounds. Luana and I shared a curious look — our first look in days — and laughed. In that laugh, I felt a jolt of terror, like our happiness was the worst thing that could ever happen to me. A premonition. I stopped laughing and told myself to calm down.

Luana was oblivious to any of this. Well, that's how she looked.

'Mãe,' she said, putting her head out of the door. 'What are you doing?'

Rita came back. Her face was shining with panic.

'It's Fifi,' she said. 'I haven't seen her for hours. I think she's escaped.'

'What?' said Thiago, shocked out of his TV stupor.

'How did she get out?' I said.

All of us looked at the window, which overlooked the back of the building, but didn't say anything.

'She's not in the playground,' said Rita, and we breathed a sigh of relief, because that's where her body would have landed, had she jumped from the TV room.

'She'll come back,' said Luana.

Thiago didn't look convinced. His lips were trembling, threatening to break into a howl.

'Yes, Thiago, don't worry,' I said, not fully convinced myself.

I'd heard that cats went into hiding just before death, but it would have been almost impossible for Fifi to escape from our fifth-floor flat. Our building, like most in Zona Sul, was a fortress: spiked walls, CCTV and porteiros — caretakers — in the lobby twenty-four hours a day, making sure that no undesirables got inside.

We joined Rita in her search, running in and out of rooms, shouting, 'Fifizinha, where are you?' We looked inside cupboards and chests of drawers, underneath beds and sofas, inside the shower, in the laundry basket and in every room. Finally, the four of us came to the closed door of Papai's study, under which a dim light peeked through. I knocked on the door. He opened it, saw us standing there and laughed.

'What are you all doing?' he asked.

'Fifi's gone missing,' I said. 'Is she in here?'

'I doubt it,' he said, looking unperturbed.

'Can we look?'

He held the door open and we walked into his study: a small room with mostly bare walls, a couple of shelves stuffed with boring textbooks and a desk spilling over with files. The four of us looked around, moving things, clucking and saying her name, while Papai sat on his chair. He never cared much for Fifi.

'I'm sure she'll come back,' he said.

It took seconds to search the room. She wasn't there. Thiago started to cry.

'Don't worry, Thi,' I said. 'Let's wait a few days.'

'She's just a cat,' said Papai.

'You're horrible!' said Thiago.

He ran out of the room. Papai's jokey smile looked strained.

'Probably got blown off the balcony,' said Rita.

'Then where's her body?' I said.

'Only Deus knows.'

'Go to the church and ask him, then,' said Papai. 'We can get another cat.'

'With all due respect, doutor,' said Rita, 'Thiago wants Fifi back, not another cat.'

★ ★ ★

The days passed, with no sign of Fifi. I made up stories to make Thiago feel better. Fifi had become the leader of a band of stray cats. They scurried around the streets of Ipanema, weaving between people's legs, catching shiny, black cockroaches with their paws.

'She eats cockroaches? That's disgusting.'

'No, she just kills them. It's a public service.'

After eating a dinner of empadinhas de camarão and coxinhas pinched from local restaurants, the band of cats returned to their home on top of the Arpoador rock between Copacabana and Ipanema. As the sun came down over the Atlantic, they howled like wolves.

'You're just making it up,' said Thiago.

'It's all true, Thi, I promise.'

★ ★ ★

A week later, Rita and Luana heard a scratch at the kitchen door. Scratch, scratch, meow.

This is how Rita told it to me. I was out playing tennis with my friend Carlito on the last day of our summer break.

The meow was so weak it barely sounded like a cat. More like the squeak of a dying mouse, caught in a trap. Rita and Luana ran to the door, taking deep breaths to prepare themselves for whatever lay on the other side. They opened the door. It was Fifi, but if they had seen that poor creature in the street they would barely have recognized her. Her silver fur was grey like the dust you find under a sofa. She was even thinner than before, a furry grey skeleton covered in dirt and scratches.

'Meu Deus!' said Rita. 'Poor little thing.'

'What happened to you, Fifizinha?' said Luana.

'Meow,' said Fifi. 'Meow.'

Which could have been interpreted in a number of ways.

$\star$　$\star$　$\star$

Meanwhile, I was dropping Carlito off in a taxi at his flat on Rua Farme de Amoedo. He was my best friend: a skinny, olive-skinned kid who always wore a white T-shirt and blue jeans — a James Dean look ruined by his messy, curly, black hair and angry, red spots.

He had worn a slightly different outfit on the tennis court at the Paissandu Atletico Clube in Leblon by swapping the jeans for some black shorts. On the way back, he stunk out the taxi with BO. Michael Jackson's 'Beat It' was playing on the radio. The driver drummed his fingers on the steering wheel.

Carlito told me about Christmas in Paris, which was 'soooo boring, cara. I spent most of the time walking in the rain, looking at old buildings with my parents. The city seemed nice, but you can't make the most of it with your goddamn parents, right?'

'Right.'

'But there was this French girl I met at my hotel. The receptionist.'

'Oh yeah?'

I was used to Carlito's schtick. He was a grand, irrepressible liar. I knew he was a virgin, and he knew that I knew.

'We did it all night, cara!'

In the rear-view mirror, the driver was looking straight ahead, not even listening. He was a middle-aged guy with a stubbly, tired face.

'What was her name?'

'We were too horny to exchange names, know what I mean? Did you meet any girls in the Amazon? A sexy Indian?'

'Not exactly, but — ' I opened my mouth, ready to tell him everything, knowing how much pleasure he would get from my story about Luana. Carlito had been slyly flirting with her for years, whenever he came round to our flat. We knew a couple of boys who'd had sex with their maids, but I didn't want to become like them — the subject of school gossip.

'No, I didn't meet anyone,' I said. 'I was with my family the whole time.'

'Boring. So, are you going to fuck Daniela this year or what?'

'Cara . . . '

Daniela Hickmann was a girl at school, one of our group. Originally from São Paulo, she had lived in Rio for a few years. I had been interested in her before Mamãe's accident. And then — nothing.

'Come on,' he said, shrugging off his joking tone. 'I know you've had a tough year, but she likes you. She's a nice girl.'

We pulled up outside his block.

'Thank you,' he said to the driver. 'Bye, André. See you at school tomorrow!'

He got out and slammed the door hard.

'Mind the car, moleque!' said the driver.

★ ★ ★

When the lift arrived at the fifth floor, I saw Rita and Luana standing at our open door, looking down at a pile of fluff. Luana had stopped ignoring me — her eyes were full of worry.

'It's Fifi,' she said.

'Meu Deus, where did you find her?'

As I approached, the fluff moved and emitted a squeak. I bent down and put my tennis racket on the floor. She purred a little in recognition.

'We found her lying right outside the door,' said Rita.

'Outside the building?'

'No,' said Luana. 'Outside the kitchen door.'

'She knew her way back to the fifth floor?'

'We don't understand it either.'

I looked down at the cat.

'Where the hell have you been, Fifi?'

The three of us worked together. Using an old towel as a stretcher, we carried Fifi on to the balcony, overlooking the beach. The same balcony where that photograph was taken of Rita, Luana, Fifi and me, when we were so young — Rita, too. But Fifi's time was up. The cat's belly was rising and falling with shallow breaths and, in the afternoon sun, you could still see specks of silver in her grey fur. Her body had stopped moving by the time Thiago came home from his football club, and the sun had gone down. The

Atlantic swished darkly in front of us and the Vidigal favela lit up the hills at the end of the strip.

Mamãe had bought Fifi when I was almost three years old. I couldn't remember life before her. I couldn't remember life before Mamãe, because there was no life. Now Mamãe was dead and so was Fifi. This is life, I thought. I understand now. Everything ends, everything continues. I felt so grown-up, thinking this. I didn't cry, but Thiago sobbed.

'How did she know which button to press in the lift?' he said.

'She just knew,' said Luana, putting her hand on his shoulder. 'Isn't that right, André?'

I nodded quickly. The cat's death had broken her vow of silence, but I could tell that she wanted to put Marajó behind us.

'Yes,' I said. 'She was always so clever.'

I can put it behind me, too.

Luana put her arms around Thiago as tears dribbled down his face.

Can I?

To this day, I don't know how Fifi got back home or where she had been. Just one of those things you'll never know, like what your parents were like before you were born, or what Ipanema looked like in the year 1500.

We scattered her ashes in the playground. After shaking the last grains out of a plastic bag, Papai made the sign of the cross, just to amuse himself.

11

I usually took the bus to school, but one day I decided to walk. I had time to kill, because I had been woken up two hours early by my mother shouting, 'Wake up, André!' — but when I opened my eyes, I remembered that she was dead.

It was April — autumn. The sun hadn't completely risen, so the temperature was low: around twenty-three degrees. Here in London, that's warm enough for men to walk shirtless down the street, but in Rio it's pleasantly cool. The city stays up late and rises early, because everyone wants to escape the heat. Maybe that's where the city's mania comes from: sleep deprivation. In the grey morning light, people moved swiftly through the streets. Driving, walking, talking, jangling their keys and opening up shops, rolling up metal blinds. Some subdued and quiet. Others, like the binmen in their orange overalls, laughing and joking.

I bought a coconut from a stall and drank its iced, sweet water as I walked to Copacabana. As the sun grew whiter and hotter, the pores opened on my forehead. I thought of Luana, starting her work day, and then I interrupted that thought and replaced it with Daniela Hickmann. We had been dating for three weeks. Just kisses — nothing more. I was hoping that she would push Luana out of my mind. Quite difficult, since we lived under the same roof.

As I arrived at school, I threw the coconut into a bin. My school was a grand old building, a peach palace surrounded by Copacabana's modern ugliness — high-rise buildings and overpriced hotels. Cars were honking and kids were running, hugging and screaming, as though they hadn't seen each other in years, rather than for a day or two. I scanned the crowd, looking for my friends.

'Oi, André!'

A nasal São Paulo-accented voice. I turned to face Daniela. Her skin and hair were golden from the weekend sun. Even her blue eyes had a touch of gold. We had been at Ipanema beach on Saturday with our friends, who had watched us keenly, like dogs watching people at the dinner table.

'Olá, Dani,' I said.

I moved in for a hug and she moved in for a kiss. I quickly corrected myself and kissed her lips. My eyes were open, hers closed and sincere. She was the kind of girl Mamãe would have loved to see me with. Her parents appeared in magazines.

Our school days started at dawn and ended at noon. The afternoons were ours. We congregated with friends on Copacabana beach, hugging each other hello, lingering on the girls so that we could feel their bikini-covered breasts on our bodies. There was Carlito and Daniela, plus Isabel and her boyfriend Rodrigo, and Gabriel. Everyone dressed either in a tight sunga or bikini. The towering whiteness of Copacabana Palace and its sunburnt gringo guests were at a safe distance. Even so, all around us, European and American tourists were toasting themselves pink while wearing the wrong sort of swimwear. We were young, nearly naked and had nothing to hide.

Carlito shouted, 'Ei, gringinhos, you look like lobsters!' and the gringos waved back, thinking he was being friendly.

He got bored with this quickly, and ran screaming into the ocean, Gabriel close behind him. Daniela sidled up next to me, slim and tanned in her blue bikini, her body at its peak of unselfconscious perfection. (Not that we knew that then.) She squatted down, careful not to put her crotch in the sand. Girls always sat on sarongs or beach chairs, never directly on the sand. I glanced quickly at the soft bulge of her blue crotch, and then looked back at the sea.

'Why so quiet?' she said.

'Am I?'

'You always are.'

I pushed my glasses up my nose. Being quiet was — and still is — regarded with suspicion in Rio, which is strange, considering the sullenness of our Portuguese forefathers. Daniela thought, somehow, that being my girl-friend would change me, but still, I was determined to make an effort, to stoke up the crush I had before Mamãe died.

'Want to swim?' I said.

'Yes.'

We stood up, shook the sand off our bodies and walked to the ocean. As the cool water rushed over our feet, Daniela yelped at its force. I took off my glasses and held them in my right hand.

'Can you see anything?' she said.

I could see a smiling blur where her face was. Behind her, the Atlantic. Behind that, who knows?

'Not much,' I said.

She took my hand and we waded in.

After the beach, Daniela and I went to my flat to get a drink — it was her idea. I felt queasy, thinking of her meeting Luana, but I couldn't think of an excuse not to go. Dani wanted to see where I lived. We took the service lift, because we were covered in sand, but walked into the flat through the guests' door.

'Hello?' said Luana, from the kitchen.

'Hi, it's me,' I said. 'I've brought a friend.'

Luana walked into the living room with her hands clasped behind her back, looking strangely formal.

'Luana, this is Daniela,' I said, forcing a casual smile.

'Hi,' said Dani, looking at Luana, then at me.

'Prazer,' said Luana, nodding. 'Can I get you anything to drink?'

Before I could say no, Daniela had already given her order: 'Yes, please, can I have a guaraná with ice?'

'For you, too, André?'

'Yes, please.'

She left the room, her uniform hanging loosely over her body. It was probably her mother's dress, I realized. Dani and I sat on a sofa, spreading the sand everywhere. She leaned in and kissed my cheek while I tried to think of something to say, knowing that Luana could hear us.

'What's up with her?' whispered Dani, rolling her eyes.

'What do you mean?'

Before she could answer, Luana had returned with two frosted glasses of guaraná with ice.

* * *

That evening, at dinner, Papai quizzed me about my day at school. I told him what I'd studied and left out the bit where I spent the entire afternoon on the beach, drinking beer with my friends, smoking cigarettes and flirting with Daniela. Shoving each other in the water, holding hands, laughing at the return of our mutual attraction.

'Just make sure you work hard,' said Papai. 'Keep your head down. Don't waste time with your friends.'

'Surely I can see them sometimes?'

'Within reason.'

Papai had been a teenage nerd — I could tell from his old photos — and was trying to mould me in his image. I had the glasses, but that's where the resemblance ended.

Thiago had put a fork through his chicken breast and was eating it in tiny little bites, like an ice cream on a stick.

'That is a disgusting way to eat,' said Papai.

Thiago continued, regardless. My father couldn't be bothered to pursue it.

'What did you learn at school, Thiago?' he said.

'About the Portuguese landing in Brazil.'

'What year was that?'

'1500.'

'And who discovered Brazil?'

'Uhhh . . . '

'Come on, this is easy for us.'

'Cabral!' said Thiago, through a mouthful of chicken. 'Pedro Álvares Cabral. Is he related to us?'

'Probably,' said Papai, slicing his chicken and taking a quick bite. He clashed the fork against his teeth, sending a shiver down my spine.

'It's a common name, though,' I said. 'He didn't even stay in Brazil.'

'Oh, André, stop ruining our fun.'

'Yeah,' said Thiago. 'I'm the king of Portugal!'

He shot his skinny arms into the air, and we all laughed.

'André, I have a proposition for you,' said Papai. 'How would you like to come to work in the surgery? Just once in a while.'

He pushed his glasses to the top of his head and looked at me intensely. I didn't have a choice in the matter and knew that 'once in a while' did not mean 'once in a while'.

'What would I do?'

'Watch operations, help the receptionist. Maybe even, you know, start assisting me.'

'Is that legal?'

He screwed up his face, as though to say: who cares? My father didn't worry about rules, other than the ones he set himself. In this sense, he wasn't unusual. The country — indeed, the continent — was run by men like him. Rules were for servants and poor people, and lucky gringos who lived in civilized countries.

'Pai, I have a lot of schoolwork at the moment. I don't know if I have time for this.'

'Stop going to the beach with your little friends and you'll have time for it,' he said.

'Do I have any say in this?'

He looked straight at me and laughed, his eyes small and mocking, his brown skin glistening with sweat. What would Mamãe have said? Matheus, leave him alone, meu Deus do céu — he's just a boy.

'Oh, it's like that?' he said. 'I offer you an opportunity and you just want to wriggle out of it and go to the goddamn beach? I would have loved to do something like this at your age but, unfortunately, I had to do it all alone.'

This was a recurring theme: how lucky we were, compared to him, though he never went into much detail about his past. Mamãe, when she was angry with him, would tell us: Papai was impossible because he came from an impossible family. She said that his father had a dozen illegitimate children and disappeared when Papai was a teenager, probably murdered. I didn't know if this was true, but it sounded exciting, like a novela.

'OK,' I said. 'I'll do it.'

'Good,' said Papai, looking genuinely pleased. 'You'll start next week.'

We didn't talk any more. All I could hear was slicing, chewing, swallowing, drinking, and outside, cars on the street, people walking and talking. Life was out there; one day, mine would begin. I ate quickly and stood up to leave. Thiago followed me.

'Run along and watch TV,' said Papai, 'because soon you'll be working with me. Playtime is over, menino.'

We went to the TV room. I was furious. Anger pumped through my heart, burning my fingers and toes. One day, I won't be under his thumb, I told myself. One day, I'll show him I'm a better man than he is. Thiago was in his own world, telling me about his school's new petting zoo.

'I stroked a baby goat,' he said.

'Was it nice?' I managed to say.

'It was cute. We should get a goat. Turn on the TV.'

I don't remember what was on — some novela — because I wasn't watching. I was looking at the TV, but not seeing it. After washing the dishes, Luana appeared and sat on her wooden chair. Her eyes lacked their usual brightness. Less lime-flesh, more trampled leaves. Still beautiful enough to make my anger turn lukewarm. I paid even less attention to the TV. She knew I was looking at her — her jaw twitched and her eyes were glassy — but still, she stared ahead at the screen. I turned to Thiago and saw that he had been watching me.

'What are you doing?' he said.

'Nothing.'

Luana glanced at us, looking uneasy, and then looked back at the TV. When the show finished, she got up, said, 'Goodnight,' and retired to the room at the back of the kitchen. She didn't even look at me when she left. Flip-flops slapping on the kitchen tiles. I counted them: um, dois, três, quatro . . . Then Thiago followed soon after, and went to his bedroom.

Living with Luana was becoming more difficult every day, and there was no end in sight. I was planning to attend university in Rio and would be living at home for many years, until I paired off with a woman. It could be six years, ten years or for ever, like Mamãe's brother, Gustavo, who in his forties was still living with Vovó and Vovô, jobless, delusional and dulled by lithium. Aunt Lia lived in fear of becoming his guardian — she was a psychoanalyst and had enough mad people in her life. But I was nothing like Gustavo. I decided to avoid Luana as much as I could. No more TV sessions, no more lingering looks. I would follow my father's orders and stay in my bedroom, do my homework like a good boy. His offer of unpaid labour was the perfect excuse to get out of the flat, even though I didn't want to do it.

That night I lay awake in bed, neatly lining up my plans, like ornaments on a shelf. And then I masturbated while thinking of Luana — her curved, pink lips, her round bum-bum, her small breasts and her nipples, which I had never seen, but which were surely as brown and hard as raisins — but after I came stickily into my right hand, my excitement faded to shame. A sound came from the kitchen, on the other side of the flat. Luana or Rita's flip-flops. *Slap, slap, slap.* Water gushing into a plastic cup.

12

When I was a kid, Europe was the dream: o primeiro mundo, the mythic first world. Despite the fact that my friends and I had all been there on holidays — and found it deeply boring, walking around art galleries and tired old streets, wearing too many layers of clothing — we clung to the idea that emigrating to Europe was like going to heaven. The specific country didn't matter. To us, Europe was itself a country — uniformly glamorous, wise and superior — though, looking back, I doubt we were dreaming of the USSR, Yugoslavia or Romania. Those countries didn't count.

Sometimes older siblings or cousins would go over for a year or two and come back blabbering about the galleries, the culture, the statues, the superiority of our ancestral home. (I have Italian and Portuguese blood, but even Portugal, when I visited, seemed entirely foreign: that brittle accent, the dour people.) Our twentieth-century explorers always came back, for some reason. Like Carlito's older sister, Juliana, who spent two years in London, living with Brazilians in a shared house, dating a Brazilian chef and skipping her English lessons: 'Meu Deus, it was incredible.'

The old world. Londres. Roma. Lisboa. Paris. But especially Londres. No dictatorships, bureaucracy, muggings or shitty currency. (That year we had a new one, the cruzado.) Most of us had been mugged at least once. I had been with Mamãe when she handed over her purse to black boys with knives. My bicycle — my seventeenth-birthday present — was taken three weeks after I received it. Rodrigo had his trainers stolen while visiting family in Santa Teresa, up in the hills. He walked back to his aunt's house in socks. Carlito once came home just in his boxer shorts. Isabel lost her grandmother's wedding ring to two boys, no older than twelve. The ring had survived Auschwitz, hidden away in some orifice, but couldn't survive a night out in Copacabana. Daniela had been mugged twice in São Paulo — once at knifepoint, once at gunpoint. Not surprising: wealth seeped from her freckles, her blue eyes; nails done, legs waxed, hair sun-bleached, walk insouciant. Our wealth shone from our faces like beacons: come and get us. No wonder we wanted to get away and live in cities where there were more of us.

I hadn't been to Europe since I was twelve, but that didn't stop me from taking part in the hagiography. We had it all planned out: midnight strolls by the Trevi Fountain, gold glittering on the girls' necks and ears, with no risk of theft; eating croissants by the Seine.

'The streets were so clean in Londres,' I said, 'and everyone sat in cafés, reading books.'

We were sitting under a tree outside our school, just after classes had ended. It had rained heavily that morning, but already the ground had dried to dust.

'Wow,' said Isabel.

Any of us could have sat in cafés reading books in Rio, but we didn't. I had forgotten that the streets of London are also flecked with chewing gum, dog shit and homeless people, shivering in the year-round cold — or maybe I hadn't noticed.

'We went to the cinema and could watch any film we wanted — nothing was banned.'

'Nothing's banned here any more,' Dani pointed out.

'Yeah, not for the last five minutes,' said Carlito. 'What did you watch?'

'*The Empire Strikes Back.*'

'That wasn't even banned here,' said Rodrigo. 'I saw it at Barra Shopping Centre!'

'Yeah, but come on — I was twelve years old,' I said. 'I wasn't going to watch *Deliverance.*'

'What's that?' said Dani.

'Only the most important American film of the seventies.'

'The seventies?' said Isabel. 'Who cares about the seventies?'

'I don't know why you're all so obsessed with leaving,' said Dani. 'I like it here.' We all looked at her, making her face turn pink. 'Why is that weird?'

'This country is a shithole,' said Isabel. 'I'm gonna go to Paris, work for *Vogue*.'

She cackled, like she knew it was a pipe dream, and that she would become a society woman like her mother; kept, stretched and gym-honed, with three empregadas and a husband who played away.

'I don't need to live in the centre of the world,' said Dani.

I wondered if people felt different living over there, walking through those old streets, knowing they were going somewhere, doing something. You would walk off the plane and feel a crackle of importance in the air. I hadn't felt it when I was twelve, but I was a man now.

'You don't mind living here for the rest of your life?' I said.

'I'd like to travel the world,' said Dani, 'but I want to come back afterwards.'

'No way, cara. I'm leaving and never

coming back,' said Gabriel. 'As soon as I get signed to Juventus.'

He laughed ironically, just like Isabel had done.

'In your dreams!' said Carlito. 'I'm leaving, too.' He picked a city at random. 'Madrid, or something. What about you, André?'

I was serious. I wanted to get away. From the suffocating humidity, palm trees on the beach, the taste of coconut water, the neatly folded clothes in my wardrobe. The view of the Cagarras from my living-room window. All of it an echo of my mother. All of them whispering, Mamãe Mamãe Mamãe.

'Londres,' I said. 'I really felt at home there.'

Everyone nodded, apart from Daniela. She was laughing at me, shaking her head. I was talking out of my arse. I hadn't felt at home in London. I was bored, cold and pissed off with my parents, trailing behind them at museums. Thiago had been two years old, the centre of attention. The highlight had been the breakdancers in the street, with their rolled-out mats — black boys shilling for coins, just like they did in Rio, but these weren't the same sort of black boys — and *The Empire Strikes Back*, which I watched with Papai at a cinema in Marble Arch. At least that's where I think it was. It's difficult to align the London of 1980 with the London of 2014. In reality, the only place I had ever felt at home, in 1986, was on Avenida Vieira Souto, between Rua Maria Quitéria and Rua Joana Angélica, five floors up.

13

Papai's surgery was in one of the few remaining houses in Ipanema. Who knows why it was exempt from the destruction of the old Zona Sul — it was nothing special. Whitewashed and squat, windows barred against robbers and too poky for its purpose. It seemed incongruous: state-of-the-art plastic surgery taking place in such an old building. ('Old' in Rio means early twentieth century.) But Papai always said that surgery wasn't that sophisticated — just butchery and common sense. A large sign was posted in the front yard, stating Papai's name and credentials, with a photo of his smiling face: 'Matheus Cabral, Cirurgião Plástico'. I vividly remember an argument he had with Mamãe over the sign, when he first bought the building.

'Who would want surgery from someone with a nose like yours?' she said.

But his business didn't suffer. Maybe his clients liked the picture's honesty. Here's my big Lebanese nose, it said, here are my tiny native eyes and my full, trustworthy Portuguese mouth. Now let's see what we can do about your ugly face. Young women mostly wanted nose jobs and breast enlargements or reductions, while their mothers and grandmothers had their faces stretched tight over their skulls. Men, too, walked the streets of Zona Sul with bandaged faces, proudly bearing their bloodied symbols of wealth. Sunglasses on top, like the Invisible Man.

I started working as the surgery's receptionist, administrator and general dogsbody, unpaid, on afternoons, evenings and even weekends — Papai was working longer hours than ever before. The first operation I witnessed was a breast reduction. I don't remember the woman's face, but I will never forget her breasts — enormous, goose-pimpled, dark-nippled — and how her skin gave way so easily to my father's scalpel, which I had passed to him. Under the skin, the woman was red meat and yellow fat, just an animal being butchered. I tasted something sour at the back of my throat and my body felt heavy, my head light, but no, of course I wouldn't give in to it in front of my father. He turned to me and nodded appreciatively, as though we were witnessing a rare work of art. I soon got used to the operations and sometimes even assisted Papai, beyond just passing his instruments. It wasn't legal, of course, but the other doctors and nurses barely raised an eyebrow when, a few weeks in, he asked me to sew a nipple back on to a breast. I did a good job, though, and the woman would never know any better — she was out cold, her tongue hanging out.

'Who needs medical school when you have me?' said Papai, slapping me on the back.

He smiled widely through his surgical mask, his eyes small and bright. I smiled back. It pleased me to please my father. I learned how to make an incision, sew someone up and mould a nose to perfection. Ahead of the curve, just like he wanted. One day, all this could be mine, whether I wanted it or not.

⋆ ⋆ ⋆

Papai had always been a workaholic, but sometimes I would wonder, what kind of person gets a nose job at 10 p.m. on a Monday? When I started working with him, the mystery deepened. Most of his employees clocked off at six or seven, but Papai and one of his nurses, Elena, worked into the night. After eating dinner at home, we would often return to the surgery, where I would sit at reception, doing admin and welcoming his patients. The patients in the evening were not like the others. They weren't registered in the appointment book. They didn't look any different when they left. No bandages, no swollen chests. Just tear-blotched faces, wincing a little. All of them women, usually alone. Papai didn't invite me into the operating theatre, and told me not to answer phone calls in the evening but put them straight through to his office.

One night, I asked him what was going on.

'I'm experimenting with some new, non-surgical techniques,' he said. 'It's best to keep them off the books.'

This sounded plausible, but dodgy — what if someone ended up deformed? That night there was just one client booked in, for 9 p.m., but she was late. I sat for an hour, bored as hell, waiting. Clock ticking, air con humming, cars beeping, distant night-time laughter from bars and people on the street. I read all the waiting-room magazines and newspapers: *Veja*, *O Globo*, an old copy of *Vogue Brasil* full of cod-philosophical interviews with high-society peruas, patricinhas, models and actresses. In the newer magazines, the big story was the World Cup, which was a week away, in Mexico. Not that I cared. (Most Englishmen, when they hear I'm from Brazil, immediately start talking about football. When they find out that I'm not interested, they back away, astonished, as though I've admitted to some terrible perversion.)

The client finally arrived: a woman in her early forties, wearing high heels, sunglasses and a blue silk scarf knotted over her dark hair. She was stinking rich, it was obvious. In Rio, only the super-rich spent enough time in air-conditioned cars and buildings to necessitate wearing headscarves. I asked her to wait while I called my father on the intercom. The woman popped Chiclets into her mouth and chewed loudly. Her face twitched with nerves. I tried not to look.

When my father came in, she said in a scratchy voice, 'Who's the kid? I thought it would be just you and the nurse.'

'It's my son. Don't worry. Shall we?'

He took her to the operating room and came back a few minutes later.

'Go home, filho. It's late.'

★　★　★

It was Aunt Lia who told me the truth, when Thiago and I were at her flat in Leblon. Lia was Mamãe's older sister. She had a world-weary glamour, with her silk blouses, grey, bobbed hair, her psychoanalyst's couch — which we liked to lie on — and her cigarettes, which she smoked all day, even through meals. She never married or had children, but she loved young people and treated most adults, especially Papai, like boring idiots. Perhaps she thought Mamãe could have done better.

We were eating pudding, a bright yellow quindim. Thiago stood up to go to the bathroom. Lia's eyes followed him until he had left the dining room.

'So your father's working you hard, eh?' she said.

Earlier, I had been complaining about the long hours.

'Yes,' I said, but not wanting to stoke her disapproval of him, I added, 'It's fine, I'm learning a lot.'

'To be honest, I respect what he's doing,' she said, and I looked up. 'You're shocked? It's the right thing to do. I'm not a Jesus freak, why should I care?'

I had no idea what she was talking about, so I kept quiet and nodded, hoping she would carry on.

'It's dangerous, but it's right,' she said. 'When your government is as shitty and self-serving as ours, you have to take matters into your own hands, don't you think?'

'I suppose so.'

'But don't tell him that I know. I found out from one of my patients, who went to him.

Just a girl, poor thing, far too young to be a mother. His name just slipped from her mouth — she didn't mean to say it.'

'Right.'

I was taken aback, but I tried to stay calm. It was hard to fool Lia, though — she was a perceptive woman. She pursed her lips, widened her eyes and leaned into me.

'You knew that, didn't you?' she said.

'Of course, of course I knew,' I blabbered.

'Meu Deus do céu, you didn't know,' she said, looking at the ceiling, then back at me. 'You didn't know, did you? Shit!'

Her hands became jittery, grabbing at her pack of cigarettes. She lit one with a silver fighter, sucked and blew smoke, and waved it away.

'Don't tell him I told you,' she said.

I agreed, just as Thiago returned to the room.

* * *

I told Papai that I knew, but I didn't tell him how I knew.

'I can't reveal my sources,' I said.

'What are you, a detective?'

'When did you start doing this?'

'It's been a few years.'

'Did Mamãe know?'

'Yes, but she didn't like it.'

'Do you really need the money?' I said. 'It's illegal.'

'It shouldn't be. We don't need more unwanted children in the world. Look at the First World — it's legal over there. We can't keep up with them because there are too many religious maniacs over here.'

'Aren't you worried about getting caught?'

'I'm not advertising it to the world. Between you and me, I've helped some very important people, which offers me some protection. Can't tell you who. *Very* important. But you can't tell anyone. Not even your friends.'

'What if one of them needs an abortion?'

'Hopefully, your friends aren't like that,' he said, looking appalled.

For an atheist, he had a real puritanical streak. Papai was a backstreet abortionist, but Rua Joana Angelica is no backstreet. He aborted the richest embryos in Rio de Janeiro.

14

Late in the afternoon, several hours after school, I was sitting with my friends on Copacabana beach. My father had given me the afternoon off to study. I took my books to the beach, but left them in my backpack. The sun was on its way down, and I was thinking about leaving. Dani had a fashionable new hairdo — a big, fluffy perm. Isabel told her she looked like a famous actress, but I thought she looked silly. I could smell her hair gel every time we kissed. A tiny black insect flew into her hair, but I didn't say anything because I didn't want to embarrass her. I doubt it came out alive.

I walked home alone on the pavement beside the beach, all the way to Ipanema. The sun goes down quickly in Rio, and already the sky was blue-black, obscured on the right by tall buildings, and on my left, reaching across the ocean, to the world. People jogging, riding bicycles, women clicking home in high heels, the air light and warm. I passed the Arpoador rock, and I was in Ipanema. The curves of the Dois Irmãos mountains were still visible at the end of the beach. The

141

favelas beneath them were lighting up as people arrived home from work. The ocean was loud and dark. People drinking and chatting, on plastic chairs, at the beach bars. Ten metres away, a mother and two children were sitting on the pavement, looking ragged. And there was my building, on the other side of the road, nestling in the middle of the block, the living-room window aglow, like a lantern in the night.

I heard Luana's voice as I stepped out of the lift; it was as soft and sweet as a peach, like nothing could faze her. She was saying something like, 'Mãe, can you pass me the — ', and I felt oddly moved that she was there, preparing our dinner. I opened the door and walked through the kitchen, greeting her and her mother. Rita and I made small talk about the hot weather. Beyond saying hello, Luana didn't speak or look at me, and carried on cooking, her head bent over the stove in concentration or avoidance, or both. I carried on talking, my voice too loud, and my lungs felt tight, like they were running out of air.

'Don't distract us, André,' said Rita, in a sarcastic tone.

'OK, OK,' I said, leaving the kitchen, laughing.

After showering, I went to the dining room.

Papai was back from work, reading a newspaper at the table.

'Hello, André,' he said. 'Did you study much?'

He raised his tortoiseshell glasses and wiped the sweat from his forehead and eyelids with a napkin.

'A bit, yes.'

'Good.'

I could hear the soft hum of Rita and Luana's voices in the kitchen, and recognize the rich coconut-and-manioc smell of bobó de camarão cooking on the stove. Soon they would bring the food from the kitchen, and I would see Luana — that's what I was waiting for. I had seen her thirty minutes earlier, but already I missed her. Thiago joined us at the table, wearing caped Superman pyjamas, all ready for bed. His hair was still wet from the shower. He sat down at his usual chair, pulled a comic out of his trousers and started reading.

'Filho,' said Papai, 'don't read at the dinner table.'

Thiago glanced up and carried on reading. My father slammed his fist on the table.

'Stop it,' he said.

Thiago put the comic on the table and looked straight ahead. Rita brought in bowls of rice and salad. Then came Luana from the kitchen, holding a heavy ceramic pot, eyes downcast. There was an orange smudge of sauce on her white uniform. She put the pot on the table, looked up and smiled at me for the first time in weeks, or months, making my stomach feel so empty. I smiled back, feeling delirious. I looked at my father, and he shook his head, almost imperceptibly. Thiago looked from me to Papai and back again, and emitted a high-pitched squeal.

'Shut up and eat,' said Papai, and we ate.

* * *

Later on, I was reading in bed with my lamp low, so that everyone would think I was asleep, but my father knew better. He entered my bedroom without knocking, flooding it with yellow light from the corridor. Still in his shirt, tie and trousers, he stood in the doorway, his hand on the knob.

'What are you reading?' he said.

'Fernando Pessoa. It's for school.'

'Good Portuguese poet. But don't get any funny ideas. Life is not as simple as a poem.'

'What do you mean?'

He approached my bed.

'Aren't you hot in those clothes?' I asked.

He waved this question away and stood over me, in the half-darkness, with his right index finger raised.

'Do not fuck around with Luana,' he said.

His voice was barely a whisper — as quiet and raspy as the scuttle of a cockroach.

'What?'

'Do not. Fuck around. With Luana.'

'I'm not doing anything with Luana.'

'Good. That's how it should be. Understand, André?'

'What are you talking about, Pai?'

'It's a line you don't cross,' he said.

'I wasn't planning to.'

'They're not like us. It's not right.'

'OK,' I said.

What had Papai seen? How could he know? Did he hear us in Marajó? Had he been standing in the corridor while we kissed? Worse still, was there nothing I could do, or even think, without his knowing about it?

My father went over to the full-length mirror and looked at his reflection. The pale moonlight (or maybe it was just the streetlight, come to think of it) shone on to his face, casting a shadow on the pronounced curve of his mouth. He took a comb from his pocket and slicked back his thick, black hair. Loosened his tie and looked back at me. My bedroom faced away from the beach but, in my memory of this moment, I could hear the Atlantic, crashing against the sand.

'Maybe we should go to Pará again this Christmas. Would you like that?' he said.

'Sounds good.'

Orange bikini, kissing in the dark river.

'Just the three of us.'

Oh.

'Until tomorrow,' he said.

'Goodnight, Pai.'

After he left, I turned the lamp off and pulled a sheet over my body, but it was too hot, so I kicked it off. I stared at the darkness, thinking about what he had said. If he found out about the kiss, he would be livid. Perhaps he would send Luana away. I must make the effort, I thought, to stop thinking about her. It's over. That's that. But as I closed my eyes, Papai's warning was soon drowned out by thoughts of Luana, of her green eyes, her bikini glowing neon under the river water. I soon fell under a heavy cloak of sleep.

★   ★   ★

I woke up exhausted. My eyes were crusty, my head heavy and my nose blocked with snot. When I lifted my head from the pillow, pain shot through my body, and I groaned. As usual, Rita knocked on my door at quarter to six to wake me up for school.

'Rita!' I whined.

'Yes?' she said through the door.

'I'm feeling unwell, I can't go.'

'OK, querido, I'll call and let them know. Do you need anything?'

'No. I'll just go back to sleep.'

I heard her flip-flops smacking down the corridor, then two people murmuring in the kitchen — Rita and my father. His heavier, clanking footsteps coming towards me. He came in without knocking and stood in the doorway, frowning at me. I felt broken and pathetic. I could barely open my eyes. My father was only five foot seven — one inch shorter than me — but he looked like an evil giant from a fairy tale. I felt feverish and mad.

'What's wrong with you?' he said.

'I'm aching all over.'

He strode over, felt my forehead with a dry, warm palm, and nodded.

'Stay in bed. I'm off to work.'

He walked out. The sun had just come up. It wasn't yet hot, though I wasn't a good judge of temperatures that day. I was sweating all over, but my bones felt like ice. The sheet was mangled around my feet. Painfully, I untangled it with my hands, pulled it over me and fell asleep. Usually, sleep is such a comfort, but not on that day. I plunged into a vivid dream. My mother bent over me, with her long, black hair. She folded a little damp cloth and put it on my forehead, cooling me down.

'Poor Andrézinho,' she said, pulling the sheet up to my neck.

'Mamãe, where have you been? I thought you had died.'

'What are you talking about, querido?'

'You — you crashed into a traffic light. I saw you at the hospital. You were dead.'

'Can't you see I'm here?'

She stroked my cheek. Her hands were warm and alive, nails manicured pale pink, wrists jangling with silver and gold. As she leaned in and kissed my forehead, I inhaled the cloying scent of her perfume — now heavenly to me. She was wearing a cream silk dress, a brightly coloured necklace and the gold watch she wore every day. Everything was perfect, even down to the mole on her left cheek.

'Yes, you're here,' I said. 'But it felt so real. A year went by . . . Papai was alone. We went to Pará without you.'

'Urgh,' she said, smacking her red-painted lips. 'Why would you go to that shithole? Your father and his obsessions. It was just a bad dream. Mamãe is here. I'll always be here.'

I looked around the room. We weren't in Rio any more but in my bedroom in Marajó, except the river was flowing right outside my window, like a Venetian canal. Luana swam past in her orange bikini, looking straight ahead, doing breaststroke.

'But we're in Pará, Mamãe,' I said.

'Oi, Luana!' said Mamãe, waving at her.

Luana stopped swimming and waved back, smiling but saying nothing. Seeing her, my mood lifted, but then I remembered what Papai had told me: do not fuck around with Luana. I turned to my mother, who was looking at me in a strange, serious way, as if she knew what I was thinking. Luana swam on.

'That girl is far too pretty to be an empregada,' said Mamãe. 'Where does she get it from? Rita's hardly a looker.'

'Don't be rude about Rita,' I said. 'You were always so mean to her.'

'Lie back, querido. Don't tire yourself out.'

I stretched out my left hand, and she took it in both of hers.

'You'll be just fine,' she said. 'All you need to do is sleep.'

'But . . . the accident. How did you survive? I saw *you*.'

'How could that happen? I'm such a careful driver.'

I sank back into the pillows, feeling my cool sweat soak into them.

'Graças a Deus,' I said, as I closed my eyes. 'Graças a Deus.'

As I fell asleep in my dream, I woke up in Rio. Helicopters whirring outside, looking for some bandido. It was appallingly hot. Mamãe was gone. No one to pat my head with a cold, damp cloth. No one to comfort me. I cried like a child, with abandon, but into my pillow, so that Rita and Luana wouldn't hear. The injustice made me want to scream. Why her? Why my mother?

'André?' came a voice through the door. Luana.

'What?' I croaked.

'Are you OK?'

'I'm fine.'

'Do you need anything?'

'No, thanks.'

Couldn't she just leave me alone?

'Let me know if you change your mind.'

I turned to my side, pulled my knees up to my chest and squeezed two more tears out of my eyes, which were feeling heavy again. I closed them and fell asleep, hoping to see Mamãe again, but this time it was a dreamless sleep, or the dreams weren't worth remembering.

★   ★   ★

When I woke, it was dark. I could hear distant voices from the bars, but they weren't shouting or laughing that much, so it must have been early evening, before they were properly drunk. The air in my bedroom was hot and stiff. A few seconds later, a soft knock. Lua. Luana.

'André? Are you awake?'

'Yes.'

'Can I come in?'

'Yes.'

The door creaked open, letting in the light from the corridor. She closed the door behind her.

'I won't turn on the light. It'll hurt your head.'

She walked over. She was barefoot — I could hear her feet padding across the wooden floor.

'Would you be able to open the window?' I said.

'Of course.'

She leaned over my bed to get to the window, and swung it open. The noises from outside — the bar people, the cars — became amplified. I saw she was holding something. A small, white cloth.

'Would you like this?' She held it up. 'My mother always puts a cloth on my head when I have a temperature.'

'Yes.'

She shook out the cloth, folded it twice and put it on my forehead. It was cool and damp, just like in my dream.

'That feels nice.'

'Good. Do you want some soup?'

'Yes, please.'

'OK, I'll bring it up.'

Minutes later, she brought a spicy chicken soup on a tray and a glass of water. I drank all the soup and downed the water. She sat on a chair by my desk, in the dark, as I ate. I could just see her outline, still and patient.

'One of your friends called,' she said.

'Which one?'

'Daniela. She was asking if you were OK.'

'What did you say?'

'I said you were sleeping. She said she might come and visit you tomorrow evening, if you're still unwell.'

She left and closed my door, and I lay in the dark, listening to the outside world.

★   ★   ★

I never get ill any more. That's what happens when you have children. As a parent, you can't play at being a child — not until you're older, and then it returns with a brute, unwanted force.

I felt a little better the next day, but not well enough to go to school, so I spent the day in bed, listening to music and trying to read Chekhov's short stories, translated into Portuguese. My headache made it difficult to keep up with all the Russian names and characters. I managed one full story, 'Gooseberries', a story within a story, about greed and disappointment, like all the best stories. I wondered how Chekhov managed it — writing in the evenings, working as a doctor all day. He must have had empregadas and a very understanding wife. Even with his empregadas, I couldn't imagine Papai having time for anything else other than work. But then I gave up on reading and turned to music. There were two record players in the flat — one in the living room and one in my parents' bedroom. Papai never used the latter, so Rita and Luana brought it to my room, put it on my desk and plugged it in. I felt guilty for bossing them around, but they were the ones who kept asking me what I wanted every five minutes.

'Can you play the Chico Buarque one — *Chico Canta?*' I said to Luana.

She had brought a pile of records into my room. Rita had gone elsewhere — back to cleaning. Constant cleaning: every day, all day.

'This one?' she said, holding up a record. The cover showed Chico in a flat cap and with a moustache, crooning into a mic.

'The third song.'

She shook the record out of its sleeve, placed it in the machine and pressed play. I thought she would then leave the room, but instead she sat on the chair, in front of the turning record. Mamãe's song, 'Tatuagem'. I hadn't heard it since Marajó.

'This is old music,' said Luana, grinning.

'Not that old.'

I closed my eyes and listened. The impossible beauty of the strings, the directness of his words. When I opened my eyes, Luana was resting her head on her palm, and her elbow on the table, looking into the distance with her milky, green eyes.

'I remember it,' she said.

'You do?'

'Of course. Dona Beatriz played it over and over again. Especially on the days when she didn't come out of her room.'

'When was that?'

'Lots of times. Sometimes she would stay in bed all morning, and only get dressed and put her makeup on before you came back from school. Someone else would run her shop for her.'

154

'I don't remember that.'

'Well, you weren't here. We could hear it coming from her room all day. My mother and I got so sick of it.'

She got up to leave.

'Don't go,' I said.

'I have work to do.'

'Luana, please. Tell me more about my mother.'

'You should ask your father.'

'You're remembering it wrong. My mother was fine.'

'You're right, I don't know anything.'

'That's not what I meant.'

She left, and the record played on, until it reached the end of side one and drifted into rhythmic, crackling nothingness.

★   ★   ★

Daniela paid me a visit, true to her word. She came into my bedroom still wearing her school rucksack on her back.

'Hi,' she said. 'How are you feeling?'

We had seen each other a few days before, but it felt like longer. All those dreams, all that stretched time.

'Better than yesterday.'

'I know. I dropped by yesterday. You were asleep. I was walking past, on the way home, and dropped in. Just to see if you were all right.'

'Thanks, I appreciate it.'

'But you were asleep,' she said again. She seemed anxious.

'How are you?'

'Oh, you know. School. Boring.'

She sat on the end of my bed. I realized we had nothing to say to each other. Maybe it was just the illness, clouding my mind. She looked lovely, with her nervous blue eyes, her blond hair in a bun, but I wished that she would go away.

'Your empregada,' she said. 'She's pretty.'

'Is she?'

'You know she is. Isn't that weird? Our empregada looks like an old bruxa.'

15

'Can I ask you something?' said Bia. 'How did your mother die?'

'You already know that,' I said.

'I know it was a car accident, but you've never told me the whole story.'

We were at a local Italian restaurant, just the two of us. It was my idea — I wanted to tell her that I thought going to Brazil was a good idea, that she should accept Thiago's invitation. After I said my piece, she brought up Mamãe. The wine, it made her bold. Esther wouldn't have approved of us drinking together.

'It's not a nice story,' I said.

'Do all stories have to be nice?'

'Why do you want to know?'

'She was my grandmother,' she said. 'I just want to know. But if you don't want to talk about it — '

'No, it's fine.'

By then, a fourth letter had come. I'd been carrying it in my pocket for three days and had memorized it from beginning to end.

André,

I'm back in Marajó, sitting on my porch.
Breakfast has finished, so I have a few
minutes to myself before I go back to
work. I thought I would tell you a bit
more about when we left Rio.

Chico settled in quickly up here
— quicker than I did. When we left Rio,
he kept asking, 'Where are we going, why
are we going there?' and wouldn't let go
of my mother's legs. She was crying, too,
which didn't help. I kept the tears inside,
but I knew I would miss Rio. I still do.
The view of the beach from the morro,
my friends and family, the constant
noise, even in the middle of the night,
when everyone should be asleep. I don't
like to be there, but I miss it. I'm sure
you know what I mean.

I missed my —

'Dad?' said Bia, laughing, waving a hand in
front of my face. 'You've drifted off somewhere.'

'Sorry. OK, I'll tell you.'

Bia folded a slice of pizza in two and bit
down. I had forgotten about my food, veal
Milanese with spaghetti. I ate a couple of
mouthfuls. It had gone cold. I sipped my
wine before refilling our glasses. How many

years since I'd last told this story? When I was young I told it regularly to new friends and girlfriends, but I hadn't had one of those in years.

'I was at the beach one Sunday. Ipanema — you remember it?'

'Everyone knows Ipanema,' she said, pronouncing it 'Ipaneema', like a gringa. 'It's, like, world-famous.'

'I don't mean do you remember it from a picture, I mean from life. It's a different thing. Especially on a Sunday. Thousands of people. Rich people, poor people, beautiful people, ugly people, tourists. Past midday, it's nearly impossible to find a place to sit.'

'Who were you with?'

'My friends Daniela, Rodrigo, Isabel and Carlito, and some others. I can't remember their names. We were sitting on the beach, surrounded by people on all sides. It was very hot. Maybe thirty-eight degrees, maybe forty, which is when it becomes intolerable. It was January, which is summer in Brazil.'

'Of course.'

The waiter came and took our plates, and then brought a dessert menu.

'We were sitting at Posto Nove, the ninth lifeguard post, which was the fashionable place to sit — all the students and socialists used to go there. These were the final months of the military dictatorship, so there were lots of radicals around, lots of protests. I was swimming in the ocean with Carlito and Rodrigo, getting swallowed up by the waves. We were playing jacaré — 'alligator' — catching the waves with our bodies.'

'Bodysurfing?'

'Yes, but often the waves just caught us. The ocean in Ipanema, it's no joke, but we weren't scared of drowning, because we were young.'

⋆ ⋆ ⋆

We swam behind where the waves broke and floated a while, watching the girls on the beach, the sun shimmering on the ocean and on the new buildings that had been springing up since we were babies. Everything was blurred, because I had left my glasses on the beach, with the girls. Carlito looked over with a wet, toothy grin.

'André,' he said. 'Daniela — she's crazy for you. Crazy.'

I laughed, and he leapt on me, pushing my head under the cool water, which rushed into my ears and nose as I fought him off.

'Stop it, cara! You think so?'

'Cara, she totally is,' said Rodrigo. 'You're lucky.'

We looked over at the girls on the sand, in bikinis and sunglasses, lying on rented beach chairs with their tanned, curvy legs bent at the knee. Sure, Daniela was the prettiest. She stalked the school corridors in miniskirts and sandals, confident of her power.

We waved at the girls, and they waved back.

'She wouldn't go out with me,' I said.

⋆ ⋆ ⋆

'And Carlito said, 'Hey, isn't that your maid?' I looked up and saw Rita, one of our maids, standing on the beach.'

'How many maids did you have again?' said Bia.

'Two: Rita and her daughter, Luana.'

I hadn't said her name out loud for years, perhaps decades. Even when I visited Brazil and saw Papai and Thiago, we never talked about her. Such an odd, familiar sensation, moving my mouth around those syllables. Lu-uh-nuh. It seemed to echo around the restaurant — perhaps I'd shouted it, by mistake? — but Bia didn't seem to notice.

'Rita was standing on the beach, looking out to the ocean and trying to find me. Like this.'

I raised my hand up to my forehead and remembered Rita, in her white uniform, shielding her eyes from the sun.

'Any dessert?' said the waiter.

'Just a couple of minutes,' said Bia, resting her elbows on the table. 'Carry on.'

★　★　★

Rita's figure was hazy in the heat, because I wasn't wearing my glasses, but also strangely still.

'I'll see what's up,' I said, looking back to check if there was a wave coming, so I could play one last round of jacaré.

There was. The wave curled behind me, as clear as glass, and I started swimming, feeling it take me. It dropped me in the shallows. A perfect catch. Pleased with myself, I walked out of the sea, rubbing my hair, squeezing the water out of it, but seeing Rita up close, I knew that something was wrong. I could hear beeping and shouting on the street, further down towards Copacabana, but it was nothing out of the ordinary.

'Are you OK?' I said to Rita.

She was standing with her arms by her sides, unmoving, staring at me, a look of blank horror on her face. I laughed, hoping to hold back whatever it was she was going to say. I took my glasses from Isabel's sarong and put them on, so I could see again.

'And she said, 'It's your mother. There's been a car accident.''

'Oh God!' said Bia, holding her hands up to her face.

'Rita had been walking out of our building when she heard the commotion, so she went to have a look. She was crying, and I just knew. I don't know how, but I knew.'

'Wow.'

'So I ran to the street, towards the noise.'

Perhaps I hadn't actually known. Time has tinkered with my memories; taken them apart and put them back together in a tidy new shape. I've been living with that memory for longer than I lived with Mamãe. But it was strange, how I started running without asking Rita for more information.

* * *

The black-and-white pavement was so hot I had to dance across it, trying to stick to the cooler white stripes. Traffic had stopped, cars were beeping. A crowd had gathered further down the street — I ran towards it. Police officers were shouting at people to stay back. Women were covering their faces. My feet didn't feel so hot any more. The world became silent. I walked towards my mother's red sports car, crushed against a traffic light by a large blue truck. But she wasn't inside. A police officer held me back.

'It's my mother's car.'

He raised his eyebrows and put a hand on my shoulder.

'Where is she?' I said.

'She's at the hospital,' he said, leading me away. 'Come with me. You should get your clothes.'

I was still just wearing my swimming trunks. I craned my head to get a better look at the car. Its smashed red paintwork was shining in the sun. There was blood on the black-and-white pavement where she had landed, ten metres away.

★ ★ ★

'My mother had crashed into a traffic light, and the truck hit her from behind. She died on impact, thank God.'

It was a white lie. The force of the crash threw her on to the pavement, and she died in the ambulance. She had suffered. But I preferred the story this way.

'That's just awful,' said Bia.

'It was.'

'Why did she crash?'

164

'What do you mean?'

'You said she crashed into the light before the truck hit her. Was there something wrong with her car?'

Was there? I can't remember.

'Yes, yes, there was a fault.'

How could I not remember? It was such an important detail. Her foot slipped on the pedals — yes, that was it.

I looked at the bottle of wine, but it was empty.

I missed my mother most of all. I didn't know anyone here. The nights are silent, apart from the animals and the thunderstorms. It frightened me, at first. But not Chico — he slept well. He ran around the forest with his new friends, climbing trees, getting lost, swimming in the river. The kids here are softer, more gentle. They went swimming every day after school, and I would watch from the beach. Chico was the palest, so the kids called him Branquinho. When they weren't little any more, they called him Branco. He grew tall, grew his hair out big and frizzy and started getting attention from girls. He was beautiful.

Beijos,
Luana

16

I was doing homework on the round dining table. After being stuck in my room with the flu for so many days, I needed a change of scenery. But I struggled to stay focused. My eyes wandered to the glass doors that led on to the balcony, to the ocean. I went to the kitchen — Luana was round the back, hanging up laundry next to an open window. Rita was somewhere else. Luana lowered the drying rack with her strong arms from the ceiling, using a pulley. Once the rack was just above her head, she tied the rope and started hanging up the clean sheets.

'Hi,' I said.

She stopped.

'Bom dia.'

The tension had lifted somewhat, since my illness. We were no longer afraid of talking to each other.

'Do you want some help?' I said.

'I don't think you're supposed to help me.'

'There's no one around.'

She didn't answer, so I took it as a yes. I went over and took a pillowcase out of the basket, shook it out and slung it over the rack. She handed me a peg. I clipped it over the pillowcase and took another from the basket. For a few minutes we stood, side by side, hanging and pinning up the rest of the sheets. Luana worked quickly, automatically, while I fussed over each individual item, trying to align them perfectly on the rack. Once we were finished, sweat was trickling down my back, under my T-shirt, and the sheets were hanging over us, damp and fragrant.

'Thank you.'

'Any time.'

'Want to drink some mate?' she said. 'I made some a few hours ago. It should be cold by now.'

'OK.'

She opened the fridge and brought out a white plastic jug covered in condensation, full to the brim with cold, sweet mate. I took two glasses out of the cupboard and she poured out the drinks until they were both full.

'Let's drink it in the living room,' I said. 'Then we can listen to music.'

'Oh, OK.'

We took our drinks to the living room. She looked around uneasily.

'Sit on the sofa,' I said.

She sat on the dark green velvet sofa. I wondered if she had ever sat there before.

Maybe only when we were out.

'Put your feet up,' I said, and dragged Mamãe's Moroccan pouf under her small, flip-flopped feet. 'Comfortable?'

'Yes,' she said, but she didn't look it. Her body was stiff and her eyes were downcast, embarrassed.

'What would you like to listen to?' I said.

'Surprise me.'

Our records were mixed up: my dad's classical music (the only thing he listened to), Mamãe's MPB and Thiago's Turma do Balao Magico collection. The only record I owned was Michael Jackson's *Thriller*. Unlike my friends, who knew all the latest rock groups from São Paulo, New York and London, I didn't keep up with music, but since Mamãe's death I had claimed her music as my own; her favourites were now my favourites.

I found what I was looking for — *Tropicália: ou Panis et Circencis*, a sixties classic. It was out of fashion by 1986, that's for sure. I pressed play on the title track — a psychedelic, chanting mess. I loved its weirdness; it made me feel free. Before the accident, I would sometimes hear it on a Sunday morning, drifting from my parents' room. Mamãe often stayed in bed late, it was true. I had forgotten all about it, till Luana reminded me.

'This is a weird song,' she said, her face

hovering between a grin and a grimace.

The album was released in July 1968, the month I was born, when Mamãe was twenty-one, nearly twenty-two, freshly dropped out of her law degree at Universidade Federal do Rio de Janeiro. Perhaps she had left me alone with Rita, who was even younger, and not yet pregnant with Luana. I can imagine Mamãe wandering the sunny streets of Ipanema, towards a record shop. Still bloated from pregnancy, but happy, I hope. Or maybe she bought it months later. I don't know.

Luana was looking straight ahead at the record player, watching the black disc go round. Her eyes blinked softly as the song ended. I got up to turn it off.

She said, 'Leave it. Let it play.'

The next song started: 'Lindonéia' sung by Nara Leão.

'Can I ask you a question?' I said.

'Yes.'

'Have you ever sat on this sofa before?'

'Yes, I have. Though I probably shouldn't tell you that.'

'How do these rules get passed on? Was there one day when someone decided that empregadas can't sit on sofas?'

'My mother told me when I was young, but I barely remember being told. It's just something you know. You can't relax in front of your employers. It's been that way since the beginning of time, don't you think?'

'Then why are you sitting now?'

'You asked me to.'

Her white uniform was bright and hard against the soft green velvet of the sofa. Bare, brown legs, still stretched out on the pouf. Above her, on the wall, hung a folkish painting of a dark-skinned naked woman, lying on a bed, surrounded by bright flowers.

★ ★ ★

Helping Luana with the laundry, and then listening to music, became a regular occurrence. She didn't need my help — in fact, I slowed her down — but she didn't refuse it either. It could be a Wednesday evening, when Rita had taken Thiago to one of his many activities and my father was working late. It could be a Saturday morning, when I wasn't needed at the surgery, or a Sunday, when it wasn't her day off. Rita would go to the market and, occasionally, take Thiago. Sometimes I would encourage him to accompany her, telling him that I'd seen a man selling puppies on the street, or I'd give him money for ice cream.

One Saturday, everything fell into place. My father was working, Rita was shopping and Thiago was at his football club, so I went and found Luana in the laundry area at the back of the kitchen, with her basket of clean clothes.

'Thiago's clothes,' she said.

'Good. I can't say I enjoyed hanging up my dad's underwear last week.'

She laughed that sweet donkey laugh and brought down the rack. I took an item from the basket — Thiago's Superman pyjama top — shook it and pinned it up. She took the matching trousers, and hung them up, too. We carried on like this, quick and silent, going through the basket. Even now, I can still smell the soap, its faint coconut scent. The damp coolness of the laundry, hovering above us. Her brown arms picking and pinning, with elegant grace. The view outside the window, of concrete buildings, humming with life, and dark mountains beyond. Soon there was a single sock left in the basket. We looked at each other and reached for it at the same time. Our hands touched lightly, a thumb to a finger, but we didn't move away. Just stayed there, feeling that small bit of skin. Then I was holding her hand. It was like our hands had their own objective, which we could only follow.

Luana turned towards me, and I towards her. A light sweat on her skin. Those green eyes. Damp laundry. My pulse was beating in every part of my body, from my eyes to my penis to my toes. Fear as well as excitement. I touched her lips with mine. Luana smelled of coconut soap and sweat, and faint perfume. A hot ray of sunshine from the open window scorched the back of my neck, until Luana covered it with her hand, pulling me closer to her, so that she could feel my erection against her stomach.

She pulled away and said, 'What are we doing? We shouldn't do this.'

'I know.'

We kissed again, for several minutes, until my lips felt raw. She put a hand on my chest and pushed me away.

'That's enough,' she said. 'This is weird.'

'I know.'

What else could I say but: I know, I know, I know.

'I'm sorry, André.'

'I'm not sorry,' I said, tugging at her sleeve.

'We can't be together.'

I wasn't intending on being together. Not then, anyway. I was on the cusp of my eighteenth birthday, kissing the most beautiful girl I had ever seen.

'Then I'm sorry, too,' I lied, and started walking to the kitchen door.

She stood there, in her white uniform, just

looking at me. In my bedroom, I jerked off and listened as she cleaned the flat, prepared food, did her job.

That evening, as she and Rita served our dinner, both of us were subdued, but only my mood was remarked upon.

'What's wrong with you?' said Papai, as he spooned salad on to his plate.

'Nothing.'

'Nothing!' said Thiago.

'I'm just tired.'

'Tired from sitting around all day at home? Are you going out tonight?' said my father.

'No,' I said.

He raised one eyebrow and gave me a confused look.

'You wanted me to concentrate on studying, so that's what I'm doing.'

'You need to get out once in a while. Have you even left the house today?'

'No.'

'Well, go somewhere. What are your friends doing tonight — that girl you mentioned?'

Luana was eating in the kitchen with her mother, with the door closed, but I wondered whether she'd heard that.

'Don't know.'

In fact, I knew exactly what my friends were doing: they were knocking back beers in Baixo Gavea, west of Ipanema. They'd invited me on Friday, at school, and I'd lied and said I was busy, because I didn't feel like it. But as we ate the rest of our food in silence, I realized that I had to get out of the flat. It was too much, being there, so close to Luana. I would stop being such a bicho do mato — a lone, wild animal — as Mamãe used to say. After we finished eating, I changed from shorts into a pair of jeans and left the flat without saying goodbye to anyone.

★ ★ ★

Nossa Senhora was a fashionably shabby bar in Baixo Gávea. Walls covered in posters and mirrors, lights low, chairs mismatched and scattered about. I felt like a tremendous square as I approached, wearing my baggy T-shirt and glasses. My friends were sitting at an outdoor table, sharing large bottles of beer in small glasses and laughing hysterically. Isabel was sitting on Rodrigo's lap, kissing his cheek. Carlito, leaning dangerously back on his chair, noticed me, squinted in the dark and gave me a wave.

'Ei, André! Pull up a chair.'

Daniela was sitting next to him, arms knotted across her body, avoiding my gaze. She was smiling in a suspicious, unreadable way. I asked the curly-haired hipsters at the next table if I could take one of their unused chairs, and they said, 'Of course, cara.' I wanted to place it next to Dani, but she didn't move to make room, so I sat between Carlito and Gabriel.

'How's it going?' said Carlito. 'I thought you weren't coming.'

'Too much studying,' said Gabriel.

'I thought I could give myself a break.'

'Such a nerd.'

'Well, at least he's gonna make something of himself, cara,' said Rodrigo.

'I'm going to make something of myself!' said Gabriel.

'I am, too!' said Carlito, raising his glass.

When the boys outnumbered them, the girls barely spoke. Sometimes I would spot them in the school corridors, shrieking with laughter, but when the boys were around they were supporting characters.

'How's it going?' I said to Dani.

'Fine,' she said, masking her feelings with a closed smile. 'And you?'

'I'm very well,' I said, thinking of the kiss with Luana.

I glanced across the street and for a moment I thought I saw her in her white uniform, but no, it was just another girl with curly hair and brown legs; she was wearing a white dress, not a uniform, and laughing with her friends. She wasn't an empregada, I could tell.

'What are you looking at?' said Dani, glancing across the road. 'Checking out girls?'

'No.'

'More beer?' said Carlito, and we all shouted, 'Yes!'

We got wasted. I had been drunk several times before — mainly during long, hot afternoons on the beach, when the cold water, sun and salty air pulls you back from reeling into oblivion — but that night I got drunker than ever before. After getting bloated on several large bottles of beer, we moved on to caipirinhas, and Carlito handed out cigarettes, all of us sucking and enjoying the mix of booze sweetness and tobacco bitterness, despite the fact that none of us was a real smoker yet. A forró band started playing inside the bar — the hipsters were in the band, it turned out — and we swayed to the music on our chairs. Isabel and Rodrigo got up and danced together on the pavement, keeping perfect time, but then they would stop and their poise would fall, and they would slump in their seats, rubbing their faces, laughing. I found myself sitting next to Dani, and then putting an arm around her, and then dancing with her, clumsily.

'You dance like a gringo,' she said.

'What do you mean?' I said, swinging her around. 'I'm the new Fred Astaire.'

'Who's that?'

We carried on dancing, until it felt like my clumsiness had given way to debonair ease. We clung on to each other, close as can be. And then we were kissing and our friends were cheering and we smiled at them, sheepishly. I looked at my watch and it was midnight. I thought, I'll just stay for a few minutes, but the next time I looked it was two in the morning. The bar was in no hurry to close. Conversation became garbled, nonsensical. Carlito was ranting about something political, something to do with the dictatorship, and Gabriel was saying, 'Cara, I don't even notice any difference — they're all escrotos.' Daniela was sitting on me and stroking the back of my neck.

Sometime in the morning, when the street cleaners started sweeping around us, I stood up and said, 'I'm going home,' and hugged everyone goodbye.

Dani said, 'I'll go, too,' and everyone went, 'Oooh!'

'Let's get a taxi.'

'No, let's walk for a bit. I feel like walking.'

Rio isn't like London; people don't walk much, especially not late at night. But we were drunk and didn't want to end the night, so we linked arms and walked east towards Ipanema, trying not to fall into the road. Even at that hour, there were cars, cabs and people in the streets. Bars still open, still going. We passed through the neighbourhood of Lagoa, where lights glinted off the surface of the dark lagoon. Sometimes we would stop to kiss against walls, and then we'd slope back into walking, bumping into trees and dustbins. We both nearly tripped over when a white cat streaked across our path.

'We had a cat,' I said. 'She ran away to live on the Arpoador.'

'What are you talking about?'

'Nothing.'

'You're such a weirdo.'

Half an hour later, we hit the Avenida Vieira Souto, the beach and the ocean, which was sloshing blackly under a fat, white moon.

'Let's walk on the beach,' she said.

'Why?'

'Why not?'

She dragged me by the hand, down the steps leading to the empty beach. The sky wasn't quite black. It would be dawn soon. I felt her soft, moist lips on mine, and laughed. We were at the edge of the beach — where it meets the pavement, two metres above us — so we were hidden from the street by a wall.

'Why are you laughing?' she said, annoyed.
'I'm having fun. Aren't you?'

I wrapped my arms around her, and she wrapped hers around me. I didn't know if I was going to come in my pants or puke into her mouth. I thought the former would be preferable, so I tried to silence my lurching stomach and dizzy brain. Dani pushed me up against the wall and got to her knees, unbuckled my belt, pulled my jeans and underwear down to my knees and put my penis into her mouth. Again, I laughed.

'Stop laughing,' she said, with my dick in her mouth, which only made me want to laugh more.

Ripples of pleasure and sickness were shimmering through my body as her mouth went up and down. I groaned without reserve and then came in her mouth, just as a voice came from the street; 'Go fuck in your bedroom, you goddamn perverts!'

Dani spat the semen on to the sand and shouted, 'Vai tomar no cu!'

My mouth tasted sour. Probably not as sour as hers. In silence, we took the steps back up to the street. No sign of the peeping Tom. Daniela's face was lit yellow by the streetlights, and she looked serious.

'Are you all right?' I said.
'Yes.'

I put my arm around her and felt her body relax. Then I walked her to the gate of her building on Rua Barão da Torre, a few blocks from the beach. Beyond the gate, through a glass door, I could see a bored porteiro, watching a tiny television. He looked up, recognized her and buzzed her in. I kissed her before she went inside. Her kiss was salty, which made me feel ill, but I swallowed down the bile until she had closed the gate, then ran back towards the beach and vomited into a gutter. Blood pounded in my ears, BAM BAM BAM, as I heaved on to the pavement and, on the other side of the road, the ocean roared like a lion.

* * *

I woke the next day with my father standing over me, shaking his head. Who knows what time I had gone to bed? All I know is that I collapsed into a dreamless sleep and woke up thirsty, with a stabbing in my head and my father's face staring down, saying, 'Wake up, wake up!'

'Leave me alone,' I said, turning my back to him.

'You're coming to work with me.'

Just the thought of it — blood, sliced skin, stitches — was enough to make the puke rise to my throat. I breathed very slowly, which only made it worse.

'You're the one who told me to go out.'

'Going out doesn't mean getting completely hammered like some animal!'

His shouting just made my headache worse.

'Please, Pai. You don't need me there. It's Sunday.'

'Fine,' he said, leaving the room. 'You smell like a tramp.'

He left without closing the door, which forced me to get up, slam it shut and fall back on the bed. I pulled the sheet over me and passed out almost immediately.

17

When I woke up, the flat was quiet. I went down to the kitchen, where Luana was cooking a feijoada. The clock on the wall read eleven twenty-two a.m.

'Where is everyone?'

'Oh, hi,' she said, looking up from the stove. 'My mother took Thiago to the market.'

I looked down and remembered I was just in my underwear. A year ago, this wouldn't have been a problem, but now it most definitely was. She turned back to the stove. Her neck the colour of doce de leite, and perfectly smooth. A stray ringlet hung out of her ponytail, just touching her white collar. The feijoada smelled rich, dark and stodgy. There's no better hangover cure.

'How do you feel?' she said. 'I heard you coming back last night.'

What did she hear? Crashing chairs, fridge door opening, vast quantities of mate being gulped straight from the jug.

'Yeah, not so good,' I said, rubbing my eyes. 'I drank too much.'

I laughed, but Luana didn't laugh with me.

She didn't even look at me — just carried on cooking.

'Did you have fun?' she said mechanically.

'I think so.'

Had Luana ever had a night like that? Maybe in Vidigal, on her days off, which were so rare that I only have vague memories of them — reheating the food she and Rita had left behind; sometimes I would peek into their empty room out of curiosity. What did she do on her days off? I wondered what she acted like when she was drunk, whether it made her wild or gloomy, or both.

'You went out with that girl,' she said, her voice softer.

'How did you know?'

'I didn't.'

'Does it bother you?'

'Why would it bother me?' she said, stirring a pot, still looking away.

Steam rose around her. It's like my mind took a picture, just then. The red tiles. The steam. Luana's hair. Her white dress. Her brown neck.

'I don't know,' I said, though of course we both knew.

Why couldn't girls just say what they were thinking, instead of expecting you to read their minds? I left the kitchen, went to the TV room and switched between channels for a while. Everyone on TV seemed to be shouting: the adverts, with people screaming at us to buy things; the presenter Xuxa in a neon-pink outfit, surrounded by kids doing a choreographed dance; newsreaders barking the news. People shot, gang leaders arrested, everyone hates the president, the usual shit. I turned it off and lay there, feeling my sweat soak into the sofa, there to remain for ever.

Lunchtime came and still no one was at home. Luana had set the table for one. The food was already on my plate — feijoada with rice, greens, orange slices and a salad — and she had placed a glass of water next to it. I opened the kitchen door and saw her sitting alone at the plastic table, already eating.

'Do you want to eat with me?' I said.

'What?'

'Why don't we eat together?'

'I'm fine here, André. Thank you.'

'I'll eat in the kitchen, then.'

Before she could say anything, I zipped back to the living room, fetched my plate, and brought it to the kitchen. I sat on Rita's seat — the one that faced the stove. Luana said nothing, just looked down and kept eating.

'It's delicious,' I said.

'Thank you.'

'I'm sorry if I was rude earlier.'

'Were you?'

I couldn't think of anything to talk about. It was the kiss, blocking the conversation, letting nothing else seep past. We ate our lunch in silence, and then I helped her put the plates in the sink.

'Need any help with laundry today?' I said.

'I can manage it.'

'Are you sure?'

Half an hour later, we were standing under the damp white cloud of laundry with our arms around each other.

When we pulled away, she said, 'Your breath tastes disgusting,' but we carried on kissing. I wanted to remove her uniform and throw it on the floor. But when I tried to unbutton her dress, she stopped my hand and said, 'No.'

'Why not? Have you ever done it before?'

'Yes,' she said.

'Really? With who?'

'I had a boyfriend, César.'

'I didn't know that.'

'You don't know anything about me.'

'Well, you don't know me either,' I said, fully aware that the opposite was true.

She shut me up by pressing her lips to mine. I felt my hands up her body, and she allowed me to place one on a small, firm breast. My consolation prize.

We carried on with our laundry-hanging and our kisses, performed more regularly and with more abandon every day. My father or Rita would leave a room, and we would kiss. In the TV room, watching novelas, Thiago would turn away for a few seconds and we would kiss quickly and silently. One time, we kissed behind the sheets in the kitchen while my father poured himself a glass of water.

Publicly, though, I was Daniela's boyfriend. Each week, I spent several afternoons at her flat, pretending to study, but really we were just feeling each other up. She taught me how to lick her between the legs. At first it seemed sort of revolting and pointless, but then I found her clitoris and learned how to make her slippery and out of control, clamping my head between her thighs, making me laugh into her. She would pull a pillow over her own face, so that her parents wouldn't hear, and even after I washed my hands and face, her sweet-rotten smell lingered. One evening, when her family was out, she guided my penis inside her, and I rocked over her for five minutes, until I started to feel that electricity.

She said, 'Pull it out, pull it out,' and I squirted on to her stomach.

I went home and had dinner with my

family, who were none the wiser. I felt too guilty to kiss Luana that night, so afterwards I went straight to my bedroom.

★　★　★

At school, I was back in the gang. Back sitting under our tree, sharing a coconut with Daniela as she laid her head in my lap. The few weeks I had spent drifting away were quickly forgotten. We were still planning our European dream-lives, but also thinking about things within reach: weekends, parties and the long winter holiday. Carlito remembered that it was my birthday soon, on the fourteenth of July — my eighteenth.

'You're not getting away with this,' he said. 'No way.'

'It's your fucking birthday, cara!' said Gabriel.

'I don't want anything big, guys.'

'I don't think you have a say in the matter,' said Daniela, looking up from my lap.

Her blue eyes and dark blond hair were shining in the afternoon sun.

'You should have a party!' said Carlito.

'A big fucking party.'

'No way.'

'Come on, it's your eighteenth,' said Rodrigo.

'What about a small party?' I said. 'Just the gang.'

They didn't look convinced. Flicking their eyes at each other, sighing with disappointment at a missed opportunity, waiting for their king, Carlito, to give his response.

'OK, cara,' he said, 'but you won't get away with it next year.'

Their gentle threats and friendly promises felt like shackles and ties. Who said we would still be friends in a year? Who said I would be in Rio? School would be over soon. What about Europe? I kissed Dani and thought to myself, it's funny that no one can hear what I'm thinking.

'You're great,' she said quietly.

The sincerity in her face made me feel silly, like an actor in a novela.

'You are, too.'

She looked thrilled, drugged. I leaned down and kissed her lips, and wished I could be back at home, sitting on my balcony and looking at the blue Atlantic coming in and out, in and out, over the pale sand.

'Want to come over tonight?' she said. 'Everyone will be out.'

'I'm going to the surgery.'

'What about after that?'

'I'm staying there till late.'

'Just get out of it,' she said. 'Tell him that

you need to study.' She winked.

I can't say it didn't tempt me. Of course it did. She was laying herself open like a platter, begging me to eat, eat, eat. But I didn't want to. Not that day.

'I can't,' I said.

'What do you do there, so late at night?'

'Just admin.'

She looked suspicious, and then she smiled.

'How boring,' she said.

⋆ ⋆ ⋆

Once we got off the bus, Dani insisted on walking me to the door of the clinic. I complied, of course. The sky was overcast, and the humidity was unbearable, like a steam room. It was hard to breathe. All I wanted to do was go home, have a shower and waste the rest of the day, lying in bed or on the sofa, watching novelas with Thiago. (What I would give now, to waste a little bit of time.) It looked like it was going to rain. I hoped it would. Dani talked too much, that was her problem. She wanted to know everything about me. She wanted to know about Mamãe: what she was like, how I felt about her being dead, how much I thought about her.

It feels pretty bad, I wanted to say.

Pretty bad, you patricinha.

Have you ever had a day of suffering in your entire life? An hour? A second?

Her perfect little freckles said: *No, we have never.*

As we arrived at the entrance to the clinic, a fat drop of rain fell on my cheek. She leaned in and kissed me. Her mouth felt dry and uninviting.

'Start thinking about your party,' she said.

'Don't call it a party.'

The rain started to fall hard; a sound like dry rice shaking in a can. I stood in the porch of the clinic, under cover, waving at Daniela as she walked off. A woman came out of the clinic, her face bandaged like a mummy, wearing sunglasses. The security guard followed her, holding a giant umbrella, as they walked towards a waiting car. I waited a few minutes longer, just to make sure that Dani was gone, before going home.

I started taking my clothes off in the kitchen as soon as I walked through the door. Threw down my soaked-through rucksack, removed my rain-speckled glasses and peeled off my jeans, socks and T-shirt into a wet heap on the floor. Rita and Luana, hearing me, came out of the living room, which they'd been cleaning, to have a look. Thankfully, my underwear was black, otherwise it would have been see-through.

'Meu Deus!' said Rita. 'You're totally soaked.'

She bounded over, fussing under her breath. Standing next to me, she came to my shoulder. I remember when I used to look up at her. When I would cling on to her legs and make her laugh. Luana was usually somewhere else, back then — being cared for by family in Vidigal. Rita was mine, all mine. She bent over and picked up my clothes. Luana was in the doorway, watching us.

'Let me take these clothes,' said Rita. 'Now go and dress before you get ill again.'

'OK.'

I enjoyed being ordered around by Rita — like old times.

'Before I forget,' I said, 'I was thinking of having some friends over for my birthday, the weekend after next. Just for some salgadinhos and drinks.'

'Sounds good,' said Rita. 'We'll arrange it all. Won't we, Lua — '

But when we looked at the doorway, Luana wasn't there.

18

I turned eighteen on the fourteenth of July 1986, a Monday. Nothing much happened on that day. Papai didn't work late that evening. Rita made her special fish and prawn moqueca, and the three of us — Papai, Thiago and I — ate it in a chattier mood than usual. My father allowed me to have a glass of Chilean Sauvignon Blanc, and encouraged me to smell it and swill it around, pretend I could taste the hint of citrus and wood. I liked the feeling it gave me as the alcohol swam into my blood-stream, making my head feel soft and unbothered. We toasted to my future.

'Almost a man,' said Papai. 'Almost.'

What was Papai talking about? I *was* a man. I was in love — what could be more grown up than that? A year earlier, when I turned seventeen, it would have seemed unimaginable — me and Luana. Luanazinha, Rita's daughter.

'André, you're so old!' said Thiago.

Seventeen was my first birthday without Mamãe. In previous years, she would have spent the day advising Rita about dinner, even venturing into the kitchen to make a nut cake with sweet baba de moca in the middle. And she would have masterminded a Sunday get-together for our extended family — really, they were just her family, because the Cabrals were hidden away up north. Second and third cousins running around the flat, playing games, trying to be friends but failing to ignite the spark. The spark of blood — it's often weak, but rarely indifferent. Uncles crowded round the coffee table on those green sofas, smoking cigarettes and talking about business. Aunts in a corner, talking about other people.

None of that had happened on my seventeenth. Papai was not Mamãe. We had eaten a semi-silent dinner at a local rodízio, filling ourselves with barbecued meat and salads and talking of little apart from how good the food was. Mamãe's presence had been everywhere: in the taste of the restaurant's food, which I hadn't eaten since before her death; in the third caipirinha Papai drank, which she would have tutted at; in the empty chair at our four-person table. Back home, my father gave me an excellent gift — a new bicycle, green and shining chrome. I had pointed it out to Mamãe ages ago — how did he know? I didn't bring it up. Anyway, I didn't own it for long. Three weeks later the bike was stolen from me at gunpoint on the corner of Rua Farme de Amoedo and Visconde de Pirajá, by two black boys with anxious eyes. I've already mentioned this before, haven't I? The smaller one was holding the gun, and it looked too heavy for his skinny arms.

'Give us the bicycle, playboy,' he said.

They were around my age, perhaps younger, their bodies thin from malnutrition.

'What are you waiting for?' said the taller one, though he wasn't even as tall as me. His voice still had the high pitch of a boy's. 'Give him the fucking bicycle or we'll blow your brains out.'

I felt oddly empty, almost on the verge of saying, 'Go ahead.' But I gave them the bike, and they rode off on it — both of them — calling me a filho da puta. My mother isn't a puta, I wanted to say, she's dead. But I didn't say anything. Just stood there like an idiot.

I didn't have a party with my friends that year. Why bother? I had drifted away to my little world of grief. But grief ebbs away. It has to, there's no other choice.

★ ★ ★

On Saturday, Rita and Luana spent hours preparing food and tidying the flat — not that my friends would have noticed. They would mostly be impressed that Papai had taken Thiago to Teresópolis for the weekend; he didn't expressly say he was going away because of the party, but that's what I assumed. I loved him for that. Later, I would end up wishing he had stayed.

I had invited my gang, and they brought a few others — people I had seen around at school, spoken to a handful of times, maybe I even knew their names (now forgotten). I suppose I wasn't forthcoming when it came to making friends. I preferred to let friendships happen to me, rather than make them happen. That party — it happened to me. I told everyone to come at eight, and they mostly came at nine or ten. They arrived at the flat in twos and threes and fours, shiny-eyed with excitement about the night to come. I felt awkward, welcoming all these semi-strangers into my home. Rita served assorted snacks, including her pasteis de carne, which I can still taste when I close my eyes; crisp on the outside, hot inside. Luana served beer and I mixed some too-sweet caipirinhas, but with vodka instead of cachaça. That was the new fashion — vodka was imported, expensive and, most importantly, European.

I'm getting ahead of myself. Daniela was

the first to arrive. She came alone, at quarter to nine. I let her in through the guests' door, into the living room, even though she had rung the kitchen buzzer.

'Hello, André.'

She was wearing a short red dress, high heels and lipstick; a girl trying to look like a woman, and almost succeeding. But she looked good. Even her frizzy hairdo was OK, or maybe I was just getting used to it. We hadn't had sex for a few weeks, but that was more because of circumstance than anything else. She gave me a wrapped present, and I encouraged her to sit down.

'No, I'll stand for a bit,' she said. 'I didn't get the chance to look around before.'

She wandered around the living room, looking at the folk art on the walls, the Bahian pots and ceramic busts. One of them was a black woman with pouting red lips.

'You have a lot of stuff,' she said.

'My mother had a shop. She sold this sort of stuff, mostly to gringos.'

'Is it still open?'

'Yes, someone bought it from us.'

Dani's flat was bare and minimalist — just some family photos here and there — but there was a wooden cross over her bed, which I often focused on when we were fucking. Her family wasn't religious; it was an heirloom from Italy.

'Are you going to open your present?' she said.

I looked down at the parcel, wrapped in blue paper with white hearts. A flat rectangle. I started carefully taking the parcel apart, separating the tape from the paper.

'Just rip it!'

I ripped the paper off, melodramatically, and chucked it on the floor, which had the desired effect — it made her laugh. I laughed, too, but I stopped when I saw what she had given me. A photograph of the gang, on one of our many afternoons on Copacabana beach. Arms around each other, smiling like the kids we were. Dani and I were in the foreground, and I was planting a kiss on her cheek. (I don't have this picture any more, but I remember it well.)

'Thank you,' I said. 'I'll put it in my room.'

'Something to remember us by.'

'What do you mean? We're all still here.'

'Yes, but . . . school is ending soon.'

'Oh, come here.'

We kissed. At that moment, Luana came into the room, her face devoid of emotion. My pulse quickened.

'Would you like a drink?' she said.

'Can I have a beer?' said Dani.

Faster and faster and faster.

'And you, André?'

BOOM BOOM BOOM BOOM.

'A beer would be great. Thanks, Luana.'

She walked away, and Dani raised her eyebrows, but didn't say anything. She's beautiful, she was thinking. More beautiful than I am. Luana came back with our beers on a tray. I hadn't seen her use a tray since my mother's parties. I took the drinks and smiled at her. Luana rolled her green eyes and left the room. I wondered if Dani had seen it, but when I turned round she was occupied elsewhere — looking at the collection of family photos on a sideboard.

'Your mother?' she said, lifting up a photo.

It was of Mamãe when she was my age. She was standing on a balcony in Paris, during her year in Europe, before she met Papai. Her hair was bobbed and voluminous, and she wore a pale dress. I couldn't tell the colour, because the photo was black and white, but I always imagined it was yellow. Behind her, the city, the Eiffel Tower, all those clichés. She's not smiling, she's looking into the distance, but her eyes are calm and happy.

'She looks like an Indian,' said Dani.

'Her great-grandmother was, I think.'

'What a stunning woman. How sad.'

The doorbell buzzed, which was a relief. It was now nine p.m., and the party began in earnest. Beers were drunk, backs were slapped, cheeks were kissed and food devoured. Luana and Rita drifted in and out of the room like benevolent spirits, carrying drinks and snacks, hardly saying a word and just nodding, slowly, when something was requested. People were going through my records, complaining about them.

'Cara, all you have is classical music.'

'I just listen to whatever's around.'

'And all this sixties stuff.'

'They belonged to my mother. We could listen to some?'

'Do you have any Prince?' said Rodrigo.

'Who's Prince?' I semi-joked.

'I'll play some Beatles, then.'

He put the *White Album* on the turntable and the chatter died down as we waited for the needle to drop. 'Back in the USSR' started playing, a song we didn't know very well, but the booze had got to our heads and, as the guitars ground in, Carlito and Gabriel started jumping around the room, pulling girls up from their seats.

'Want to dance?' Dani said to me.

'I'm such a bad dancer.'

'Come on, we've danced before. You weren't that bad.'

She winked at me. I took her hand and led her to the space between our round dining table and the green sofas, which had become the dance floor. Luckily, there was a girl for everyone, so no one was left out. I stood in front of Daniela and took her in my arms, but it wasn't possible to dance as a couple to 'Back in the USSR', so we broke away and started shaking our bodies in time to the music, laughing till our faces hurt. We slow-danced to 'Dear Prudence', and then sat back on the sofa. People drifted away from the dance floor, to the coffee table, where more food had been laid out without us even noticing it. Dani went to the bathroom, and the guys started talking.

'These are so good,' said Rodrigo, stuffing a pastel de carne into his mouth.

'You know what else is good?' said Carlito, cocking his head towards the kitchen.

They high-fived, and Rodrigo said, 'Tell me about it, cara.'

'What are you talking about?'

'Are you a eunuch?' said Carlito. 'Do you not have a dick?'

'Your empregada, man,' said Rodrigo, a little too loudly, but still almost drowned out by the music. 'She is a gatinha.'

'Really?'

'What a waste,' said Carlito. 'She's too pretty to be an empregada.'

'I don't go for black girls,' said Gabriel,

sitting on the arm of the sofa and muscling in on the conversation, 'but I'd make an exception for her.'

'Where d'ya think you got your hair from, cara?' said Carlito.

'Shut the fuck up!'

'Have you ever tried to . . . you know?'

'Fuck her?' said Gabriel.

I was glad that the lights in the room were dim, because I could feel my face was hot, probably red.

'Of course not.'

'OK,' said Carlito. 'In that case, I'm going to give it a go.'

He got up and straightened out his T-shirt. 'How do I look?'

'Like a faggot!' said Gabriel.

'Good, that's the look I'm going for.'

'Carlito,' I said, but he didn't listen, and wandered off towards the kitchen.

Seconds later, I could hear Carlito in there, talking excitedly, but I couldn't make out what he was saying. Sometimes he would pause — that must have been when Luana was speaking — but her voice was too quiet to reach me.

Dani and Isabel changed the record to *Thriller* and then came over and sat with us.

'What are you morons talking about?' said Isabel.

201

She was wearing a short black dress, her dark hair in a high ponytail. Something was different about her — I wasn't sure what. I hadn't seen her since the start of the holidays, two weeks earlier.

'You all look very excited,' said Dani.

'It's nothing,' I said.

'We were talking about the empregada,' said Rodrigo, looking straight at his girlfriend, teasingly.

'What about her?' said Isabel. 'Which one?'

'You know which one,' said Dani, seething.

'Going crazy over an empregada? You losers.'

'You look different, Isabel,' I said. 'What is it?'

'You noticed!' she said, beaming.

'Noticed what?'

She turned to the side, so that I could see her profile, and ran her finger from the top to the bottom of her nose. I had never really noticed it before, but I suppose she'd had a small bump, right at the top. The rhinoplasty was perfectly done, but it made her look sort of ordinary.

'Look!' she said. 'My eighteenth-birthday present.'

'Very nice.'

'Done by your father.'

'Seriously?'

'Yeah, he did my sister, too.'

'Why didn't you tell me you were going to him?' I said.

'Why would I?' she said. 'Do I need your permission?'

'I work there, that's why.'

'I asked for it to be done when you weren't there,' she said. 'I didn't want you in the room, watching me.'

'Do you think I should have one, too?' said Dani, turning in profile. Her nose was small and freckled, like a child's.

'Oh, stop it, Dani,' said Isabel. 'You know you're perfect.'

Luana came in from the kitchen and started clearing beer bottles away. Carlito followed her, grinning at us and doing a little victory dance, as though he had conquered her. What had he said to her? Had he tried to kiss her? She's mine, I thought, how dare he! My face burned and sweat trickled down my back, under my clothes. I wanted to punch him in the face, but instead I just clenched my fists and smiled at him, as though nothing was wrong. Luana's face was flushed and her eyes bright.

'Ei, moça!' said Isabel, shouting to her across the room.

Luana looked up.

'Yes?'

'Can I get another beer? This one's too warm.'

Luana's green eyes flicked over the cold beers on the coffee table which she had brought out five minutes earlier.

'Those are all warm, too,' said Isabel.

'OK,' said Luana, taking the beers from the table. 'I'll put them in the fridge and get you another one.'

Isabel watched her leave the room, a smirk twisting her mouth. I realized that I barely knew her at all. She was just a friendly face in the school corridors, on the beach, talking nonsense on nights out. I didn't know what she was made of. Dani sat beside her, impassive. Luana brought back a cold beer and Isabel took it from the tray, carrying on with her conversation, not even turning to acknowledge her. I watched as Luana shuffled back to the kitchen, and I felt a pang of love for her, shot through with pity. She must loathe us, I thought. I would. This was the way of the world. Everything was an accident of birth. I wanted everyone to leave, so that I could hold her.

Time sped up. The hour between nine and ten had been stretched by sober awkwardness; the hour between ten and eleven felt like twenty minutes, and the next hour like five. I looked at my watch and it was one in the morning, and the end of the night seemed within reach. I hadn't seen Rita in hours. She'd probably gone to bed, to their room behind the kitchen, and left Luana to serve us.

'We should go to a bar,' said Carlito.

Everyone looked quite comfortable where they were, sitting on the sofas or on the floor, swaying out of time to the music.

'Really?' said Rodrigo, looking sleepy-eyed. 'I'm tired.'

'Dude, it's only one-thirty,' said Gabriel.

'Come on, that's early!' said Carlito. 'Don't you think, André?'

'Don't look at me, cara.'

'Such a nerd. Come on, everyone,' said Carlito.

'I'd like to go,' said Dani, standing over the coffee table, draining her beer.

'Who else?'

'OK, OK,' said Rodrigo.

Soon, everyone was reanimated by the idea of going out. People were standing, getting their things. The Michael Jackson record was playing again, right from the start. I opened the glass doors and stood on the balcony, watching and listening to the waves rolling towards us.

'André?' said Carlito.

'No, I'll stay.'

He stood next to me, looking at the beach.

'Just gonna stand here, writing poetry about the ocean?'

'Come on, cara, I'm tired.'

'I'm just kidding. Happy birthday.'

We hugged and back-slapped.

'Thanks.'

I wasn't looking at Dani — she was just inside the flat — but I could feel her disappointment jabbing me from behind. She came outside and put her arm around me.

'Are you sure you don't want to come?' she said.

'No, I'm all right.'

Carlito went inside, to leave us alone.

'You're like an old man.'

'Yeah, maybe I am.'

She looked into my eyes with an embarrassing intensity.

'That's why I like you,' she said.

I kissed her, because I didn't know what else to do. I hoped that Luana was in the kitchen, where she couldn't see us. When I drew back, Dani's eyes were still closed. What on earth she was thinking of me, I don't know, but I didn't deserve it.

'Let's hang out next week,' she said. 'Or tomorrow.'

'Sure. Wait and see how our hangovers are.'

She kissed me on the lips.

'Bye, André.'

The other kids slowly, surely, picked their things up and started filtering out of the flat, leaning on each other, singing bits of Michael Jackson. It was now two in the morning, but the bars would be open till the sun came up. I kissed all the girls on both cheeks, even Isabel, who went one further and gave me a hug. When I closed the door on them, I felt relief, but then I stood on the balcony and watched them walk out of the building — talking, laughing, shouting — and felt a pang of envy that I couldn't be more like them. The living room wasn't too messy. Just a few beer bottles here and there. The ashtray, which had been overflowing a few minutes ago, had been wiped clean. Luana had already started cleaning. She was filling her arms with bottles, her head down, avoiding me.

'Have you been clearing up after us all night?' I said.

'It's my job.'

'Do you want a hand?'

'There's not much left.'

I picked up four bottles from the coffee table, carried them to the kitchen and put them on the counter.

'It's late,' she said, as a hint.

'So why are you still working?'

She shrugged.

'Are you upset about Isabel?' I said.

'Who's Isabel?'

'She's just jealous.'

'Jealous of an empregada? I don't think so, André.'

'Everyone was talking about how pretty you are. That's why Carlito went to talk to you in the kitchen.'

She didn't say anything.

'What did you guys talk about?' I said.

'Why do you want to know?'

'Did he kiss you?'

She laughed, incredulous.

'Why? Would you be jealous?' she said.

I wrapped an arm around her back and tried to kiss her neck, but she pushed me back, roughly.

'Stop it,' she said.

'You're beautiful.'

'I'd rather be like your ugly friend, even with her bad manners.'

'You wouldn't.'

'Of course I would!' she shouted.

She put her hand to her mouth.

'Shh, don't wake Rita,' I said. 'Come, let's talk in the living room.'

'Only for a minute.'

I took her by the hand and led her into the other room. The music was no longer playing.

Luana sat down, kicked off her flip-flops and curled her legs on the sofa. Her head rested on a hand. I sat next to her, and she closed her eyes, like she wanted to disappear. I don't really know what she wanted. I leaned in and kissed her, brought her chest to mine. Her heartbeat was quick and light. She put her arms around me and I pushed myself on top of her. Her eyes were still closed. I unbuttoned her white uniform, popping the silver buttons one by one, until it revealed a greyed-out bra and pants, and her brown, smooth belly, which I hadn't seen since the beach in Marajó. Finally, she opened her eyes. We stood up and stripped until we were both naked, standing in front of each other. Her breasts were small and surprisingly white, never seen by the sun. Her hair neat and black.

Luana lay back on the couch. Underneath, she was ten shades darker than Daniela. I lay on top and she guided me, with her hands, inside her, and stretched her neck back, over the side of the sofa. Nothing else mattered. We were done for.

19

Oi André,

After Chico left school, he moved to Belém. I wanted him to go to university, but he wanted to work. He did all kinds of things: manual labour, emptying bins, cleaning, being a porteiro. Jobs that he was too good for, but I kept my mouth shut. Then he went to catering school, worked in a few restaurants and got a job as head waiter at one of the best restaurants in the city, right on the river, in an old building that used to be a palace. The proudest day of my life was when I had dinner there with my husband and daughter. I almost cried when I saw Chico in his black-and-white uniform, but I didn't want to embarrass him in front of his colleagues. They called him Carioca, even though he hadn't been to Rio since he was a boy and had lost his accent. He was a northerner, like your father.

After the restaurant closed we stayed behind and chatted to Chico. He was proud of himself, I could see it — giving instructions to the other staff, smiling, standing upright. He had authority, he was a man. He told us, quietly, that he was applying to be the restaurant's new manager. 'Who knows,' he said, 'one day I might open my own restaurant?'

Chico introduced me to one of the cooks, Iara, a girl who looked like an Indian. I praised her for the mouth-numbing pato no tucupi we had eaten, and she blushed, telling me that her grandmother taught her to cook. I knew then that she was involved with Chico. To be honest, I've never liked jambu. It's like eating an anaesthetic. Some things, you never get used to. I'm still a carioca, after all.

My next letter will be the last one. It will be the hardest one to write. If you have any humanity left, it will be hard to read, too. I hope it will make you suffer, like I have done.

Luana

The penultimate letter arrived on Bia's nineteenth birthday, in November. I read it quickly at work, between seeing an old man with a guttural cough and a toddler with a cold. I read it again, after the mother and child had left, but it was like reading through a pane of dirty glass — I couldn't take it in. I decided not to think about it.

By then, Bia was in Brazil. I spoke to her that evening, after work. I was in the kitchen, on my laptop — blinds drawn to the darkness — and she was lying on a hammock in the sunshine, somewhere in Bahia, talking into her phone. (Soon it would be Christmas. Who would I spend it with?) Her face was tanned, her eyes excited. She told me about the two weeks she spent with Thiago and Jesse, in Ipanema and Ilha Grande, an island off the coast of Rio — how much fun they had.

'Why don't you come and meet me?' she said quickly, towards the end of our conversation, as though she wasn't sure about asking.

'Meet you? Where?'

Her face froze for a few seconds — bad Wi-fi on the beach. I just heard ' — ém' and then the connection dropped.

I spent the rest of the evening doing paperwork, preparing for the next day at the surgery, for the endless five-minute appointments with local hypochondriacs, idlers, depressives and overprotective mothers. Where you from? some of them ask. What you doing here, bruv — isn't it like paradise over there? All them beautiful women. Do you speak Spanish, then? Or Brazilian?

Before bed, I washed down a Zopiclone pill with a small glass of whisky and lay in bed listening to the traffic going down Albion Road. Counting the cars as the pill took effect. Forty, forty-one, forty-two, and under the water I went. Luana swimming ahead. My legs wouldn't work. The river pulled me down.

20

When there were other people at home, Luana and I barely talked or made eye contact. But when the flat emptied, we would run to my bedroom, pulling off clothes as though our lives depended on it. A couple of times we fucked in the tiny room she shared with her mother, underneath Rita's porcelain Virgin Mary — but this made both of us feel awkward, and Luana's bed was even smaller than mine. Sometimes I would bunk off school and stay at home with her, just for the hour when I knew Rita was out shopping. Papai worked all hours and often wanted me at the surgery in the afternoon, so I would cough down the phone, pretending to have a cold. The third time I tried this trick, there was a note of disbelief in his voice.

'Of course, you're always ill, how could I forget?'

Sex was anxious and quick, but afterwards we would linger in bed, talking, the sheets twisted around us.

'What would our children look like?' she once said.

Her question made my insides squirm, but

I tried not to show it.

'Little mongrels.'

She smiled and her eyes creased into slits. I traced her rosy-brown lips with my finger, the way they slid down in the middle, into a deep V.

'No,' she said. 'They'd be more beautiful than the rest. I'm sure of it.'

At the other end of the flat one of the front doors was creaking open. We leapt simultaneously from the bed and pulled on our clothes.

'My mother is back early. You're not supposed to be here.'

'I'll hide and let myself out.'

'OK,' she said, tying back her hair and smoothing down her uniform. 'How do I look?'

'Like the prettiest girl in the world.'

'Lua?' said Rita. 'Where are you?'

She ran out of the room, towards the kitchen. I didn't think it then, but now I wonder whether Rita could smell it on her.

*   *   *

Luana's seventeenth birthday in November passed without fanfare at our flat. She and Rita spent the weekend at Vidigal. Who with? Family, I suppose. Friends from the favela, who they never spoke of. Rita's sister Jacinta, who worked for Vovô and Vovó, would certainly be there. They had eight other siblings, so it was probably a big party. Up in the hills, overlooking the beach, all the way to the Arpoador. The best view of the city, so I've heard. The spring sun hammering down. I imagined her dancing on a terrace with some other guy — someone like her. Inevitably, he would be a good dancer, not like me.

When they returned, their smiles were strained, like they didn't want to be here. Papai gave Luana a bunch of flowers, a belated present. She put them in a vase and kept them away from us, in their bedroom, until, one day, I found them in the bin, dead and dry.

⋆ ⋆ ⋆

Throughout those months, I had kept up my relationship with Daniela, more or less. She anchored me to my group of friends in a way I knew I couldn't manage by myself. We were both planning to study medicine at the Universidade Federal do Rio de Janeiro, but I imagined that soon I would have a new gang, the friends I had always been looking for. Become my true self! What a ridiculous notion.

'Are we all right?' she said over the phone,

the week before the end of school. We were both taking a break from revision.

'What do you mean?'

'Sometimes I feel like we're not really dating.' She paused. 'Are we?'

'What are you talking about?'

'We haven't had sex in three weeks,' she whispered.

'We have a lot of work to do, Dani.'

'Every time I suggest we go to a motel — '

'That's tacky.'

'It's what everyone does.'

'I don't want to do what everyone does.'

* * *

Dinner was over. The plates had been cleared away, apart from mine, which sat alone, half finished. I'd lost my appetite, so I took it to the kitchen. Rita was there, doing the washing-up. I don't know where Luana was. Maybe with Thiago, watching TV. Rita and I didn't speak much, not like when I was a little kid. She used to hug me every day and tell me she loved me at least once a week, calling me Andrézinho and querido. I was nothing to her any more.

'Shall I take your plate?' she said, looking up from the sink.

'Thanks. Where's Luana?'

'Why?' she said, a little abruptly.

Did she know? Did she?

'Oh, nothing,' I said. I couldn't think of a single excuse for needing Luana. 'I'm going to watch some TV. I've been revising too much.'

I smiled, but she didn't.

'That's what she's doing,' said Rita. 'Watching TV.'

Rita never watched TV.

★ ★ ★

Luana and Thiago were sitting on the sofa, side by side. She had her arm around him, and his head rested on her right shoulder. I felt a jolt of jealousy, and then shook it off and sat on the hard wooden chair by the door.

'I thought you didn't watch novelas any more,' said Thiago.

'Sometimes I still do,' I said.

Luana turned her head and gave me a small smile. I didn't know what she was thinking, not at all.

'Did you have a good birthday?' I said to her.

'Yes, a friend from Vidigal had a barbecue for me. It was really fun.'

She used the masculine, amigo — a boy.

Her boyfriend? Thiago watched us inquisitively, looking from my face to hers, and then back at the screen. He was now eight, and sharper than before. I wasn't following the novela's plot. People screaming, overacting, professing their undying love — the usual thing.

The show ended, but I didn't notice. I only realized when Thiago stood up.

'I'm going to bed,' he said, marching out of the room, his wavy hair bouncing in time.

'Goodnight,' said Luana and I, in unison.

'I'm going, too,' she said.

'Already? It's only nine.'

'Nothing else to do.'

'Just sit with me for a bit,' I whispered, knowing that my voice would carry all the way to my father's study if I didn't keep it low.

'It's not normal for a boy to sit with his empregada, just talking. I don't want my mother to lose her job.'

'What about your job?'

'I'm just a hanger-on. One day I'll go and find another family to look after.'

'Really?'

'Yes, and then you can carry on with your life.'

I looked at the door of the TV room, which was open just an inch or two. Beyond it, the corridor was dark. I looked back at Luana and took her hand.

'We should go away together,' I said.

'What?'

'After my exams. To Marajó — the blue house.'

'What excuse could we give for both of us going away? Especially me — when do I ever go away? I barely even get time off.'

'We could try a motel.'

'What if someone sees us?'

'Let's carry on as we are, then,' I said.

I stood up to leave. She stayed on the sofa.

★ ★ ★

Sometime in the night, I heard the door of my room open. Or rather, I felt it: a change in the air. I had been dreaming about Mamãe — we were shopping for clothes at Barra Shopping, but I couldn't find the swimming trunks I wanted. All of them were painfully small. Mamãe looked gaudily beautiful, like a film star. As we walked through the empty mall, all I could think was: she's not dead. Why did I think she was dead when she's so obviously alive? It hurt to look at her.

When I saw a figure standing in the darkness, I wanted to scream, but, like in the worst nightmares, no sound would come out.

Then I realized it was just Luana, wearing the lilac, flowered dress that she wore in Marajó — now relegated to nightwear — with the light from the corridor illuminating her curly hair. She closed the door, and I couldn't see her any more but I heard her moving towards my bed. Her smell of coconut soap and skin gave me a hard-on.

'What time is it?'

'Shh,' she said.

The soft thud of her dress, as it dropped to the floor. Bare feet padding on the wooden floor. I felt her slip into my single bed next to me, her body cool and dry against my dream-sweat. She wrapped her legs around me. Naked skin, smooth and plump to the touch, one thigh on either side of my body. We kissed quietly but with desperation. From her mouth down to her breasts, down and down. In the dark, she could be any girl, not just an empregada. She was wet and warm, rankly sweet like an overripe fruit. She turned over on all fours and I entered her from behind. When the bed started creaking, we moved to the floor — me sitting, and her on top.

And afterwards.

'What will happen to us?' she said.

'I don't know.'

'You'll find another girl at university, and

I'll still be here, cleaning up after you.'

I heard her sniff in the dark, and realized that she was crying.

'Hey, hey, don't cry.'

'Life is so simple for you,' she said, between quiet sobs. 'I don't even love you, I just envy you.'

'What do you mean?'

She left the room without a word. I didn't sleep much after that. Things became slowly visible in my room as darkness lifted — my desk, the cartoon characters on my sheets, the framed photo of Mamãe with the hummingbird on my bedside table — and I thought, that's it, the day is lost. I'll be too tired to study. Meu Deus, I'm fucked. I stared at the ceiling until the room went from grey to yellow, and then got up for breakfast. It was five-thirty, but already my father was sitting on the living-room sofa, reading the paper and drinking a coffee.

'You're up early,' he said.

'Couldn't sleep.'

I could hear Rita and Luana in the kitchen. When Luana came into the living room, her face showed no sign of what we had done, or what she had said. She wasn't in uniform but in a denim dress that looked brand new. She looked fresh and awake.

She put a pot of coffee on the table, said,

'Good morning, André,' and disappeared back into the kitchen.

'Why couldn't you sleep?' said Papai, rising from the sofa and heading over to the table. 'Nervous about the exams?'

'Maybe.'

'Thinking about Mamãe?'

That made me feel guilty. Maybe I should've been thinking of her, but I hadn't been. Only in my dreams.

'Yes.'

'It's been nearly two years,' said Papai. 'Can you believe it?'

'No,' I said.

I stared at my plate. I was so tired. Rita came in from the kitchen and arranged the fruit, bread, cheese and ham on the table, wordlessly. Her dark brown skin was shiny in the morning light. Papai and I ate in silence, and then I took the bus to school. Soon it would be over. My limbs felt like lead. I couldn't follow one train of thought without another barging in on it. Thoughts of Mamãe, eclipsed by Luana, eclipsed by Daniela, eclipsed by how tired I felt, how much I would like to lean against the dirty glass and close my eyes.

★ ★ ★

Later that evening, my father was sitting on the sofa wearing his work suit, reading a book and listening to Puccini's *Madam Butterfly*. It was on so loud I wondered how he could concentrate on the book. Rita and Luana were in the kitchen, talking and cooking.

'Revising hard?' he said, looking up, over his glasses.

He was reading a French translation of *Anna Karenina*.

'Yes.'

It was a lie. After school, I had gone to Daniela's flat while her parents were out, and we had fucked in her air-conditioned bedroom, surrounded by soft toys. My tiredness lifted once I saw her lying on the bed, her long blond hair swept to one side. Just as we were about to finish, her empregada, Dada, called her to the kitchen, and she shouted, 'Wait, Dada! One minute!' as she moved up and down, sitting on top of me, her face pink and sweaty.

'You'll be at university soon, if all goes well,' said Papai. 'Are you excited?'

'I suppose so. First I need to pass the exam.'

He raised his eyebrows and grimaced at my self-doubt. Then his face softened, as he gestured towards the book, still in his hand.

'You know, this was one of your mother's

favourite books,' he said. 'Have you read it?'

'No.'

'It's all rather hysterical.'

'I don't know the story. Can you even read French?'

'More or less.'

'Maybe that's why you're not enjoying it.'

He put the book face down on the coffee table. Twenty pages in, at most.

'Could be,' he said. 'She was fluent, though. She studied in Paris when she was a teenager — did you know that?'

He looked up at me, his face heartbreakingly sincere and open. His upper lip twitched.

'Yes, of course.'

She had talked about it a lot, always showing people that photo with the Eiffel Tower. But I couldn't really imagine what my mother had been like in Paris, at eighteen. How could she even exist without me, let alone enjoy her life?

'You haven't been coming to the surgery very much lately,' said Papai.

'I know, I've just been — '

'Don't worry about it. You'll be at medical school soon, learning from real teachers. It was just something I thought you would enjoy, working together.'

'I did enjoy it.'

He waved this away. His olive skin hung off his face, like an old man's, and was peppered with black moles — too much sun in his youth. His hair was still mostly black, but with a few grey strands.

'I'm glad you did,' he said.

He walked out of the room, towards his study, at the furthest end of the flat. I picked up the book. The pages were browned and dog-eared, the spine cracked. Inside the cover was Mamãe's maiden name, written in her curled, elegant handwriting: Beatriz Maria da Silva Melo. I closed my eyes and sniffed it — sweet old paper and glue — put it back on the table and went to the kitchen to get a glass of water. Luana and Rita were sitting at their plastic table, chopping vegetables. Back in the laundry area, Mickey Mouse sheets were hanging from the ceiling rack.

'Hello, André,' said Rita.

'Hi, Rita, how was your day?'

'Not great. I went to see my friend in hospital. She's not well.'

'What's wrong with her?'

'Too much work, too little money. A hard life, she's had.'

'She's got cancer,' said Luana, looking up from her chopping board. 'It's gone to her bones.'

'But she has very nice employers. They're

going to pay all her bills until she's better.'

'It's not going to get better, Mãe. It's in her bones.'

'I'm praying all day, in my head. It might just be a test for her.'

'I hope your prayers work,' I said.

'Se Deus quiser.'

Luana sliced a tomato in two and the knife hit the board hard, like it could go right through.

21

After our last day at school, I came home the next morning so drunk I felt sober. For one night, we forgot that the exams were still ahead of us. The gang had ended up at Rodrigo's cousin's house up in Santa Teresa, an old mansion with a swimming pool. On the terrace, we heard gunshots from the favela nearby, and then saw the sun rise over the city. Rodrigo, Gabriel and Carlito dive-bombed into the pool in their underwear, screaming, and the girls were laughing, and lights were pinging on all over the city.

Back at home, long past waking-up time, I opened my bedroom window to let in the air, and lay back in bed. I hadn't even said hello to Luana and Rita in the kitchen — too drunk and tired. But then there was a knock at my bedroom door.

'Come in,' I said.

She was in her white uniform, her feet in white rubber flip-flops. Her face a caramel blur, because I wasn't wearing my glasses.

'Good morning,' I said, pulling the sheets up around me, just in case Rita suddenly showed up, but then I heard the vacuum cleaner turn on at the other end of the flat, and relaxed. Luana closed the door behind her.

'Did you have fun?' she said.

'Yes. School's over.'

'Good for you. I need to talk to you.'

'Come here.'

She walked over to my bed and sat down on it, and I wrapped my arms around her, feeling for her breasts, searching for her neck with my lips. She winced. I probably smelled bad.

'My period hasn't come,' she said.

My lips stopped searching and went numb.

'What? In how long?'

'It should have come four weeks ago.'

'How can that be?'

'You're the doctor — you tell me.'

'You haven't done a test, though?'

'I can feel it,' she said, putting her hands on her stomach. 'I can feel that it's there. I don't know how.'

I withdrew my arms and flopped back on to my bed.

'Fucking hell.'

Luana lay down next to me, nuzzling her face on my chest. She put her arm around me. I felt a small puddle of tears forming where her head was lying, but she wasn't making a sound.

'What are we going to do?' I said.

'You know how, don't you? At your father's surgery?'

Papai had sworn me to secrecy, but I had told Luana about his night-job.

'You want to kill our baby?' I said, raising my voice a notch, and then remembering who we were, where we were. 'I don't know how to do it. Anyway, it's out of the question.'

'I'm your empregada.'

'We could have it,' I said. 'We could get married.'

Is that what I wanted? No, but it was something to say. I put my hand on hers and looked down at her tearful face. Just for a moment, I glimpsed a smile, but Luana twisted it into a frown.

'Don't be stupid,' she said. She squeezed her eyes shut and shook her head.

Rita's vacuum cleaner turned off. Luana stood up and smoothed down her uniform.

'Splash your face first,' I said.

Five minutes later, two vacuum cleaners hummed from opposite ends of the flat.

*   *   *

That morning I lay in bed, drifting in and out of sleep, praying, asking for forgiveness, asking for my sins to be reversed. None of this would have happened if Mamãe hadn't died. Grief, it had unhinged me — I didn't know what I was doing. If only I could go back, do things differently. Break it off with Luana. Never have kissed her. Spent the day with Mamãe, instead of going to the beach with my friends. She'd still be alive, or maybe we'd both be dead. I fixed all of it in my head.

I could buy an abortion — from another doctor, obviously, not from Papai — and we could pretend to forget. Soon I would be at university, and then I would leave home. Perhaps move to Europe, like I had always wanted. I would marry and have children with someone like Dani, but not Dani, and Luana would work for another family, just like she had said.

I ate lunch alone, at the dining table, listening to Luana and Rita chatting in the kitchen. You would never know something was wrong from the bright, lively tone of her voice. We had both become so good at pretending. I went for a walk by the beach — keeping my head down, in case someone recognized me — and climbed the Arpoador rock between Ipanema and Copacabana. Surfers were still out, jumping on their boards, being dragged under waves, coming up spitting — even as the sunlight faded and the sea turned grey. I remembered the river in

Pará, how wide it was, so that you couldn't see the other side. I walked home and had dinner, and tried to keep my mind off Luana — which was impossible, because she was serving the food.

Papai noticed something, though, because he said, 'Why are you so quiet?'

'I'm just tired. We were out pretty late.'

'The end of childhood. It's a bittersweet thing.'

'I don't think that's it.'

'Have a rest, then.'

But I had to go out that night to the Lovers Motel in Copacabana with Dani. She had planned the whole thing.

'I'm going out tonight,' I said.

'What about your work?' said Papai.

'I've been studying all day.'

I hoped that Luana and Rita couldn't hear us. When I was younger I never worried about them hearing me, as if they didn't exist.

'Don't tire yourself out,' said Papai. 'You're only at the beginning, filho.'

'Beginning of what?'

'Your life. Everything.'

Yet it felt like the end. I left the table while he and Thiago were still eating. My father's eyes followed me out of the room like a dog following a bone; I could feel them on the back of my head.

The motel was a short cab ride away, but I was meeting Dani for a drink first in Ipanema, on the beachfront. I needed it. What I didn't know was that she had also invited Carlito, Rodrigo and Isabel along for drinks. I saw them as I walked up to the bar, and composed my face into a pleasantly surprised expression.

'Hey, cara!' shouted Carlito. He blew a smoke ring into the air and smiled as it wafted away.

'How's it going?' I said, sitting next to Daniela and planting a kiss on her cheek.

'You can do better than that,' she said, turning her face and kissing me on the lips, with tongues. Everyone else on the table went, 'Wooo!'

'Well, at least someone's getting lucky tonight,' said Rodrigo, whose eyes were sleepy and red.

'Shut up, you babaca,' said Isabel.

'Come on,' said Carlito. 'Have a drink. It'll cure your hangover.' He put forward an empty glass and filled it to the top with frothy, cold beer. 'Let's forget our worries.'

'What worries?' said Dani, who already looked drunk.

'The Vestibular,' said Rodrigo.

'I'm not worried,' she said.

She took my hand in hers and smiled

toothily, like we were in an American movie. Everything would be OK in the end. (No it wouldn't, no it wouldn't.) Carlito proposed a toast.

'Saúde!' he said.

'Sexo!' said Dani, which made everyone laugh.

We stayed for an hour and then Dani tugged me on the arm, looking up at me with those blue eyes, which seemed more dull than dreamy — the gold all gone — and said, 'It's time to go.'

'Don't stay up too late,' said Carlito, his dark curls shaking with laughter. 'You have to study tomorrow!'

Dani and I walked down the street holding hands, sticky with sweat. We passed a popcorn seller and a delicious buttery smell filled the air.

'Pipoca!' he shouted.

'You want some?' I said.

She shook her head. I was the one who wanted some, but we kept walking.

'Why did you tell them where we were going?' I said.

'Why not?' said Dani.

'Because it's private.'

'Come on, they're our friends. Are you embarrassed?'

'No, just — '

'Stop talking, André, otherwise I'm going to change my mind.'

We caught a cab to Copacabana, where prostitutes were stationed at each street corner, in miniskirts and high heels. Half of them were girls, the other half were something in between. Lovers Motel was on one of those corners, a neon heart buzzing over the front door. We got out of the car. A girl was standing outside wearing gold hot pants, a bikini top and white platform heels.

'Want some company?' she said blandly.

Close up, she looked around seventeen. A black girl with sloppy red lipstick and skinny legs, not yet grown.

'No, thanks,' I said.

'No worries, have fun.'

Daniela dragged me into the lobby, muttering, 'Don't speak to the prostitutes.'

The door went *ding!* as we walked into reception, which was lit by a single bare bulb and staffed by a neatly dressed middle-aged man. He looked like a bank clerk or a primary-school teacher, not a sex-motel receptionist. He had seen thousands of teenage couples like us, playing at being grown-ups, unable to find anywhere else to fuck. When he opened his mouth to speak, I saw that most of his teeth were gone.

'Welcome,' he said.

I needed to leave.

'We've got a reservation,' said Daniela.

I needed to leave, but I stayed rooted to the spot.

'What's the name?' said the receptionist.

Yes, we could get married, Luana and me. Papai would get over it, in the end. It wasn't the end of the world, just because she was an empregada, just because we were young. We could buy a flat with my inheritance from Mamãe. I would go to medical school and Luana would stay at home with the baby.

'Senhor and Senhora Cabral,' said Dani.

Luana Cabral, that would be her name.

Dani turned and winked at me. I opened my mouth to say that I needed to leave, but I didn't say anything. The receptionist took a key from the wall, dangled it over Daniela's open hand and dropped it. On the keyring, there was a wooden heart. How many dirty, sex-covered hands had touched that key? Hopefully, he cleaned them when they were returned.

I needed to leave.

'Room fifteen,' said the man. 'One flight up.'

I didn't leave. I followed Daniela up the darkened stairs, feeling the walls because I could barely see. She was giggling, as though all of it — the darkness, the toothless man, the teenage whore — added to her excitement. Inside the room, she flicked on the lights, which were bright and white, before changing her mind, turning them off and switching on the red bedside lamp instead. Outside, it had started to rain hard and loud — jungle rain. Even this had been a jungle, once upon a time. So long ago, it didn't matter any more. The motel's neon sign was just beneath our window, and its red light flashed into the room every other second. Daniela pulled the blinds down, but I could still hear the rain and see a glimmer of red neon. The air conditioning was broken, and sweat was tickling my neck and the sides of my body, running from under my arms.

'We should've brought a drink,' she said, sitting on the bed.

I sat next to her, stiffly. She put her hand on my leg and I laughed — at myself, I think.

'What's funny?'

'Do you think Rodrigo and Isabel have fucked on this bed?' I said.

'I doubt it.'

'And how many whores, on this very bed?'

'André, don't ruin it.'

'Sorry.'

'Wait here,' she said, darting off to the bathroom.

I stayed on the bed, noticing the

sticky-looking green walls, the way the mattress sagged, the 'erotic' framed drawing on the wall, of a naked woman with her arms wrapped around herself. I heard — from the room next door — a female howl of ecstasy, and wondered what the woman's lover had done to achieve that. I'd never made someone howl. Not even close. I remembered Luana and thought, yes, I will leave now, but then Dani came out of the bathroom, naked. She walked languorously, like a model down a catwalk, her face haughty and confident. She stopped a few inches in front of where I was sitting, small white breasts hovering at my eyeline. I grew hard. How easy it was to forget. Dani walked forward an inch and I took one of her breasts in my mouth. She was less shy than Luana, more theatrical. Louder, bossier, unafraid of telling me what to do. I tried not to think about how many people had fucked on those sheets, whether their DNA could really come out in the wash. At times I thought I could smell Luana on my fingers, but that was impossible — we hadn't had sex in a week. Afterwards, we lay in silence for an hour. I pretended to sleep, hoping that Daniela would get up and leave. Luana, I thought. Luana. The couple next door pierced the silence with torture-chamber screams.

When we left, we saw that it was an old white guy and a tall transsexual with an eerily perfect body. A hooker, of course. No man can fuck his wife like that.

22

On Sunday, Papai came back from work just after lunch. Luana and Rita were in the kitchen, eating the same feijoada that Thiago and I had just finished eating. Papai entered my bedroom without knocking, as usual. I was at my desk, trying to study.

'How are you?' he said.

'I'm well.'

He was like a stranger again — back to working seven days a week. Long gone was the Papai who walked down the street in Marajó, his hands on our shoulders. And he was stranger still for not knowing that I had destroyed my life, in this very room.

'How was work?' I said, which was not the sort of thing I ever asked him.

'Fine, fine.'

'You're working on Sundays again.'

'We need the money.'

'Do we?'

'The way the economy is going?' he said. 'Of course we do.'

It wasn't the whole truth. He was the one who needed it — he needed to work, to avoid living, at all costs. I don't blame him. Work is easier than life.

'We should go back to Pará sometime,' he said. 'Our house in Marajó is just sitting there.'

'I would like that,' I said, though I knew we would never go again.

He nodded unconvincingly and turned to leave.

'Pai,' I said, almost wincing, 'I want to tell you something.'

'Tell me,' he said, closing the door behind him.

'I don't know how to say this.'

Luana was a few metres away in the kitchen, preparing our food, like she always did. Nothing would look out of place, but everything had changed. Our child was growing inside her.

'Go on, this sounds interesting,' said Papai, with a small, innocent smile.

Be quiet, Luana would say. Not now, not like this.

My mouth was full of saliva. I swallowed it and shivered with disgust.

Yes, now.

Perhaps Papai thought I was going to reveal my plans to become a plastic surgeon, to take over the business, like he always dreamed I would. No, that wasn't going to happen. I wasn't a good son, I couldn't do anything right. I hadn't planned on saying anything until that very moment, and now I didn't know what to say. I felt like I was going to vomit — or scream, 'Help me, Papai!' — so I reached, desperately, for a white lie.

'I'm only telling you this because she's afraid to tell you herself,' I said, as quickly as possible, before I could change my mind, 'but Luana got involved with a man and needs our . . . help.'

His eyes shot up, his smile vanished. I could feel the blood in my face, like fire on my skin.

'Which man?'

'Someone from Vidigal. No one we know.'

'What do you mean, 'needs our help'?'

He knew what I meant, but was just wasting time, trying to delay the truth. I could see it in his face; his wrinkles were instantly deeper, the carved lines of an old man.

'She's pregnant,' I said.

'She's pregnant,' he echoed, not as a question, but as a statement. And then his features sharpened, his eyes went black. 'Who the hell did this? I'll cut his fucking throat.'

My face was still burning. I looked at my father, terrified but unable to look away. He walked over to my bed, opposite my desk, where I was sitting, sat down and rested his elbows on his knees. He started shaking, from head to toe, like a tree in a storm, with his hands over his face. It was terrible. I had never seen anything like it, not even when Mamãe died.

'Papai?' I said. 'Are you OK?'

He clasped his hands together, trying to regain control.

'How — how could this happen?' he said finally.

'I don't know.'

'Is there something else you want to tell me?'

'Like what?'

'Like the identity of this . . . this man?'

'No, I don't know who he is. She had no one else to turn to.'

'What about Rita?'

'I don't know. Maybe she was afraid.'

'You're lying,' he said.

I didn't respond. He looked at the wall above my head with drooping, troubled eyes, pondering something — a memory, a question — and then shook his head.

'There's something you should know,' he said. He moved his eyes from the wall to my face. He shook his head again. 'I thought I would never tell you this. I didn't think I needed to. But since you're lying to me — '

'Pai, I'm not lying.'

His face glimmered with sweat, but he had regained composure.

'Have you ever wondered why I paid for Luana to go to a decent school?' he said.

'Because you're a good boss.'

'Do you know any other empregada who was allowed to raise her child at work?'

'No, but — '

'I told you not to screw around with her.'

'I didn't screw around with her.'

'Don't lie to me!' he shouted, spitting everywhere. 'I can see it in both your faces. You think you can hide anything from me? My own children?'

'She's not your child. You can't control her.'

'My children,' he said, looking up at me.

We sat in silence as the truth overwhelmed me, making my head spin, burning in my stomach and getting stuck in my throat. The sour taste of bile, at the back of my tongue. I gripped my chair. What parallel universe had I stepped into? Had I known, it would never have crossed my mind to . . . Or would it? It was the most shocking thing anyone had ever said to me, but if you saw us, in that room — if you had been a cockroach on the wall — you would have just seen two miserable people, a middle-aged man and his son, having a staring match. The silence rippled between us. It was something I could almost touch, something that could throttle me, if I didn't speak. Say something, say anything.

'What the fuck are you talking about?' I said.

He didn't respond. It was too shameful to repeat, too revolting to explain. He stared at the ground, completely diminished. I'd never seen him like that, so pathetic. A bead of sweat pinged from his face on to the wooden floor. I thought of Mamãe, dying in the ambulance. I thought, briefly, of my father in bed with Rita (how was it even possible? I couldn't imagine her with anyone, let alone him), but I immediately buried this image — it was too much.

'Pai?' I said.

Again, he didn't respond. My body filled with adrenalin. Sweat poured from my head, my armpits, my back, like rain into a gutter. I had to do something, I didn't know what. I jumped to my feet and lurched towards him, but I couldn't do it — I couldn't hit Papai — so I kicked my wooden bedside table, shattering the lamp, kicking, kicking, until my schoolbooks were on the floor and the table in pieces.

'You escroto,' I said under my breath, feeling thrilled and terrified, because I had never spoken to him like that. 'You filho da puta.'

'Stop it,' he said, in a weak voice I had never heard before.

'Who are you?' I shouted, inches from his face. 'Who the hell are you?'

He didn't answer. He didn't know.

'What about Mamãe?'

'She didn't know. It was a mistake to keep them here, I can see that now. I just wanted . . . ' He sighed and shook his head. 'I wanted to see her grow up.'

Several cars beeped outside. Someone shouted. People were stuck in traffic, trying to get somewhere. The world was going on, but for me it had ended. Fix it, Papai. Fix it, I wanted to say. He stayed with his eyes on the floor, his collar soaked with sweat. I sat back at my desk, my head down.

'Does Luana know?' I said.

'No. Rita swore she wouldn't say anything.'

'What are we going to do?'

'I'll deal with it. They need to leave as soon as possible. This baby — '

'I know,' I said.

'It can't be born.'

He got up to leave. I couldn't believe what had just passed between us. I hoped that it was a nightmare, that I would wake up in my bed, hearing Mamãe's voice in the next room.

'I know that Mamãe was ill,' I said. 'It was your fault. You made her that way.'

Papai didn't react. He just walked to the door.

'I could see it in your eyes, both of you,' he said. 'A while ago, in Marajó, but I hoped I was wrong. I — I hoped that you were just becoming friends.'

He left the room. I put my head in my hands and wept. Snot ran into my mouth, salty and thick. I listened to Papai's heavy footsteps going down the corridor. My humiliation was complete. It was the plot of a cheap novela. I sat in silence, straining to hear his conversation with the empregadas, but the kitchen was too far away. Already I could feel Luana's absence. Coconut, perfume and sweat. Sweetness and rot. What kind of baby would it be, if it lived? A mangled, incestuous mess, fifty per cent Matheus Cabral.

The kitchen door slammed. I went to the living-room balcony and saw Papai, Rita and Luana — five floors down — walking out of the building, opening the gates, walking down the street. Behind them, the sea was unusually still and the sky was bright. Both searingly blue, unreal. Thousands of people on the beach, unaware of me watching them. They were an odd sight: a man in a suit followed by two empregadas, neither of them carrying anything or pushing a pram or holding the hand of a child. What a comfort Rita had been, when I was younger. How many years had passed since I last held her hand? That's what I longed to do, as I watched them walking away, casting long shadows across the mosaic pavement: hold Rita's hand and hear that everything was going to be OK.

★ ★ ★

The living room was growing dark, but I didn't turn the lights on. I stayed on the balcony for several hours, watching as the street lamps turned on, all at once. Thiago came outside and asked, 'What are you doing?' but I couldn't respond. I tried to hug him and he pushed me away — he was getting too old for that — and returned to his bedroom. People left the beach. I heard American voices, talking too loudly, saying repeatedly that something was 'amaaaazing!' I longed to be them, with their simple lives. The beach bar across the road was still busy, people drinking away the dregs of the weekend, before work began again the next day.

Out of the darkness came a figure in white: Rita, walking back alone. I leaned back from the balcony, so that she wouldn't see me. I couldn't see the expression on her face as she approached the building. I went back to my bedroom. A few minutes passed, in which she would be taking the service lift, the shitty one with no mirror. I heard her greet Thiago. His high voice saying, 'Rita!' and something else, which I couldn't make out. She was being professional, that's all it was. Poor Thiago. He loved Rita just like I had done at his age, and he was going to lose her. Somehow, I fell asleep. I don't know how long for, but I woke when Rita poked her head into my bedroom. In the darkness, I couldn't see her expression.

'Dinner is ready,' she said, as though nothing had happened.

'I'll come in a minute.'

I went to the living room after splashing water on my face. Everything was set out on the table — fried fish, rice and salad — and the kitchen door was closed. I couldn't hear any voices behind it. I ate with Thiago. He was reading another one of those comics, eating noisily and wriggling his legs under the table. I covered the fish in lime juice, but it tasted like nothing. My senses had dulled.

'Finished!' shouted Thiago, putting his fork down.

He sprinted to the TV room and, a few seconds later, the television came on — a comedy show with canned laughter. I heard him giggling along. Rita came into the room to collect the plates. She had an odd, faraway look. I longed for her to hold me in her arms, for her to tell me what a wonderful child I was.

'Wasn't it good?' she said. 'You hardly ate any.'

'It was great,' I said, feeling my body go cold with fear.

'Not hungry?'

'Yes, just not hungry.'

She avoided my gaze and concentrated on the plates. Her smile had gone and hatred emanated from her averted eyes, her expressionless face, her quick movements. I could feel her judgement, burning me. But she was a good actress — she always had been. I stood up to help her clear the table and she jumped in surprise.

'Hey, don't do my job for me.'

'Was it your job to sleep with my father?'

Her head shot up and she squinted. She had never looked at me like that before, with such contempt. Then she looked back down and stacked the plates and bowls, one on top of the other.

'You think you and your father are the first?' she said. 'You're not the first.'

'What do you mean?'

'Lucky that times have changed. We're not owned by you, and neither is the baby.'

'It's gone, though, the baby. Hasn't it?'

She didn't reply.

'Hasn't it?' I said.

Rita walked towards the kitchen, holding the plates, her flip-flops smacking against the floor. A bead of sweat ran from my armpit to my waist, under my T-shirt. At the door to the kitchen, she paused and looked back.

'I'm a real Christian,' she said, 'not like your father.'

'She's going to have it? Please, Rita, I need to know.'

'Just forget about it. Forget about us. That shouldn't be too hard.'

She went into the kitchen and started humming a song, as though she were in a bright mood. Maybe it helped her to forget. I needed to forget, too. Just for one night. So I phoned up Daniela and asked her to come out with me.

'Sorry, I'm studying,' she said.

'Just take a break — I want to see you.'

'I can't. We've already gone out two days in a row.'

'Come on, I just want to have some fun.'

'What happened to you?' she said, laughing. 'Usually, you never want to come out.'

'Fine,' I said. 'Don't worry about it.'

'Sorry, amor!'

I winced at that word.

After hanging up the phone, I walked out of the flat. I didn't tell Thiago or Rita that I was going out. I walked down the road, away from the beach, and went into a little bar that I'd walked past thousands of times but never entered. The kind of bar you'd find on any corner in Ipanema — at least you would in 1986. Inside, the usual array of men and women, but mostly men, were sitting at chairs and tables that spilled out on to the pavement, drinking cold beers, eating, smoking and laughing. Most of them were a bit bedraggled, middle-aged or older, apart from a little girl having dinner with her parents. Outside it was hot, but inside it was hotter, and an ineffectual fan twirled on the ceiling, stirring up the hot air. I sat outside and ordered a chopp — draught beer. People glanced over at me, drinking alone, but soon returned to their conversations, which veered from hushed and urgent to hysterical and deafening. I finished my beer quickly and ordered another. That one went down nicely, too. I tried to ignore the faint smell of piss that hummed up from the pavement.

When I was halfway through my fourth chopp, I saw them walking down the street:

Papai and Luana. She was still wearing her uniform, but it was rumpled and her face was tired. She walked uncomfortably, an arm around my father's arm — the strangest thing I had ever seen. So she had done it. Rita had lied. I raised the menu over my face, so they wouldn't see me, but they didn't even look over. They just walked on.

At some point in the night, I found myself sitting at another table, laughing uproariously with a trio of guys in their fifties and sixties, all of them dressed casually in T-shirts and shorts but the smell of money hung around them — something about their portly confidence, their nasal Yiddish accents and the brusque way they ordered their drinks. One of them, the oldest, had a concentration-camp tattoo on his left forearm and curly white hair sprouting from the neck of his T-shirt. I couldn't remember sitting down with them or being called over — I was suddenly just there.

'What do you senhores do for a living?' I said.

'This and that,' one of them said.

'We make money,' said the tattooed man, laughing.

They ordered steak sandwiches and more cold chopps, tipped fries on to my plate, which I gobbled up, and regaled me with stories about cops and robbers.

'One time, a guy tried to mug me by throwing a coconut at my head. I just kicked it back and it knocked him out. Like goddamn Zico or something.'

'Lies, lies, lies!'

'I swear! A coconut! I had to call an ambulance for him, poor thing.'

'What about you, menino — you ever been mugged?'

I was unbelievably drunk, but somehow I managed to show off a little, telling stories about all the people I knew who had been shot in bungled robberies. (Most of them were acquaintances or acquaintances of acquaintances.) One of them was true, though: one of my teachers had been shot dead in front of his house in Humaitá by a teenage boy who made off with his cheap watch and almost-empty wallet. This was years before, when I was Thiago's age.

'Rio de Janeiro,' said the tattooed man, shaking his head. 'What a shithole.'

I glanced again at his arm, and he noticed.

'Ever seen a tatuagem like this before?' he said.

'Sorry, I didn't mean to stare. No, I haven't.'

'Don't worry. People are always looking. I thought of having it removed, but what's the point? It's not like I'm going to forget about it.'

He looked down at his drink, his lively mood diminished. His friends were silent, heads shaking with sympathy, heard it all before. The man showed me a black-and-white photo of his mother, which he carried in his wallet — a brunette with sad eyes, as though she knew what was coming. He was from Poland, he told me, but had no intention of ever going back. His eyes were moist. They were pale, like hers. My mother is dead, too, I nearly said, but I didn't. We drank more beer and talked about something else.

★ ★ ★

I woke up to the sound of the ocean, and something poking me in the ribs. When I opened my eyes, an old black guy wearing ragged clothes was standing over me, holding a rubbish-picking stick.

'Menino, wake up,' he said, in a raspy voice. 'Wake up.'

My face was in the sand, my body sweaty and stiff. I licked my lips and tasted salt. My right foot hurt. I vaguely remembered the bedside table. Why had I done that? Oh.

'Leave me alone,' I said.

'Are you alive?'

'Unfortunately, yes.'

I sat up and looked ahead. It was early morning. I could tell, because the sky was white, the beach empty and the breeze almost cool.

'What are you doing, sleeping out here?'

'I don't know. I don't remember.'

'You should go home before your mother starts to worry.'

I forgot for a second, but then remembered.

'My mother is dead,' I said.

'Sorry to hear that. So is mine.'

Well, of course she is, I didn't say. You're old.

A grey foamy wave curled in the sea, several metres high, and went *smash* on the sand. It all looked so dirty — the water, the sand, the sky.

'Don't worry about it,' I said. 'Can I just sit here for a bit?'

'Of course. I was just checking you weren't dead. Sometimes we find bodies here.'

'Really?'

'Usually drunks. They drown and get washed up. Sometimes murder victims. Last week, we found two kids — ten years old, maybe younger, both shot dead. It was terrible.' He paused. 'Well, at least you're alive. I'll leave you now.'

'Thank you.'

When I stood up, I realized that my shoes had gone. Either lost, or taken, while I slept. My wallet, too — gone — but I still had my keys. No memory of the night beyond drinking with those Jewish guys. No memory of whoever took my things. I walked home barefoot, limping. People stared at me because I looked too rich to be a tramp. When I walked into my building, the porteiro, Marcelo, looked me up and down, mildly horrified.

'Are you OK, André?' he said.

'Yeah. I think so.'

'You're spreading sand all over the place!'

'Sorry about that. I can help you to clean it, once I've had a shower.'

'Forget it. I'll do it,' he said, looking cross. 'But you'd better use the service lift.'

★ ★ ★

The flat was silent. Everyone still asleep, I thought. I threw my clothes in the laundry area, on the ground, had a cold shower and walked around in my boxer shorts, already sweating again. There was a heatwave coming, I could feel it. It was December — summer again. The air was heavy and damp, the flat filled with sunshine, traffic and birdsong, seeping in through slightly open windows — just the way Rita liked it.

'Fresh air cures everything,' she used to tell me when I was little.

After I'd thrown a tantrum, she would take me out for a walk towards the Arpoador, buy an ice cream for me and a coconut for herself. I always dodged the black bits on the black-and-white pavement. Even in my sandals, I could feel their heat. Then we would reach the Arpoador, dip our toes into the sea and watch the surfers being whipped around.

'Feel better?' she'd say, and of course I did.

Maybe the empregadas were out shopping. My father at work. Thiago asleep, perhaps. I looked into the TV room, the living room, the kitchen, and Luana and Rita's bedroom behind the kitchen, which was bare and neat — two little beds, made up with hand-me-down cartoon sheets. The porcelain Virgin Mary, still looking down over them. One of her hands had snapped off, leaving a hole.

'Rita?' I said, walking through the corridor. 'Luana?'

I didn't know it yet, but they had gone. I would realize that later, when I came home from lunch with Dani — where I mentioned nothing, absolutely nothing — and noticed that my bed was still unmade. And then my father came home. He told me that they'd moved back to Vidigal, that the baby was dead, that I should move on with my life and we need never talk about it again.

That was hours later.

In the morning, I knew nothing.

I was just a hungover teenage boy in need of breakfast.

I went to the kitchen and moped around for a bit, opening and closing the cupboards and the fridge, poking at the different meats, fruits, breads and jars of beans. I took a bread roll, butter and ham out of the fridge, sliced the roll open and made myself breakfast for the first time in my life.

23

A few weeks after Rita and Luana left, the
new year came along — 1987 — and with it,
dreams of escape. Daniela broke up with me,
telling me she wanted to start university with
a clean slate. We had sex one last time and,
afterwards, she cried. But she was happy, she
said. It was just overwhelming that everything
was changing. Papai and I were in silent
agreement never to speak about Luana, but
she seemed to be in the air, swirling around
us. He hired a new empregada, Edilene, who
was nice enough, but a stranger. I had passed
the entrance exams for UFRJ but, secretly, I
was planning a new life. A one-way ticket to
Madrid — the city was randomly chosen;
what mattered was the continent. Most
importantly, since I had turned eighteen I
had access to my inheritance, American
dollars kept in a Swiss bank account. Papai
had plans for that money — for my future
— but it was under my name. I thanked
Mamãe every night before bed, the way most
people thank God.

I knew that Papai would be against it, so I
didn't say anything. I chose one of Edilene's

days off, a Monday. Unlike Rita and Luana, she had every Sunday and Monday off. Papai was at work, Thiago was at school. I posted letters to Dani and Carlito, explaining nothing, and left another two on the shining, round dining table, for Papai and Thiago. It was Thiago I felt the sorriest for. I was abandoning him to be raised by a man he barely knew and an empregada he didn't know at all. I said I would return soon, and disappeared without a backward glance.

*   *   *

I rarely stayed at the flat again. When I went to Rio I would usually book a hotel, once I could afford it. It upset Papai. I could hear it in his frail voice, during long-distance phone calls, whenever I was planning a trip. After he sold his surgery and retired, he became old — older than his actual age. Grey, plump and living alone with his empregada. (I can't remember the name of his last empregada, the one after Edilene.) I visited him at home, but refused to stay the night. Every wall and piece of furniture screamed: the past, the past. The sofa where we had watched novelas, the kitchen where I would watch Luana cook, the round dining table, my single bed, now permanently stripped. The flat hadn't changed, but we had. When Thiago was a teenager, he came to stay with us in London and I told him the whole story. Most of it didn't surprise him, but he started crying when I told him that Luana was Papai's daughter; he'd had no idea. At the end of his trip, he didn't want to go back to Rio. But he did, and he grew up, moved out and lived elsewhere, alone. Papai disapproved of him: the way he spoke and moved, the amount of time he spent on Rua Farme de Amoedo with other young men and, above all, his career as a psychotherapist, inspired by Aunt Lia.

I slowly lost touch with most of my friends. Sometimes, when I visited Rio, I would run into them in the street in Zona Sul. We laughed, remembered the old days and made plans that never transpired. I had coffee with Daniela a couple of times, but it felt like there was a wall between us. She wanted to talk about the past, and I didn't.

'When we were going out,' she once said, 'I thought you had a crush on your empregada.'

'What are you talking about?' I said.

She laughed.

'You did, I could tell.'

A few years later I saw her walking on Rua Visconde de Pirajá, hand in hand with Gabriel. They didn't see me. I kept walking.

I saw Carlito on a few of my trips to Rio

but, each time, we seemed to have a little less in common. He worked for his dad and lived at home, looked after by his mother and their empregada. He surprised me, a couple of weeks after my wedding, with a long-distance phone call. He must have got the number from Papai.

'You got married?' he said, before even saying hello, the same old friendliness jangling in his voice. 'Where was my invitation, cara?'

We hadn't spoken in a while.

'It was a small wedding,' I said. 'We only had two guests.'

'What a drag, sounds boring!' he joked. 'OK, you're forgiven, but next time you're in Rio I want to meet this gringa.'

'You will, you will.'

And he did, some months later, when I took Esther to Rio for the first time. She was charmed by Carlito, like everyone always was. We talked for hours over sushi in Copacabana. I was glad to have her there, to show him that I had turned out all right.

By the time he died in a botched mugging — a single shot to the head — we hadn't spoken in over a decade. Thiago told me about it in an email. I didn't know who to send my condolences to. I didn't know Carlito's wife and children — didn't even know their names — so I addressed a card to his parents and sent it to their old flat on Rua Farme de Amoedo. I told Esther and she burst into tears, even though she had only met him once. She encouraged me to go to the funeral, but I couldn't do it. They wouldn't want me there. I had abandoned him.

24

I

I was standing at a phone booth in Saint-Germain-des-Prés, Paris. The wet European winter was giving way to spring: blossom on trees, young people laughing in the streets. But I still wore my winter coat. I found Paris enchanting, for the same reasons that everyone else does. I dialled my old number and listened to the foreign tone, those long rings. It rang twice.

'Alô?' said Papai.

Hearing his voice, I felt like I needed to take a shit. A joyful panic.

'Pai, it's me,' I said.

Silence. For a moment, I wondered if he had forgotten the sound of my voice.

'It's me — André.'

'I know who it is.'

He sounded out of breath. There wasn't even a hint of warmth in his voice.

'I'm in Paris,' I said.

'Well, that's very nice for you.'

'Don't you want to ask me anything?'

'Such as?'

'I don't know. It's been a while. How are you?'

'What do you want to know, André? Have we been worried about you? Yes, obviously. Thiago is devastated. And so are your friends. Daniela came over the week you disappeared, looking for you, and collapsed on the floor of our living room. Is that what you want to know?'

'Did you tell her?'

'No, of course not.'

'It wasn't an easy decision.'

'It sounds easy to me, giving up on life and gallivanting in Paris. That money was for your future.'

'This is the future,' I said.

'No, it's your youth. When are you coming back?'

'I don't know.'

I wanted to ask about Luana — did he know where she worked, now? — but it was too early for that. Some other time.

'André, you did a stupid thing, but it's over. Do you hear me? It's over, filho. We are your family. We're waiting for you.'

'Is Thi there?'

'No, he's out. I'll tell him you called. He'll be sad to have missed you. Where have you been, anyway? Just Paris?'

'Madrid, Barcelona, Andalusia, the Sierra

266

Nevada, all over Spain. And then Portugal. It's cold, not the right time of year.'

'They have winter over there,' said Papai, his voice softening. 'You didn't think of that, did you?'

'Not really.'

'What's your phone number?'

'I'm on a pay phone.'

'But where are you staying?' he said.

He sounded so old and sad. He was only in his forties, though. Maybe it was just in my mind. I gave him the phone number of my hostel.

'But I won't be there for long,' I said. 'I'm going to keep moving.'

'One day you will stop.'

'One day, yes.'

'Pelo amor de Deus, keep in touch.'

II

London was cold, even in June. I stayed at a hostel in King's Cross. Back then, the area was full of prostitutes, homeless people and cars passing through. I was propositioned every time I left the tube station, but I preferred the company of an Argentinian girl at my hostel, Violeta, who was travelling with two friends. She had curious brown eyes, dark hair and a round bum-bum that reminded me of girls in Ipanema. We communicated in Portuñol, fucked in the showers and saw the sights together: the British Museum, the V&A, the Natural History Museum, the river, the Tower of London, the river — I always wanted to return to the river. It was nothing like the Amazon. Thinner, shorter and dirtier, with old buildings on either side. History in London goes further back. It's easier to get lost, to slip yourself in.

We spent two weeks like this, idling. Violeta's friends got sick of us and flew out to Granada for the next leg of their trip. All of them rich kids, like me, wanting to drag out their youth for a bit longer. None of us was thinking much of home. At the end of our month together, Violeta left at dawn, leaving me a note and a taste of my own medicine. I flew back to the continent.

III

The Berlin Wall. The French Alps in summer. White yachts shining on the Côte d'Azur. Venice, Sicily, Florence. Rome was as hot as Rio but somehow less bearable. I stuck to the shadows and cooled my arms in water fountains. Drank a beer, alone, by the Trevi

Fountain — what a cliché — but *La Dolce Vita* was one of Mamãe's favourite films, and nothing feels like a cliché when you're nineteen. In Athens, I bought contact lenses and left my glasses at the bottom of my bag, till they snapped in two. The Acropolis, the Ionian Islands, Corfu. There weren't many Brazilians in Europe, back then — with their suffocating stink of home — but I avoided the few that I came across. Italian girls reminded me of Brazil. I went back to Italy. My English improved. Whenever I thought of Luana, I distracted myself. I got drunk. I read books and went to museums. I swam in the Mediterranean, in rivers and lakes and crowded swimming pools. I smoked weed for the first time. I went to bed with other girls. The gap between the past and the present expanded, until I barely thought of her any more.

At the beginning of autumn, in Venice, I met two girls at a bar. One dark-haired, Irish and slightly buck-toothed, the other blond, German and healthy-looking. Both in their twenties — older women! They were travelling around Europe, wasting time, no end in sight. Around two a.m., I came back from the bathroom and the German girl had gone somewhere else — how disappointing — and then the Irish girl invited me back to her room.

My head clamped between thick white thighs. Her voice light and high. Birds were waking up, light was filtering in through the Venetian blinds. Venetian blinds in Venice! When I let go inside her, the room blurred and sparkled. She fell asleep quickly — a pale, curved mass, rising and falling. I can't remember her name. I doubt she remembers mine. I walked back to my hostel, on bridges over dark green canals, marvelling at my adult life, pushing back feelings of guilt and shame. It was early morning in Europe, and I was young and knew everything.

IV

A telephone booth in Byron Bay, a few hundred metres from the ocean. I was wearing shorts, flip-flops and an old T-shirt. It was February, the following year. The tail-end of the Australian summer. Since leaving Europe, I hadn't come across a single Brazilian. Not in Thailand, where the girls weren't interested in me — unless I was prepared to pay. Nor in Goa, though a hotel worker did try to speak to me in a strange, mangled Portuguese. The colonial buildings looked the same as the ones at home; the weather was the same, too. One day, as I walked through Old Goa, I felt I could taste Rio in the air — green and wet, a sweet hint of rot. I didn't stay long.

'Where are you now?' said Papai.

'Australia.'

'Australia?! Last time I spoke to you, you were in Italy.'

'That was ages ago.'

Several months felt like several years. Nowadays, months are like hours.

'Is everything OK?' I said.

'The country is a mess,' he said.

'What do you mean?'

'The inflation, it's out of control. You don't watch the news?'

'They don't report on Brazil.'

I didn't watch the news. I barely watched TV.

'The country is falling apart,' said Papai, becoming excited. 'Our money is worth nothing. Every week, everything goes up in cost.'

'That sounds terrible,' I said, but I was barely taking it in. 'How's Thiago?'

'It's a shame you missed his birthday. You didn't even call.'

'Didn't he receive my present? I sent one from India.'

'India?!'

'A wooden elephant.'

'It didn't arrive.'

Thiago was nine years old. In a few months, I would be twenty.

'Pai,' I said, 'I've got something to tell you.'

I winced, remembering the last time I had confided in him. I could still feel the shame in my bones. It was part of me; it would never go away.

'What?' he said.

There was a crackle on the line. I looked up at the street, to compose myself. A family of blond hippies walked past, hand in hand: mother, father and toddler son dressed in ethnic prints with beads dangling from their hair. The father lifted the child in the air and they all laughed.

'I'm not coming back to Rio,' I said. 'I'm going to live in Londres.'

'Eh?'

'I'm going to medical school there.'

'That's ridiculous.'

'You don't have to worry about sending me money — I have enough.'

'You think this is about money? Meu Deus do céu.'

I remember it so clearly: the slice of ocean at the end of the road, shining between low buildings, and my three American friends, Alex, Jess and Jason, walking towards me, smiling. I had met them at a hostel. They barely knew each other but, unlike me, they were magnetically drawn to their country-men. Jess resembled Luana, somewhat, with her black ringlets and pale brown skin, but she was nothing like her — tall and athletic, with an upper-middle-class confidence.

'I don't know what to say,' said Papai. 'You're an adult — it's your life.'

I was barely listening. I was looking up, squinting at the sun and waving at my friends.

'Hey, André!' said Jess. (I had become accustomed to people pronouncing it 'On-dray', instead of 'Un-dreh'.) 'Still talking to your dad?'

I held my hand up and mouthed, 'One minute.'

The Yanks were holding up plastic bags full of cold, canned beer. I felt stupidly happy, because in seconds I was going to put the phone down and slip back into my dream.

'Maybe it's for the best,' said Papai.

'What do you mean?' I said.

'You going to Londres. This country is finished.'

I hope so, I thought. Then I'll never have to return.

'Pai,' I said, 'I'm sorry, but I have to go.'

* * *

Later that night, after the beer was drunk, I kissed Jess on the beach, soundtracked by waves and bongos (remember, nothing felt like a cliché). The next day she travelled back to Sydney to fly home, and we promised to stay in touch. The kiss throbbed in my memory for several months, as I travelled up the east coast of Australia and down the middle, then through New Zealand. By the time I arrived in New York, I was bursting with anticipation.

We spent five days together at her studio flat on the Upper West Side. The first time we had sex was desperate and quick — high expectations had made us nervous. But the second and fifth and tenth times were wonderful, already tainted with sadness because we knew that we would never see each other again. What is Jess doing now? Probably tapping at a computer in an office, like most people. I can't look her up, because I don't remember her surname. There were no emails back then. I threw away her letters after I moved in with Esther, so my memories are incomplete. But I still remember her strong body, tied together by knots of muscle, honed by years of ballet and 'soccer'. Her pink-brown lips open and gasping for air.

The large Brazilian flag above her bed, which she had bought for the World Cup in

1986. Her amused dismay that I couldn't remember the winning country from that year: Argentina, Brazil's number-one rival. Walking through Manhattan in the summer. Jess in a short print dress and sandals. Her confidence brazen and lovely. The smell of rubbish, slowly rotting in the sun.

On our last night, after we had sex, Jess put Miles Davis's *Kind of Blue* on the record player and went to the kitchen to get a glass of water. The room was dark and the kitchen light. Cars outside, beeping. *Der-dum der-dum der-dum der-dum. Der-dum.* Her naked outline stood in the doorway — strong legs, curved hips, short, curly hair — already lost to me, even though I was still there. *Der-dum der-dum der-dum der-duh-dum. Der-dum.* Already lost, so we fucked again. The room went blue when the sun came up.

Already lost.

When I masturbate in the shower, these are the memories I return to.

What was Luana's surname?

25

Oi André,

This is the last one. I'm sorry that I'm doing this to you. No, actually I'm not sorry at all. Your father said you wanted nothing to do with us, but he's dead and I'm too old to care. You will know, because I'm telling you.

It was a year ago, in December. That's why I'm in Belém, at the moment — because it's been a year. Iracema and Jorge are here, too, all of us together.

This is what happened to Francisco. Iara told me everything. One night, everyone from the restaurant had gone home, apart from Chico and Iara. As I suspected, they had been dating for a few months — she admitted that to me, afterwards. They were sitting on a bench at the end of the garden, overlooking the river. Who knows what they were doing there, long after their shifts had ended? You can only guess. Iara says they were chatting. Apparently, Chico hinted that he wanted to marry her, but maybe that was wishful thinking on her part. They barely knew each other. She says that he invited her to Marajó to meet me. Chico's never brought any girl home — that's not his style.

They were about to leave, to go back to his flat. He said he needed to pee first. He stood up and walked towards the river. So Deus sabe why he didn't use the toilet in the restaurant. That's not how I raised him, to piss out in public, on to a tree, into a river or whatever the hell he was doing. Iara watched as he walked away, until she couldn't see him any more — he'd gone behind some bushes. It was dark, but night was fading. The river was black. I asked for all the details. I wanted to know exactly how it felt, so that I could pretend I had been there. That he hadn't been alone when he fell in.

Birds were singing, Iara said. The sun was coming up and she could see the river once again. She shouted his name, but he didn't reply. It happened so quickly, she said, or maybe she was too drunk to notice the time passing. Both of them were drunk. They never found his body. The river moved fast. He was swept out to sea. Maybe to Londres, to the father he never met.

I thought you should know. Please respond: info@casadaluana.com.br
Luana

Querida Luana,
It's good to hear from you, but I'm not sure I understand. My father told me that our child was never born.
Beijos,
André

André,
He was alive for twenty-six years. His name was Francisco. But you already knew that, didn't you?
Luana

Luana, what on earth are you talking about? My father said that you had an abortion.
André

Really? You believed him? And you never tried to contact me to check that it was true, or even just to see if I was all right? Matheus told me you didn't want to know about Chico. I was angry for so many years. I'm still angry. That's why I sent the letters.

My father [our father, I want to say] never told me a thing. He took you to the surgery — I thought you had the abortion. In fact, I saw you, walking back together. You had our son? And he's dead? Are you serious?

I write again, before she replies:

You're right. I should have got in touch. I never imagined that he was lying, but perhaps I should have assumed it — he had been lying for years. But even if he hadn't been, I should have called. I'm so sorry. I was a kid. I didn't know what to do.

I'm at work at the moment. A new patient comes in every five minutes, so I put away my phone, bring up their records and pretend to be interested in them. I'm well versed — no chance that they'll notice. Good to see you again, Mrs Gregson, you fucking hypochondriac. Yes, yes, here's a prescription, take two a day and it should all clear up in no time.

In my inbox, her name appears as Luana da Cruz. Her married name.

I was a kid, too — a kid with a baby. You ran away to Europe, while I raised him alone. My mother helped, but I was alone, just as she had been. I'm glad that you're sorry, André, but I can't forgive you.

Yes, we went to the surgery, but I didn't go through with it. My mother was so against it. We stayed there for hours, just talking. Your father was trying to convince her. After she left, he told me about their affair. It was insane. We both cried. Everything fell apart. He told me, that's why you have to do it, because the baby might be sick. But I couldn't do it, so he let me go. He gave us money and helped us to find new jobs. I can't believe he did this. No, that's not true. I can totally believe it.

Here are two photos of Chico — one is from his fifth birthday, in Rio, and the other is from a few weeks before the accident.

Hi, Azim. I'm fine, and you? My kids are great. How are yours? Usually, I like to chat to Azim, who runs a corner shop I visit nearly every day, on Albion Road, and whose eldest daughter is in Hannah's class at school. He tells me that he can't sleep at night. I go to bed and just lie there for hours, awake. And then I wake up and work work work at the shop — you know — and I get so tired, but still can't sleep. Poor Azim. I do my best to make sympathetic noises, but my mind is elsewhere — on the two photos I looked at for five seconds before he came in through the door. A small, olive-skinned boy with black ringlets, a finger in his mouth and little, white, grinning teeth. A green football-field cake sits on the table in front of him, but he's not looking at it — he's looking at the person behind the camera, with a child's simple, absolute love. In the other photo, the same face is rearranged and hardened for adulthood. Still smiling, but with less abandon. He's dressed in a waiter's starched white uniform. His hair is close-cropped. He wears wire-rimmed glasses. The love in his face is mellow and grown. He reminds me of my brother — the delicate shape of his face. I love him immediately, this boy. So what should I do? says Azim. I'm desperate, Dr Cabral. Please, I say, call me André.

He was muito bonito. I'm in shock. I'm at work. I don't know what to do with myself. So you live in Marajó?

Why didn't I look for her? I had assumed that she wanted me out of her life. A new beginning. That's what I had wanted, anyway, but as the years passed I realized that there are no beginnings, there are no endings, other than the beginning and end of your life. If I had known, I would have called her. Wouldn't I? Yes, yes, yes, I would.

I've lived in Salvaterra for twenty years — I wanted to get away from the favela. Didn't you know that either? Jorge and I opened a pousada recently. We used to run a restaurant.

I picture my son — one of those light-limbed, lanky favela boys — running up to the top of Vidigal, in just shorts and flip-flops. The kind of boy I passed on the street without a second glance. Skipping, skipping, skipping. Taking two steps at a time. Yellow sun on his bare, brown back. When he reaches the top, he admires the glowing, turquoise Atlantic; lush, green mountains surrounding the modern ugliness. Francisco. Chico! I want to shout his name. I would have done anything for you. I wouldn't have left. What was Papai thinking? All those times I visited Rio, Papai had said nothing. Even when Chico had still been in the city. My son and I had breathed the same air and looked at the same beach — he from Vidigal and I from my father's window. Had I passed him on the street? I

cover my face with my hands, my body
shaking, trying to push the tears back inside
before my next patient comes.

Did my father ever meet him?

Only once, when he was a baby. It was
too much for him, the filho da puta.

Luana, I didn't know anything. I don't
know what to do.

26

Five minutes after I email Esther telling her that I'm going to Brazil, the phone rings.

'Thank God,' she says, which was the opposite of what I thought she'd say. 'I've been worried sick about Bee. I've hardly slept since she left.'

It's dark outside. It's always dark in December, the cold light emerging for just a handful of hours. I've never got used to it; perhaps I never will. A draught blows through the old windows of my kitchen.

I hear Esther inhale and blow.

'You're smoking?' I say.

'Just vaping. At least it's not the real thing.'

'I'm not judging.'

'I forgot how fucking good it is.'

We laugh. Some of our happiest memories are fogged in cigarette smoke: smoking in bed, at pubs, on the street after our wedding; in Parisian cafés, on our first holiday — two young tourists in love.

She coughs and I return to the present.

'How are you, Esther?'

'I'm all right.' And then she surprises me by saying, 'I miss you.'

'I thought you hated me.'

'Oh, I do,' she says, in an ironic tone.

'You should've picked a husband from a progressive country. Sweden or Denmark. They would have been taller and more handsome, too.'

She laughs, and I feel a small glow of optimism in my stomach. It reminds me of when we met, and how easily I made her laugh back then.

'Remember the Fitzroy?' I say.

'Of course. Why did you think of it?'

'I don't know. When you laughed — it reminded me of what we were like when we met.'

'Things are easier when you don't know each other.'

'Esther, you're so cynical. We were in love.'

She doesn't say anything, but in the silence I can hear that she agrees.

'You showed me Venus, remember?' I say. 'You were depressed about Christmas.'

'I was so melodramatic.'

'You had a point.'

I pause and think, yes, I will do this. I take a breath. Oh, my heart, it hurts in my chest.

'Look,' I say, 'there's something I want to tell you.'

'I know all about it,' she says.

'About what?'

'Your affair with that girl at work.'

'What?'

'That young doctor, the one who used to call you all the time.'

I can almost see her, sitting in our kitchen, the nervous flush rising up her throat. That's what I like about Esther, her passion, the way she jumps to conclusions, the way she would jump on me, when we were young.

'Annie?' I say.

'Whatever her name is, I know all about it.'

'Esther, I haven't been with another woman since the day we met. Did you really think — '

'What is it, then?'

'I can't do this over the phone. Can I come round?'

27

When I step off the plane in Rio, it smells like home — warm and humid, the smell of damp soil. The air is heavier here, too.

*   *   *

The night before last, I went to our house on Winston Road and told Esther the whole story. We were in the living room, next to the Christmas tree, which was covered in blinking lights. Esther's eyes were wide and disbelieving, yet relieved, somehow, that we were getting to the heart of something. I showed her Luana's letters, and she read them twice. They left her in tears, shaking her head. She was crying for Luana, not for me. Afterwards, we sat in silence for ten minutes — I watched the wall clock throughout — after which Esther, with perfect timing, opened her mouth to speak.

'You have to go and see her,' she said. 'Your — your sister.'

I flinched. My sister. Papai's daughter, sure. But my sister? No one had described Luana that way before. Yes, that's what she was.

'You think so?' I said.

'She raised your child. Your *son*,' she said, rolling her eyes in disbelief. 'You owe it to her.'

She looked up and sipped her glass of red wine. She rubbed her eyes and ran her hands through her curly, dark hair, which was now chin-length, going silver at the temples. But the girl I loved was still there, hiding behind her face.

'What a mess,' she said. 'God, how I wish you'd told me this years ago.'

'You wouldn't have married me.'

'Nonsense. That's your problem, André, you try to paper over all your flaws. We could have got through this.'

'*Could* have?'

'I've met someone.'

She proceeded to tell me about the man, some Oxford-educated divorcé. They'd been dating for five weeks — the girls didn't know about it yet.

'Is it serious?' I said.

'I don't know. It hasn't been long enough for me to find out all the bad stuff about him.'

'Is there good stuff?'

'Well, he cooks me dinner, so it's a start.'

She avoided my eyes, looking guilty. You never cooked me dinner, she wanted to say.

You never helped me with the children. You never quite mastered it — being English. We said goodbye and kissed on both cheeks, like friends.

⋆ ⋆ ⋆

The cab drops me off in front of our building — Thiago's building — on Avenida Vieira Souto. The porteiro comes out of the building and tries to carry my luggage inside, but I tell him that I can do it myself. Really, I just want to stand here and look at the beach. What a familiar and beautiful sight. Ipanema on a Monday afternoon, two days before Christmas Eve. Thirty-five degrees, according to the street clocks, and not a cloud in the blue-and-gold sky. The Cagarras Islands, beyond. Small snatches of conversation as people walk past on the black-and-white pavement.

'Did you see Clarice the other day? Meu Deus, she's a mess!'

'Come on, let's go to Lojas Americanas and buy some sweets.'

'Ai, Mamãe, look at that dog, it's so cute.'

It's comforting and disquieting. The sound of home. Odd, really, that this has never occurred to me before: Rio will never be my home again. What rash decisions we make, when we're young.

On the fifth floor, when I ring the kitchen doorbell, I hear small dogs yapping on the other side. My brother's voice, telling them, 'Get out of the way!' with a fatherly tenderness. The living-room door opens, a few metres down the hallway, so I walk over. I'm now a guest, deserving of the special entrance. It's been six years since I last saw my little brother — an embarrassing length of time, but it vanishes when I see him. He is only slightly changed. His wavy hair is a bit longer and there are faint lines around his eyes. He's still a young man, just about. Could have had any girl he wanted, but he didn't want one.

'André!' he says, leaning down for a hug.

My face barely reaches over his shoulders. The dogs come out — a Yorkshire terrier and a dachshund — and start hopping up and down.

'We're all very excited, as you can see. How was the flight? Was it boring? Let me take your suitcase. Come inside.'

He leads me into the living room, which has been remodelled since Papai died. White walls, teak furniture, modern art, that view over the beach. Like something from a magazine.

'It looks different,' I say.

'We redecorated a few years ago. Do you like it?'

'I don't even recognize it.'

'I'll take that as a yes.'

'It's wonderful.'

Thiago's partner, Jesse, walks in from the back of the flat, flip-flops smacking on the wooden floor. He's an American with red hair and burnished, freckled skin.

'André, welcome home!' he says in English. We shake hands.

'How many years has it been?' he says. 'Two, three?'

'I'm afraid it's been six. Far too long.'

'Let me show you your room.'

'My old room?'

'No,' says Thiago, in his sweetly accented English. 'We're putch-ing you in my old room. Is that OK? Your room is now where I work.'

'Of course. I don't mind, Thi. I'll stay wherever you put me.'

'Bom,' he says, slipping back into our language. 'Let's show you around.'

Thiago leads me out of the living room, his hand on my shoulder. I'm overwhelmed by his presence. I want to hug him again, but I don't — too English, these days. Perhaps I always was. Jesse trails behind us, carrying my luggage, the dogs almost tripping him over.

'Oh,' says Thiago. 'How could I forget? André, this is Kika and Biba. Say hi to your uncle André.'

★ ★ ★

Ipanema beach is quiet, apart from the tourists, bums, nut-cases and students; girls sitting near Posto Nove on fold-out chairs, wearing bikinis, oblivious to their perfection, reading Freud, Marx or anatomy books. Perhaps not oblivious, but pretending to be. Girls like Daniela. I once hung out with such girls, but now I'm just another sagging middle-aged man, watching them from the corners of my eyes. My brother and I slather ourselves in suncream and sit on hired chairs, facing the Atlantic, wearing swimming trunks and sunglasses — he's still young enough to wear a sunga. I'm drinking a sweet, icy caipirinha from a plastic cup, and Thiago sips sparkling water. I'm the one on holiday, after all.

Whatever happened to Daniela?

'She's this super-famous dermatologist,' says Thiago, and I realize I've said the question out loud. 'All of the actresses and models go to her.'

'You know her?'

'I see her now and again. I didn't know her

when you were going out, but I met her through friends. She's married to this journalist called Guilherme Soares — you know him?' I shake my head. 'You know how it is, everyone knows each other here.'

'Londres isn't like that.' I add awkwardly, 'You should visit us sometime.'

'That would be great. I miss your family. That was a long time ago, huh, when I was in Londres? Twelve years?'

'Something like that. Why did you never come back?'

'I'm waiting for my invitation!'

He laughs, with that charming, open smile, perfect teeth. I can see myself reflected in his aviator sunglasses, an older man with a scrappy black beard. Maybe I should start shaving again.

'You don't need an invitation, Thi.'

'Even so,' he says, his smile a bit softer, 'it would be nice to get one.'

'Consider yourself invited. Where's Jesse's family from again?'

'Minnesota. It's incredibly boring. I won't go any more — they don't approve of me.'

'Fuck them,' I say in English.

'Saúde,' he says, holding up his water, and we clink plastic to plastic.

'Want to swim?'

'Let's do it.'

Thiago asks a group of students to watch our things, and then we walk to the water.

'Ai, it's cold,' says Thiago, as we dip our feet in.

'Come on, it's not that bad.'

I walk ahead and dive in. When I come up, squinty-eyed, Thiago laughs.

'You look like a turtle, popping its head up.'

'Come on!'

Thi wades in. Dark water dances around his body. When a wave approaches him, he dives in, and we swim together, away from the shore. Not talking, really, just looking ahead at the islands. The waves are mild today, just perfect. A gentle rocking. We float together, facing the beach: the long stretch of yellow sand, Vidigal at the end of the strip, and the tall blocks of flats, including Thiago's.

'Que delicia,' he says. 'I can't remember the last time I did this. I hardly ever come to the beach.'

'If I lived here, I would come every day.'

'I should make an effort. Jesse comes all the time. I'm always working. He's a kept man!'

We both laugh.

'How's it going, the work?' I say.

'It's good. I have too many patients. Everyone wants to go to therapy these days. Even my cleaner wants me to find someone for her.'

'You don't have an empregada?'

'No, just a cleaner. She comes twice a week. How's your work?'

'It's all right,' I say. 'Quite boring. Maybe Papai was right — I should've become a surgeon.'

'Why didn't you?'

'Didn't try hard enough. Or maybe I just wanted to piss him off.'

If I close my eyes, I can almost shrink Thiago back down to four feet, pretend that he's seven and I'm seventeen, taking him out for a swim.

'This is paradise,' I say.

'So why did you leave?'

'Come on, you know why.'

A large wave curls over us, growing in size. We dive underneath it and it throws us in the air, towards the sun. Thiago slicks his hair back with his fingers.

'Papai was never the same again,' he says.

'Don't make me feel guilty, Thi. It's not like I cut him out of my life. I visited as much as I could.'

'You were his favourite, you know.'

'That's not true.'

'He saw himself in you.'

'For all the wrong reasons.'

We float in silence, diving underneath waves that seem to get bigger and bigger.

After the fifth or sixth, Thiago says, 'Hey, remember jacaré? Let's try to catch a wave, like we used to.'

'OK.'

We bob up and down as a couple of small waves pass us by. A bigger one gathers water twenty metres away.

'This is the one, André!'

We both wait with one arm in the air, preparing to launch into a front crawl. I feel the water rising up behind me and start swimming, swinging my arms and feeling myself being lifted up and carried along. In the corner of my right eye, I can see my brother, also riding the wave. It tails off in the shallows, where we stand with the water sloshing against our legs. Both of us laughing like children, feeling the adrenalin in our blood.

After playing jacaré a few times, we swim out again, beyond the waves, and float.

'So what happened with Esther?' he says. 'Bia says you've separated.'

'She told you?'

'Yes. Why didn't you tell me?'

'I don't know. I was embarrassed.'

'What happened?'

'She's been unhappy with me for a long time, and now she's found another man. She says I have no feelings. Apparently, this gringo has more feelings.'

'Are you getting divorced?'

'Not yet,' I say. 'I'm hoping she'll change her mind.'

'Does she know about — you know?'

'I told her a few days ago. She wasn't that shocked, strangely. It seemed to be a relief.'

I pause, wondering whether to tell him more.

Before I can stop myself, I say, 'Thi, did you know that Luana had my son?'

'What?' he says, his mouth hanging open. 'I thought she'd had an abortion.'

'Papai lied to me.'

'Are you fucking serious?'

'A boy called Francisco. He's dead.'

Thiago gasps.

'He drowned in Belém last year, in the river. He was twenty-six.'

'Meu Deus, that's unbelievable.'

I look away from his shocked face, to avoid the shame. A wave comes, and we dive underneath it. As I emerge from the water, I look up at the pale, bright sky. Thiago touches my arm. He says my name. When I look at him, it's not shame I see but pity.

'You have a son,' he says, shaking his head.

'I had a son.'

'Francisco?'

'Yes, Chico. I'm going to go see Luana. She lives in Marajó. Do you remember it?'

'Vaguely. Are you sure it's a good idea to go up there?'

I look at the beach, at the students playing with their phones, at the food and drink sellers, walking up and down, shouting, 'Guaraná! Mate! Água! Cerveja!' and 'Queijo na brasa!' and 'Abacaxi!' and 'Camarão!' My eyes follow a drink seller, an old black guy, as he makes his way down the beach.

'It's not like that,' I say. 'There's nothing between us. I just want to hear about my son.'

I think of Luana, aged sixteen. Her thin, brown limbs. Lime-flesh eyes. Of course I'm wondering, will it be the same, but I hope, in my heart, that it's not. The Luana I loved is long gone.

Back on the beach, we walk to our chairs.

'Want another drink?' I say.

'After that revelation, I think I'll have a beer.'

I walk up to the barraca on the beach, where another old black guy is sitting on a plastic chair, under the shade. When he sees me walking towards him, he stands up.

'What can I get you, senhor?' he says.

'Another caipirinha and a Skol.'

'Was it good, the last caipirinha?'

'It was perfect.'

'Good, that's what I like to hear.'

He slices a lime into quarters and starts

smashing them in a cup.

'Where are you from, senhor?' he says.

'I'm a carioca. Can't you tell?'

'You sound kind of different. Like a paulista.'

'Oh, come on — anything but that! I live in Inglaterra, in Londres.'

'Londres. That's far from home.'

He dribbles cachaça into the glass, and then sugar and ice.

'Have you ever been?' I say.

He hands me the caipirinha and I thank him.

'No, senhor, I've never left Brazil, but my youngest daughter is moving to Paris soon. Met a gringo and he's taking her away, so I'll have to visit them at some point.'

'Paris, eh? Lucky girl.'

'Those gringos love our women, don't they? And our women love them, too, for some reason. He's rich — that could be the reason!' He laughs, showing the gaps between his remaining teeth, opens a coolbox, takes out a beer and hands it over. 'Oh, he's all right. They've offered to take me away, too, for my retirement, but I could never leave Rio. I was born here and I'll die here. I live right over there.'

He points at Vidigal, at the end of the beach. My babá was from Vidigal, I want to say. And my sister. But I don't say anything. I tell him to put it on the tab and walk back to my brother.

'What took you so long?' says Thiago.

'I was talking to the guy at the barraca. He was telling me about his daughter — she married a gringo and is going off to live in Paris.'

'Gringos love girls like that.'

'Like what?'

'Neguinhas da favela.'

'That's what he said.'

He pulls out a packet of cigarettes.

'You still smoke?' I say.

'Don't tell Jesse. I have one every other day.'

My brother doesn't look like a smoker — he's slim, tanned and healthy. He obviously goes to the gym. Me, on the other hand: my gut protrudes, my skin hangs, I've got the beginnings of man-boobs.

'You want one?' he says.

'Oh, come off it. I quit years ago.'

A white lie. I had my last cigarette five months ago. I remember the exact date, like I remember my daughters' birthdays: 10 July 2014. A few weeks after Esther kicked me out and four days before my forty-sixth birthday. A final attempt to become the man she wanted me to be.

'Oh go on, then,' I say. 'But don't let me have another one during my trip.'

'Sim, senhor.'

Thiago lights two cigarettes in his mouth and passes one over to me. I take a drag and blow, lingering on the greyish taste, which is both unpleasant and wonderful. It's been so long, the nicotine gives me a headrush. I can taste smoke and salt on my lips, and feel cachaça swimming in my blood-stream, making my limbs heavy and relaxed. It's midday and the sun is at its highest. In front of us, my beach and my ocean. They would always be mine, no matter how long I stayed away.

'It's so beautiful here,' I say.

'It is, isn't it?'

'I didn't appreciate what we had.'

'You live in Londres. Everyone wants to be there.'

'Different place, same person.'

Tears prick behind my eyes. At least I have my sunglasses on. I swallow hard, to keep them from flowing. I breathe heavily and Thi puts his hand on my shoulder. I know he's doing it to make me feel better, but his tenderness pushes me a little further to the edge.

'I look back and think, *who was that?*'

'You were young,' he says. 'These things happen.'

'Especially in our family.'

'That reminds me,' he says. 'I found something really strange recently.'

He drains his beer and calls over one of the can-pickers. A black guy in his forties, stout and sweaty from walking up and down the beach, looking for empty cans to sell. Slim pickings compared to the weekend. Thiago hands his beer can over and thanks him.

'I was going through Papai's papers a few months ago,' he says, 'and came across his birth certificate. His mother's name was crossed out with a black pen.'

'How odd. I wonder what it means.'

'We'll never know. Everyone's dead now.'

We never met Papai's parents, but I've seen a couple of photos. Posing stiffly in a photography studio, overdressed for the Amazon heat. Not even a hint of a smile. Papai often said they had aristocratic lineage, but that didn't mean anything; they were born after the end of the empire, when the family's titles turned to dust.

'You know, Papai's father, Felipe, had children all over the place with other women,' says Thiago.

'Oh yes,' I say. 'Mamãe mentioned that sometimes.'

'There were seven or eight of them, maybe more. Papai couldn't keep count. People would always be telling him that they'd met one of his half-siblings.'

Papai never talked about this with me, but evidently he had spoken to Thiago. I feel a pang of jealousy. In my absence, they had become close.

'One time,' says Thiago, 'when Papai was training to be a doctor in Belém, he treated a young black woman, and when she learned his name, she said she was married to his brother. Papai said, 'I don't have a brother. I'm an only child.''

'Cabral's a common name,' I say.

'This woman knew our grandfather's full name, where he lived, everything. Her husband was Papai's half-brother.'

'What a filho da puta.'

'Makes me glad I didn't have children,' says Thiago. 'Less chance of fucking them up.'

'Makes me glad that I had daughters,' I say, forgetting for a moment about Chico, but then I remember and feel a dull thud in my chest.

'Shit,' I say. 'Well, I guess I'm a filho da puta, too.'

I laugh, though it isn't funny. Thiago looks ahead, his eyes hidden by his sunglasses.

'Do you ever think of having children?' I say, to change the subject.

'No, but Jesse wants to adopt some street kid.'

'Really?'

'Oh you know, these gringos,' he says, stretching his arms over his head. 'They love saving people.'

28

It's the first day of a new year. Last night, we celebrated at home: Thiago, Jesse and me, and some of their friends. Dinner and cocktails, made by caterers. We watched the fireworks from the balcony, slept for four hours, and then Thiago drove me to the airport. When we hugged goodbye, I didn't want to let go.

As the plane comes down, I notice that the word 'God' is painted on the wing in English. Beyond the wing, the sky over Belém is cloudy and the buildings tall and grey, the river brown and smooth. It doesn't look familiar. All these cheap sky-scrapers — did they exist back then? I idly calculate how long it's been since my last visit. Nearly thirty years. My last visit? My only visit. I've thought of Pará so often it seems absurd that I've only been here once before. My head hurts.

★   ★   ★

I had been in Rio for ten days, but I didn't look up any of my old friends. It had been too damn long. What were they to me? What was I to them, but someone they used to know a long time ago? Aunt Lia had died of lung cancer some years earlier, and her brother, mad Gustavo, was long gone. I had lunch with a few second cousins and their molly-coddled, under-achieving children. Other than Thiago, no one in my family seems to have a job, but everyone has money. They spend their days at home playing with stocks and shares online, empregadas cleaning around them, bringing them lunch. The old Brazil, still going strong, but for how much longer? Empregadas have rights now, so fewer people can afford them. Everyone complained about the president and the things she's done. It's so bad here, they told me, as an empregada took our plates away. It's never been worse. We should've moved to Europe, like you did.

I went to the beach every morning, and was taken out by Thiago and Jesse nearly every night. At times, I envied their child-free lives. They took me to restaurants in Zona Sul and bars in Lapa, and to exhibitions at shiny new museums. Rio had changed.

On Christmas Eve we had dinner at their friend Luciana's mansion up in Santa Teresa, overlooking the city. The area had cleaned up, Thiago told me. It hadn't returned to its nineteenth-century heyday, but it was relatively safe.

'Yes,' said Luciana. 'I never hear gunfire

any more. I can't even remember the last time, to be honest, but I always sleep wearing ear plugs, so I wouldn't know.'

Luciana was an elegant, lively woman in her forties who reminded me of Mamãe. Thiago and she couldn't work out how they knew each other — they just did. She had long, dark hair and a husky, humorous voice; her expressive hands and wrists shimmered with gold jewellery. Only her wedding finger was bare. She was a jewellery designer — a typical non-job for a rich carioca — but she cooked the meal herself, no empregada in sight. After dinner, we drank cocktails next to her pool. Luciana lit a citronella candle to keep away the mosquitoes, and then a cigarette. I knew Thiago would be wanting one, but he abstained so as not to offend Jesse. Down below were the twinkling favelas, almost within reach. Cicadas droned around us.

It reminded me of our end-of-school celebration in December 1986, when we saw the sun rise from Rodrigo's cousin's house in Santa. I was fairly quiet during dinner — I didn't think anyone wanted to hear about the life of an almost-divorced GP — but I'd had a few drinks by then, so I told them about the party.

'The view was so similar,' I said. 'My

friend's cousin must have been your neighbour.'

'Who was your friend?' said Luciana.

'Rodrigo Morais.'

'Rodrigo!'

'You know him?' said Thiago.

'He's my cousin — it was my party! Ai meu Deus, André Cabral, of course! I remember you. Where have your glasses gone?'

'I wear contact lenses. You're still living here?'

'I came back eleven years ago. Zona Sul just didn't compare. I'm a Santa girl at heart, I need to be up in the hills. Plus, my mother got lonely after my father died. Better lonely together than lonely apart — but she's dead, now.'

'I'm sorry to hear that . . . You're really Rodrigo's cousin?'

'Yes! Am I that forgettable?'

'No, it's just been so many years.'

'Saúde,' she said, and we raised our glasses.

Though I didn't recognize Luciana, I remembered her well. Lulu, as we called her, was younger than us by a year or two, already beautiful, with her waist-length hair and morena skin. As Rodrigo's priminha, she was off limits to us, which heightened her appeal. That morning in 1986, she had passed out on one of the sunbeds in a foetal position, just wearing a bikini, her curves new and unripe. I couldn't see fresh, young Lulu in chic, chain-smoking Luciana, her olive skin creased from decades in the sun. She didn't recognize me either. Was I better or worse?

★ ★ ★

That was last week. At the airport in Belém, I look around, searching for my daughter. Two months is nothing for me but, for a teenager, it's enough for a transformation. I spot her: a lanky, tanned young woman walking towards me, in T-shirt, shorts and flip-flops. Her hair in a pony tail, aviator sunglasses pushed back. Despite her bronzed skin, she looks so English.

'Dad!' she says. 'Over here!'

A few men turn to look at her, this tall, lovely gringa. I want to tell them to look the other way, but Bia is oblivious. She runs up to me like a child and hugs me tightly, so that I have to drop my bags on the floor. Her eyes glitter with the mania of someone who hasn't seen a familiar face in a while.

'How are you, querida?'

'I'm so excited that you're here!'

I'm a little nervous, not entirely used to being alone with my children. I picked them up from friends' houses, took them to music classes and read stories to them at night when Esther was too tired. But she did everything else: dressing them in the morning, telling them to do their homework, having hysterical, screaming arguments, while I was the neutral go-between. Sometimes I felt like a trespasser in a house of women.

Outside, we catch a cab to the hotel. The air is steamy and the sun harshly bright, but inside the car it's as cold as a fridge.

'Rua Henrique Gurjão, por favor,' says Bia, her accent confident and foreign. She booked the hotel, and has already spent a night there, after arriving from Maranhão by bus.

'I hope you'll like the hotel. It's quite simple.'

'Anything's fine for me. How was Maranhão?'

She talks excitedly about the Lençóis Maranhenses, a national park of white sand dunes and lagoons. In pictures it looks unreal, a beach from another planet.

'Have you ever been?' she says.

'No, but I'd like to go. I think my grandmother was from Maranhão.' I remember how her name was crossed out on Papai's birth certificate. 'I never knew her, though.'

'Really? God, it's unbelievable.'

She sits back, blinking at the sunlight.

'What is?'

'I barely know anything about you,' she says.

'This isn't me — I'm not from here.'

The driver — a sturdy man in his late thirties, with a native face — glances at us in the rear-view mirror.

'Where are you from?' he says.

'Inglaterra,' says Bia.

'But the senhor looks Brazilian.'

'I'm Brazilian, my daughter is English,' I say. 'We live in Londres.'

'You're a carioca?' he says.

'Yes.'

'How come you moved to Londres?'

By this point, I don't think Bia can understand much, but I can see that she's concentrating, breaking the sentences down in her head.

'To study,' I say, 'and then I met my wife and didn't come back.'

'You're a lucky guy, living over there. I have a cousin who managed to get a Portuguese passport, so he moved to Inglaterra. He couldn't get a job in Londres, so he went to Manchester instead.' It's funny to hear that word — Manchester — in the back of a cab in the Amazon. 'He works as a taxi driver, too. He says it's unbelievably cold but he loves it.'

I lean back in my seat.

'He has a cousin in Manchester,' I tell Bia. 'Can you believe it?'

'Urgh, I know where I'd rather be.'

'In Belém? Not a chance.'

★ ★ ★

We're in the city for just two nights. Belém wasn't interesting to me in 1985, and now it's just depressing. Those old colonial houses in the Cidade Velha are older still. Once, they housed hopeful men who got rich on sugar and rubber, but now some of them are just walls with no windows, roofs or floors. Shoddy memorials to a golden age. Our hotel, like Bia said, is simple, but clean, and half empty, with not a single foreign guest other than my daughter. The new Brazil that gringos are clamouring for — sex and beaches, art and wealth — hasn't quite reached the Amazon.

We eat fried fish with lime and acai at the riverside market, followed by cupuacu ice cream. Then we walk around, sweating in the sun, feeling sorry for all the panting, passed-out animals on sale: rodents, parrots, rabbits and chickens. Some of them look half dead, their little tongues hanging out. That night we see a solo guitar performance at the pink Theatro da Paz, which I remember from last time — a grand European theatre dropped into the Amazon, but with wicker seats instead of red velvet. Rain pounds the roof, like thousands of fists.

On our last evening in Belém, we eat pato no tucupi at a restaurant housed in an old Portuguese palace. Bia chose it from her guidebook. Apparently it's famous. Is this the one? Is this where he died? No, there must be several restaurants by the river. Our table is outside, ten metres from the water's edge. The jambu works its magic, making our mouths go numb. Even with the garden lit up, the river is black and endless. No line between sky and water. I don't say what's on my mind. I can feel my heart again. We drink beer, and I watch Bia smoke a cigarette. I know that she smokes, because I sometimes smell it on her, but I've never seen it myself. There are worse things in life than smoking when you're nineteen, and few better. I don't ask for a drag.

29

It takes a moment to figure out where I am. A white room, a fan whirring fast and loud above my bed. The hotel room in Belém.

★   ★   ★

As a child, I was frightened of fans. They seemed precarious to me, especially the old ones at my grandparents' flat in Rio, which always seemed on the verge of spinning off the ceiling, turning us into sliced salami. Aged six, during lunch, I once laughed out loud at the thought of the fan falling down and slicing Papai's head off — and I told everyone about it.

'Oedipus complex,' said Aunt Lia, smiling and nodding as though it was the cutest thing I'd ever said.

★   ★   ★

After showering and dressing, I go downstairs and knock on Bia's door. A low murmur comes from inside.

'Bia, we have to catch the boat — time to get up.'

'Hmmm, OK.'

'See you in the lobby in twenty minutes.'

'All right, Dad!' she says, muffled by the walls but obviously irritated.

The hotel doesn't serve breakfast this early, so I go and sit by the swimming pool, in the courtyard, surrounded by little palm trees. The sun is barely up, but it's not cool. Later, it will be humid as hell. A cleaner walks past, holding a mop and bucket.

'Good morning, senhor,' she says.

'Good morning.'

'You're up early.'

'I'm getting the boat to Marajó.'

'Have you been before?'

'Once, a long time ago.'

'It never changes.'

'That's good to hear.'

'Look,' she says, pointing at the pool.

A yellow bird with black wings and black-ringed eyes is hopping towards it. It opens its wings and flies, dips momentarily into the water and then rests on the side, shaking its wings, before taking another dip.

'They come here every morning. Ei, amarelinho, you love your chlorine bath, don't you?'

The bird looks at her and cocks its head. Another bird, just like it, flies down and also takes a bath. The cleaner reaches into her

315

pocket and pulls out a bag of seeds.

'So that's the reason they come,' I say, as she scatters seeds on the paving stones.

She laughs.

'They started coming for the pool, but they returned for the food,' she says. 'Have a good time in Marajó, senhor.'

* * *

The ferry to Marajó has two types of tickets: air-conditioned and open-air. I spot some gringos heading straight for the air-conditioned section, on the top floor of the boat, but Bia and I stay outside in the heat, for the better view. We drink small cups of strong coffee and sit on plastic seats near the side. The sky is pale and golden, the clouds clearing, the sun getting ready to make us sweat.

'It's amazing that you can't see the other side,' she says. 'It's like an ocean.'

We stand up, leaving our bags on our seats, and lean on the deck rail, looking out. The same river as thirty years ago, but Bia didn't exist back then. I can barely remember what it was like to be childless. I have the memories, but I don't remember how it *felt*. As though I was always aware of Bia and Hannah, waiting around the corner, for me to become their father.

'Everything's bigger over here,' I say. 'The river, the jungle, the land, the portions — '

'The people,' she says.

'The people?'

'They seem to take up more space and time.'

'Is that a good thing?'

'In London nobody has time for anyone.'

I step back from the side of the boat and look at my daughter. There's an air of unhappiness around her, in the downward planes of her face. Probably my fault.

'Even at your age?'

'At any age,' she says, a bit abruptly. She reaches into the pocket of her khaki shorts and pulls out a pack of Hollywoods, takes one out and lights it.

'You're going to university soon, and it's not going to be like that.'

'It's going to be a lot of work.'

'Work is good for you. My relatives don't work enough. They're idle.'

'They're happy.'

'Brazilians are good at performing happiness. It's what they do.'

'Why did you leave, honestly?' she says.

'It's in the blood.'

'What do you mean?'

'Most of my ancestors weren't from Brazil. They were from Portugal, Lebanon, Italy. All that moving around the world — it's hard to stop.'

Bia nods, her face shiny and bright. Her tanned arm, leaning against the rail, is thin and muscled. It has become unbearably humid. We sit down. She reads a book — John Updike's *Brazil,* which is terrible, but I don't tell her — while I flick through her copy of *Lonely Planet Brazil.* Seven hundred pages of places that I will never visit.

'Bom dia,' says someone, and I look up.

It's one of the gringos I had seen scurrying off to the air-conditioned lounge — a man about my age, with grey hair, shorts, T-shirt and a bumbag. He leans over us, one foot hiked up on a chair. His white face is red from the heat.

'Bom dia,' I say.

But he's not a gringo — just one of those strange southerners who doesn't seem Brazilian. Not just in his German pallor, but in his foreign manners.

'Did you know that there's a room with air conditioning up there?' he says.

'I'm aware of that.'

'You two should sit there, not down here.'

'Should I?' I say.

'I was surprised that you and your daughter stayed down here, so I thought I'd come and tell you about it.'

'We chose to sit here.'

I look around at the other people on the open deck. Their bags of produce. Their dark, work-worn faces.

'You'll be more comfortable up there,' he says.

'We want to sit here and enjoy the view. Thanks, but we're going to stay here.'

His eyebrows come closer together. Against his pink skin, they're as grey as dust. His mouth hangs open, perhaps in embarrassment or just because of the heat.

'OK, no worries.'

He slopes back to his first-class lounge on the top floor, walking with an exaggerated casualness, as though our exchange had been nothing.

'What was that?' says Bia.

'Some idiot gaúcho.'

'What's a gaúcho?'

'A southerner. Descended from Germans — you see how they look like gringos? But in all my years in London, I've never seen a gringo behave like that. He's one hundred per cent Brazilian, that filho da puta.'

'What the hell did he say?'

'He thinks we should sit upstairs with the other white people.'

'Are you kidding?'

How did he come to the decision, one hour

into the trip, to come and rescue us from the commoners? The man obviously felt a kinship with me, not so much for my whiteness — I'm hardly white — but for all those other signifiers: Ray-Ban sunglasses, deck shoes, an iPhone in my shirt pocket and a daughter who speaks to me in English.

'What a cock,' she says.

* * *

Unfortunately, I do have one thing in common with the gaúchos: a taste for rustic boutique guest houses. We're staying at the same one, Pousada Laranja in Salvaterra. They send a minibus to collect us from the ferry so we don't have to contend with the local taxis and the same smell of jungle and chicken shit as thirty years ago. But this is beside the point. There is a small piece of paper in my pocket and on it is the address of Luana's pousada, which she emailed to me. I wrote it down, despite the fact that I had already memorized it, as though putting it on paper made it more real. Casa da Luana, number ten on Rua Decima Segunda. I looked it up online, but it didn't have a website yet — just two reviews on TripAdvisor and a photo of a buffet breakfast. I found Salvaterra and its numerical street names on a map: Rua Primeira, Rua Segunda, Rua Terceira, Rua Quarta, and so on. She is on the twelfth road and is expecting me later today. Last night, in Belém, I told Bia that I was going to see an old friend in Marajó. She seemed unbothered. Perhaps she was relieved not to be invited or maybe she was just too tipsy, after several rounds of beer, to point out that her old dad didn't have any old friends, anywhere.

Pousada Laranja is right on the beach: a cluster of pastel orange huts surrounding a small pool, should guests tire of swimming in the river. Our van delivers us just before noon. The poor gaúcho, sitting at the back of the bus, seems the most eager to get off, to run away from me. For lunch, Bia and I eat an excellent fish stew, right on the sand. There was no pousada here in 1985. Some things have changed, but not the river — it's just as endless and gently murky. I remember swimming out from this same beach, leaving Papai and Thiago far behind me. Floating on my back, thinking of the past, but I had no past back then. Somehow I'm the same person, in crummier packaging, accompanied by this lovely girl, who I created.

Another thing that hasn't changed: it's burningly hot. I can already see red patches appearing on Bias face.

'You should wear factor thirty and above,' I say, as a waiter starts to clear our plates from the table on the beach.

'You shud wear fack-tor tirty,' says Bia, mimicking my accent. 'OK, I'm not twelve.'

'When you're my age, you'll be thanking me, because you'll still be a beautiful lady and not a wrinkled old prune.'

'I'll never be your age.'

'What does that mean?'

'Nothing. Just wishful thinking.'

She takes a sip from her coconut.

'Dad, are you OK?'

'Yes, why?'

'Your mouth is twitching.'

I touch my mouth. A small throb.

'I'm just tired from all the travelling,' I say. 'I should probably get going.'

'Where are you going?'

'To see my friend — I told you last night.'

'Did you? Oh yeah, you did. Who is he?'

'She.'

'She?' she says, grinning. 'An old girl-friend?'

Her teeth are white and straight, contrasting with her reddening skin.

'No, no. Just an old friend from Rio. What are you going to do?'

'Hang around on the beach.'

'Wear a hat,' I say.

She rolls her eyes, takes her phone out of her bag and starts to untangle her blue earphones.

'I'll meet you back here,' I say. 'I want to go for a swim before the sun comes down.'

'OK, Dad. Have fun.'

I fix my Panama hat on to my head and wander off, through the huts, past the swimming pool, wave at the gaúcho, who's standing in the pool (stupid man — who swims in a pool when you can swim in the Amazon River?), and he waves back, and I reach the street. There are few shadows to hide in, because the buildings are so low — just sharp, yellow sun.

'You won't get lost,' Luana assured me, evidently unaware of my appalling sense of direction. 'Anyway, you already know it.'

No, I don't really know Salvaterra. The streets look familiar, but only vaguely, like when you recognize someone in your dream but then wake up thinking, who the hell was *that?* An old black woman in a long white dress walks past, holding a pink umbrella. Sweat streams into my eyes, stinging them with suncream.

'Good afternoon,' I say.

'Good afternoon, senhor!'

A small, golden-brown dog starts following me, moving slowly, its tongue hanging in the heat. I pat it on the head. It's a puppy and still beautiful, despite belonging to nobody. Boys cycle past on bikes that look like they've been rescued from a dump. They're whistling, joyous. The dog runs after them. People have thrown open their windows and doors, and the same unfamiliar song is playing on the radio, out of each house; something old and melancholy, a woman singing a love song. When I reach Luana's street, I stop and try to breathe. I'm sweating like a horse. (I remember riding horses in Teresópolis with Mamãe when I was eight years old, before she got pregnant with Thiago, and when I reached down to pet the creature's neck, it was warm and damp, pulsing with life.)

I walk up the road, but can't see any house numbers. A boy is sitting by the side of the road, playing with a dog — a brown-and-black vira-lata of no discernible breed — teasing him with a little stick.

'Good afternoon,' I say.

'Olá, senhor.'

'Do you know where number ten is? It's a pousada.'

'Luana's pousada?' he says, and my heart nearly bursts out of my chest. I manage a nod. 'Right over there, the blue house.'

He points across the street, a few doors down. The blue house. Of course, Papai's house. A sign hangs on it: 'Casa da Luana'.

Hers now, not his. When Papai died, I noticed that the house wasn't in his will, but Thiago said it had been sold years earlier — that's what Papai told him. The garden overflows with bright flowers — pink hibiscus, yellow and purple orchids, others I can't identify, in every shade — many more than I remember. I walk to the entrance, take a handkerchief from my pocket and mop the sweat from my face. A young woman comes out, holding a small child on her hip. For a few seconds, I stop breathing.

'Good afternoon,' she says, leaving the door open for me.

But it's not Luana, because Luana is no longer young. I walk inside.

★   ★   ★

Rita's daughter. Our empregada. My father's daughter. The mother of my son. My sister. My Luana. I recognize her instantly, sitting at the reception of her pousada, in what used to be the hallway. I see her before she sees me. She's looking down at some papers on her desk, wire-rimmed glasses sitting on her nose. Her face is thinner than it had been — exquisite. She wears a black vest, her ringlets loose, lightened at the ends by the sun. She pushes her glasses back, over her

325

hair, and raises her head. Her eyes are still green, but of course they are.

'Can I help you, senhor?' she says.

'Luana.'

Her mouth stays open. It still has that deep Portuguese curve; my father's mouth. She smiles, but only for a second, puts her glasses back on and stands up. Blue jeans and gold rubber flip-flops.

'Hello, André.'

How many years I've spent pushing her to the back of my mind. But Luana is here, she's real, it happened. She's my sister and I loved her and it's disgusting and no one has ever come close. She's standing in front of me, waiting for me to speak, but I can't, because I'm terrified. She frowns, looking at me from head to toe. I feel self-conscious, old and ugly. She is still beautiful, but with a weariness that suits her, makes her elegant, a woman. I don't know how to greet her. A kiss on each cheek? A hug? A handshake? I wait for her to make the first move. We stand for a few seconds, looking at each other. She puts out her hand, and I shake it, and then she smirks at the formality of it. She takes a step back, away from me.

'Where are your glasses?' she says.

'I wear contact lenses. And you, you're wearing glasses.'

'I had bad eyesight, even back then — I just didn't know it.'

Why didn't I remember that? The way she squinted at the TV when the novelas were on — why didn't I notice? Both of us half blind, like our father. The air between us crackles with strangeness.

'Do you want a drink?' she says.

'Some water would be good. I'm not used to this heat any more.'

'How about a cold beer?'

'Even better.'

'Let's sit outside on the porch.'

★　★　★

We sit in the shade on wicker chairs, side by side, so that we don't have to make eye contact. Luana arranged the chairs this way. She mostly stares at the road, as though I am unbearable to look at.

'How's Londres?' she says, sipping beer from a frosted glass.

'It's fine,' I say, looking at her, but she doesn't meet my gaze. 'Well, it's home. I've been there for a long time.'

I look back at the road. No cars, no walkers, but on the other side an old couple sits on their porch, watching us, hopefully too far away to hear our conversation. Tiny hummingbirds swoop down into Luana's garden, moving from flower to flower.

'I know,' she says. 'Matheus told me all about it.'

'Did you see him often before he died?'

'No, not much. After I left Rio I never saw him again, but we wrote to each other a couple of times a year. I think it was better that way. He was never my father, not really, but I'm grateful to him for giving me this,' she says, gesturing at the house. 'I wanted to leave Rio — it wasn't a good place for . . . for a boy to grow up — and I liked it here. So we moved up here and I started working in restaurants, as a cook and waitress. That's how I met my husband, Jorge — he owned one of the bars on the beach. Sorry, am I talking too much?'

She presses her lips together and laughs in a way I've never seen before, light and relaxed, but then she stops herself and looks back at the road.

'No, of course not. It's great, what you've done here.'

'We just opened it this year, the pousada,' she says.

'After . . . ?'

'Yes. I wanted to do something new.'

She pauses and drinks her beer.

'Did you leave Brazil because of me?' she

says, turning her head and looking straight into my eyes.

Her confidence is unnerving. I look away — at the old couple, still watching us, not talking. The man lights a cigarette and the woman fans herself with a piece of card.

'Yes,' I say. 'It seemed easy, running away — a simple solution.'

'Was it worth it?'

'My wife has just left me, so no, perhaps not, but it was worth it for my daughters. I made the same mistake that people have been making since the beginning of time, thinking that you can change yourself just by going somewhere else. Meu Deus, I sound like a self-help book.'

She snorts — the old laugh. It's a lovely thing to hear. There's a small gap in her front teeth that I don't remember and, when she smiles, I see a sliver of pink tongue, in between. Another new thing: she has dark brown freckles on her cheeks, brought out by the northern sun.

'I wouldn't have left if I'd known about Chico,' I say. 'You know that, don't you?'

She doesn't react — just drinks her beer. What is she thinking?

'What's she like,' she says, 'your wife?'

'She's a doctor, too. Her name is Esther. She's . . . she's great.'

Luana purses her lips, as if to say: sorry you fucked it up.

'And your daughters?'

'They're called Hannah and Beatriz.'

'Like Dona Beatriz.'

'She looks like her, too. She's here with me in Marajó. She's going to study medicine.'

'Like my daughter.'

'They're cousins,' I say, only just realizing it.

Luana tips some more beer into her mouth and then refills her glass from a bottle. I see a glint of gold on her hand.

'I would have liked to become a doctor,' she says.

'Really?'

'Yes, or a lawyer or something. Something *good*. I envied you, you know, but in the end I've been happy here, raising my children, living with my husband.'

'Where is he, Jorge?'

'He's in Belém today, but he'll be back later. We go quite often, especially with our kids . . . with Iracema living there.'

Our kids. For a moment, she must have forgotten, but she brushes aside this lapse with an efficient smile. It must happen all the time. I can't imagine how it feels, losing a child. I lost him before I found him.

'And Rita is still in Rio?' I say.

'Yes.'

'Tell her I said hi.'

'No,' she says, 'I won't. She wouldn't like us meeting like this.'

She looks across the road and exhales heavily, trying to stay calm. We don't speak for a few seconds.

'I'm sorry. Forget I said it.'

'You think you're still Andrézinho, don't you? Andrézinho da Rita,' she says, imitating the sweet voice her mother used when talking to us. The voice she used, too, I realize, but her voice has changed. It's low and firm, no longer sweet.

'I'm so sorry, Luana.'

'Good. I'm glad you're sorry.'

I've barely had a sip of beer. The glass is warm in my hand. My mouth is dry, so I take a gulp. The moment passes and Luana carries on telling me about her life. She has become a talker in the last thirty years, or maybe she always was and I just didn't know. She tells me about Jorge, who she met during her first month on the island, two decades ago, when she worked at his bar. He's quiet and modest, she tells me, and he loved Chico, who was eight years old when they arrived. Chico loved him, too — when he went into catering, he was following in Jorge's footsteps. Jorge, the perfect father. Jorge, the perfect husband.

'I know that's not much of an achievement to someone like you,' she says, 'but for a boy from Vidigal — '

'He must have been very dedicated.'

'He was going to do so much more,' she says. 'I always knew it.'

I'm proud of him, I want to say, but I can't. I have nothing to do with his achievements. All I gave him was my blood. I wonder whether he called Jorge 'Papai', but I don't ask.

'What was he like, Luana?'

'Come and see. I can show you.'

We go inside. Unlike our flat in Ipanema, the original character of the house is almost entirely intact. I wonder, in fact, if I recognize the paintings on the walls. Luana leads me to the back, beyond the kitchen. The TV room, where we first kissed, was now locked and labelled 'I' with a ceramic sign, though I can hear televised laughter from behind the door. Luana has extended the maids' quarters into a self-contained flat, where she lives with Jorge, but we only go as far as the living room.

'This is him,' she says, picking up a photo of her family standing in front of the blue house. Luana with her arms around an older black man, a chubby teenage girl and a young man, who's taller than all of them. Olive skin, paler than Luana's, cropped curly hair and, unmistakably, Thiago's toothy, dazzling smile.

'What a beautiful boy,' I say.

'He looks like Thiago, don't you think?'

'I was just thinking that. Did he use Jorge's surname?'

'No, mine,' she says. 'Nazaré.'

'Francisco Nazaré.'

She nods, still looking at the photo.

'When was it taken?' I say.

'Two years ago.'

He doesn't know that he's going to die. He doesn't know that he'll never have children or marry, or see his sister become a doctor. He'll never meet his father, and he doesn't know it. It's the wide smile of an innocent child. My child. I excuse myself, because there are tears in my eyes. I feel Luana's arm around my shoulder, and then I am in her arms, holding her. Her body feels smaller and harder than it did in my dreams, the body of a stranger. I feel a shudder and know that she's crying. She says I don't have to hide any more, but I can't do it — I can't cry in front of her — so I take a few breaths and hold it in.

'I'm sorry for everything, Lua.'

She steps back, lifts her glasses and wipes her eyes.

'You were too young to know what you were doing,' she says, 'and I was too young to stop you.'

'But you liked me, too, didn't you?'

She was the one who came into my room.

'Let's not go over it,' she says. 'Maybe some other time.'

There will be no other time — this is it.

'Something good came out of it, and that was Chico,' she says. 'For twenty-six years I had the most wonderful son. I wish you had met him, because you would have loved him, too. That's — that's why I sent the letters. I wanted you to get to know him. I wanted you,' she says carefully, 'to know how it felt to lose him.'

'Thank you,' I say.

'Did they upset you, the letters?' she says, looking hopeful, and who could blame her? While I tried to bury the past, she had lived with it every day. It had a name, it was a person.

'Yes,' I say, 'very much. I read them hundreds of times.'

'Good. I'm glad.'

They drove me mad, I want to say. My life is ruined.

But instead, I say, 'Luana, will you come to the beach with me? I want to introduce you to Beatriz.'

She looks shocked for a second, but she's good at masking her feelings — years of being an empregada, a waitress, of tending to her clients and employers.

'I won't say anything,' I say. 'I just want you to meet her.'

She smiles and says, 'OK, I'll come.'

We walk under a Mickey Mouse umbrella, like friends, like siblings; our bodies not close enough to be mistaken for lovers. Luana tells me that Jorge knew all about my visit, about me. Chico had known about me, too. Even Iracema was raised knowing that a doctor from Rio was her brother's papai. Sometimes I forget that I'm walking with Luana through the streets of Marajó. I catch myself and feel amazed, remembering how we walked the same streets as kids, without the slightest idea of the future. Just today and tomorrow, the beach and the river.

When we reach the beach, I see Bia standing in the shallows. I call her over.

'Meu Deus,' says Luana. 'She looks exactly like Dona Beatriz.'

Bia looks perplexed and moody, the same way she looks just before an argument with Esther. When she sees Luana up close, though, she smiles and holds out a hand. Luana ignores her hand and kisses her on both cheeks. Bia still hasn't learned the etiquette.

'This is my daughter,' I say in Portuguese to Luana, and in English I say, 'Bia, this is my old friend Luana.'

'Nice to meet you. How do you know each other?'

'Luana's mother was my nanny. We grew up together.'

'What did you say?' says Luana.

'Just a bit of the truth. Not all of it.'

'Are you ever going to tell her?'

'I think so. But not today.'

★ ★ ★

We wade into the river, my daughter and I.

'She's very pretty, your friend,' says Bia, as the water climbs our legs.

'Yes, she is.'

Luana stays on the shore and orders a Coke from the beach bar. She tells us she'll wait for us; that afterwards, we can walk to the blue house to meet Jorge — he'll be back from Belém. What on earth will he think of me?

Bia is a strong swimmer and is soon far ahead — just a black dot in the water, which is cool, calm and heavenly. Will I ever swim here again? No. Just in my dreams. I lie on my back and float, like I did back then, and I almost feel the same. Just flesh and bone and water, just another animal, another Indian swimming in the Amazon. And then I look at my arms — covered in white sun spots — and my slack belly, and I call to my daughter, because I'm worried that she has gone out too far. I swim back to the shore with Bia several metres behind. The splash of her front crawl reassures me.

When I get out, I look for Luana, but I can't see her at the beach bar. She's not at her table. I walk over to the young man who runs the place. He's standing behind the bar, typing into his phone.

'Hello,' I say. 'My friend was sitting over there — do you know where she went?'

'Who, Luana?'

'You know her?'

'Yes. She paid the bill and left, senhor.'

'She isn't in the bathroom?'

'No, I saw her walk that way.'

He points away from the river, to the road.

'You're friends with Luana?' he says, somewhat incredulously.

'Yes, we knew each other in Rio.'

'She's probably just gone back to her pousada — you know it?'

'Yes,' I say. 'It's OK, I'll see her later.'

He goes back to his phone.

Maybe we took too long in the river and she needed to go back to work. Yes. She might call later and explain everything, and then we can see each other again tomorrow, and talk more about Chico. I'll sit in her living room and imagine him sitting beside me. He'd be twenty-seven now — still a young man, stupidly young — smiling Thiago's smile, telling me about his job in Belém. I'd buy him a ticket to London. He'd get to know his British sisters. They'd love him, even though they would share no common language.

A Coke bottle and a glass sit on a white plastic table, both of them almost empty. There's a pale smudge on the glass, where my sister's lips touched it. The grainy pattern of her mouth. Behind me, my daughter is wading out of the river. I can hear her bare feet pounding the sand. I pick up the glass and hold it up to the sun, to look at Luana's mark — to memorize it — and then I place my lips over it, and swallow the last drops of warm, sweet liquid.

Acknowledgements

Thank you to Emma Paterson at Rogers, Coleridge & White, Mary Mount at Viking, John Glynn and Nan Graham at Scribner, Julia Sauma, Ardashir Vakil, Rachel Seiffert, Romesh Gunesekera, Michal Shavit, Alex Christofi, Matt Smedley, Beatriz Bastos, Ana Abreu, Ana Paulina Sauma, Maxim de Sauna, Gabriel Sauma and, most of all, Tim Goalen.

We do hope that you have enjoyed reading this large print book.

Did you know that all of our titles are available for purchase?

We publish a wide range of high quality large print books including:
Romances, Mysteries, Classics
General Fiction
Non Fiction and Westerns

Special interest titles available in large print are:
The Little Oxford Dictionary
Music Book
Song Book
Hymn Book
Service Book

Also available from us courtesy of Oxford University Press:
Young Readers' Dictionary
(large print edition)
Young Readers' Thesaurus
(large print edition)

For further information or a free brochure, please contact us at:
Ulverscroft Large Print Books Ltd.,
The Green, Bradgate Road, Anstey,
Leicester, LE7 7FU, England.
Tel: (00 44) 0116 236 4325
Fax: (00 44) 0116 234 0205

Other titles published by Ulverscroft:

TRANSIT

Rachel Cusk

Faye, a writer, has returned to London with her two sons, and purchased a dilapidated council flat. While the boys stay with their father, she pursues the renovation of the place, determined to create a family home from the squalid and neglected building. Along the way, a series of encounters with others — from Gerard, her former partner, to a garrulous and profound hairdresser; from a phlegmatic ex-army builder to a dryly self-deprecating author on a literary festival panel — will give her much to ruminate on . . .

THE EVENING ROAD

Laird Hunt

Meet Ottie Lee Henshaw: young and white, who navigates a stifling marriage, a treacherous boss — and, on one summer's day in 1930, an odyssey across the countryside to witness a dark and fearful celebration . . . Meet Calla Destry: young and black, desperate to escape a place where the stench of violence hangs heavy in the air, and to find the lover who has promised her a new life . . . Every road leads to the bedlam of Marvel, where people are gathering for a death carnival — the lynching of two men. And, along the way, lives will collide and be changed forever.